UNTIL
THE DAY
BREAK

BY

LOUIS BROMFIELD

Harper & Brothers Publishers

NEW YORK AND LONDON

To
all those brothers regardless
of race or creed, color or
nationality, who have died
fighting the Anti-Christ

Until the Day Break

UNTIL
THE DAY BREAK

IN THE HOUSE IN THE RUE WASHINGTON SHE SAT
watching d'Abrizzi, and listening with only half
her mind to what he was saying. He sat in a big
chair that was all gilt and mauve brocade and the
squat heaviness of his body and the compressed
swarthiness of his face gave him the look of a toad
comfortably ensconced in Byzantine luxury. He
was a Levantine with the blood of Armenians and
Turks, Italians and Greeks flowing in the coarse
blue veins which rose above the surface of the skin
on the hairy hands. His lips were thick, rather like
half-inflated inner tubes, and the heavy black eye-
brows were joined above the shrewd, pupilless
black eyes. Certainly he was a monster of ugliness,
a grotesque, but the eyes redeemed something of
the ugliness, for they glittered with a light of
extraordinary intelligence, and there were moments when they turned soft and seemed to change
color like the eyes of a hurt deer, and sometimes
they could be kind eyes.

As she listened, wondering what he was leading

I

up to, she thought of him with kindness bordering upon affection. He had done much for her; without him she might be in the gutter now or a nonentity married to a husband in the suburbs who had to rise at dawn to catch a train to the office, or she might even be dead. Then she heard him say, "This morning they sent for me. I had an interview with a Major von Wessellhoft. They insist that we reopen the revue. They want it to seem that their being here has changed nothing. They want the world to get the impression that Paris has accepted them and that the people desire, as he put it, to collaborate."

"What a nerve they have!" she said casually. "Are you going to do it?"

"I haven't much choice in the matter. Either I do as they say or I have to get out, without a penny. I have to give up both theaters and all my property. Everything I have in Paris."

"I must say it's tough on you."

He looked down at his hands for a moment, studying them, as if they were not a part of him, as if he had only now discovered them. It was a trick he had. She knew it but she paid no attention. Then when he noticed that she was absorbed again in the task of putting lacquer on her nails, he looked up and stared at her for a moment. She was aware of the stare but she was used to that too.

Without looking up, she said, "Go on, Léon. What is it? There's something else you want to tell me. Is it about Nicky? Is he dead?" It required an immense effort to say the words. She stopped lacquering the nails and looked up at him, squarely, almost coldly. "I can take it," she said.

"No. It's nothing about Nicky. I haven't heard anything about him. It's about you."

"Me?"

"Yes. The Boches were very insistent that you return to the revue."

"I haven't the slightest intention of returning."

"They pointed out that you were a good star and very popular and well known and beloved in Paris."

"I'm an American. I have an American passport. They can't make me do anything."

"No," he said quietly, "if they try to force the issue, they can't do anything."

She laughed. "Any one of the girls can take off her clothes and walk down a flight of stairs just as well as I can."

D'Abrizzi grinned. "No, they can't or I wouldn't be paying you what I'm paying. They just don't look the same. No French girl does."

He leaned back and lighted a very black cigar. For a moment he kept puffing at it thoughtfully. She knew this trick too. When he wanted something he would take all the time in the world. He would go round and round the point coming in upon it slowly in a spiral fashion. She kept lacquering her nails and heard him saying reflectively, "I'd never thought about that. A French girl when she takes off her clothes in public always turns coy and dirty, and after a while she just gets bored and hardened and is lousy at the job. Every time you come down the stairs in the Alhambra . . . every time in more than ten years . . . it is always like the first time. And you aren't either coy or bored. You walk down them with a kind of magnificence, like a goddess. There's nothing dirty about it any more than there is about the Venus de Milo. Anyway most French girls—European girls, for that matter—haven't got good bodies. There's always something wrong somewhere about them . . . no magnificence."

She laughed and looked up, "Poetic, I call it." She laughed and said, "Come on, Léon. What is it you want?"

They were talking in French, which she spoke now as easily as she spoke English and in much the same direct, picturesque idiom . . . the idiom of Broadway or the Place Clichy; it was in the end the same thing.

He said, "*I* want you to be with the show when we reopen."

"No. I'm going back to America. I'm sick of it and I'm scared."

"Of what? You can take care of yourself."

She put down the lacquer brush and began polishing her nails. Without looking up, she said, "Do you realize I haven't even got a servant in this mausoleum I rented? They all ran away before the Germans came."

"I can find you servants."

"No. And it's fourteen years since I've seen Times Square."

He looked at the end of his cigar. "Is it that long?"

"It's fourteen years since you picked me out of the line at the Ambassadeurs."

He whistled softly.

"I'm thirty-two years old," she said.

"That doesn't matter in Paris. Look at Chevalier. Look at Mistinguette."

"Well, look at them!" Then she stopped polishing and a look of interest came into her deep blue eyes. "Why did you pick me out of twenty-four girls, Léon? I've always wanted to ask you that."

He laughed, "Why am I in show business? Why am I a success? Why have I made a fortune?"

She realized suddenly that outside darkness had come down and that the light must be shining out of the windows. That was against the blackout rules and might make trouble. Luckily the light was on the side of the garden and not the street. Rising, she crossed to the window and unfastened the heavy gold cords which tied back the brocade curtains. She had rented the place from an Argentine who had gone home when his supply of funds had given out. He had furnished it for a Roumanian mistress and everything in it was heavy and lush and over-elegant. The gold cords were like ropes of metal.

The heavy curtains fell together of their own weight and as she returned to her chair she heard him saying, "Paris has meant a lot to you, hasn't it?"

She sat down. "But for Paris," she said, "I'd be in a burlesque house back home or on the street. I haven't got any illusions. I may be the nuts in Paris. Back home I'd be in the third row. There's too much competition there."

He looked again at the end of his cigar. "I'll have to go to New York sometimes. If it's all you say it is, it must be something."

"It is . . . and more, honey."

"But you still like Paris?"

She looked up and a curious light came into her face. "Like Paris . . . I love it! I owe it everything I've got."

"They've been good to you here."

"I'll say so."

"And yet you want to leave it now?"

She looked at him. "If I could be of any use, if I could do any good, I'd stay. I've thought and thought but there isn't anything I can think of. No, I'm going home."

He did not answer her directly. He said after a minute, "One of the reasons I'm staying . . . maybe the principal reason . . . is that I can't imagine living anywhere else. I wouldn't mind losing everything. I'm smart enough to begin all over again somewhere else . . . only I'd be homesick always." He fell to studying the end of his cigar again, and again she knew that he hadn't said yet what he meant to say. But he did say an extraordinary thing. He said, "I was born in Alexandretta. Before I was born, before I ever saw Paris, it was my home. It's that way with a lot of people." The look of kindness and warmth which sometimes redeemed his ugliness came into the black eyes.

She thought for a moment and then answered him, "I see what you mean. It's kind of like that with me."

"And Nicky," he said suddenly.

"What do you mean 'and Nicky'?"

"You're going to walk out and leave him?"

"Yes, Léon, I think it's better that way." And then a change came into her voice. "Anyway I don't know what's become of him. He's probably a prisoner or dead."

At the change in her voice, he looked away from her and presently said, very casually, "I suppose you can dine with me tonight?"

"I haven't anything else to do. What about curfew hours?"

He grinned, "That's taken care of. That's part of a bargain. I have a pass for myself and one for you." He took a wallet out of his jacket and extracted from it a pass, stamped and made out in her name. "All you have to do is paste a passport picture in the blank space. We're entertainers. They need us. They didn't make any objections as neither of us was born French. But don't lose it. Having it is a great advantage. You can go and come as you like."

With astonishment she took the pass from him and examined it. Then she looked at him, "But I'm going back to America just the same."

"It doesn't matter. You can use it till you leave. Where do you want to dine? Some small joint?"

"No, I don't feel like it. I couldn't bear to see Germans sitting around."

"Where shall we go?"

"Some place in Montmartre . . . Luigi's."

"Luigi's is fine. Have you got champagne in the house? We might not be able to get any."

"Yes, but only in the wine cellar."

"Can I get it?"

She stood up. "No, it's not easy to find. I'll go with you." She opened the drawer of the vulgar brass and marquetry table and took out two keys. "The Argentine," she said, "must have had an awful lot of wonderful wine the way he locked it away. There isn't much left now."

When he stood up his bristling black head scarcely came above her shoulders. "Have you ever seen the wine cellar here?" she asked.

"No."

"It's something."

She went before him out of the room and down the curved stairway which led to the hall and the heavy street door below. In the hallway she opened a small door and switched on a light—a single glaring electric bulb at the foot of a worn stone stairway which had the appearance of great age.

Belowstairs the cellar, an immense room, had a vaulted stone ceiling. D'Abrizzi stopped and looked about him. "But this is much older than the house," he said.

"The Argentine said the cellar was part of an old monastery. They just built the house on the top of it."

He took the cigar out of his mouth. "It's plenty old," he said, with sudden awe.

The room was dusty and filled with a clutter of old and broken furniture, packing cases and rubbish. She moved away from him among the columns which supported the roof and after a moment he followed her. She came to a wooden door set in the stone and with one of the keys she unlocked it. When it was swung open, a stone-vaulted gallery appeared dimly. When she switched on another light, the vaulted gallery emerged; it was perhaps forty feet in length and eight feet wide. At the far end there was another door of steel. This too she unlocked.

Inside, beyond the steel door, the rows of bottles lay in wooden racks in the shadows on either side of the gallery. She pointed to a wooden box. "You'd better stand on that," she said, "the Lanson is on the top row."

With the aid of the box, he was just able to reach the rows of bottles she indicated. He treated the two bottles he brought down with reverence. "That should do us," he said.

"I should hope so."

Then they went back again, closing and locking the doors and turning out the lights. The steel door of the inner room swung shut easily, the lock snapping into place.

"He certainly took good care of his wine," said d'Abrizzi. Again on their way back, he stopped in the middle of the cellar and stood for a long time looking about him.

Luigi's was a small restaurant in an impasse a little way from the Place Clichy. Not many foreigners knew of it and very few Parisians save those in the world of the theater. To them it was a kind of haven. In hard times they came there— jugglers from Poland, young girls from Lyons and Lisieux and Dijon who hoped one day to be *vedettes*, Roumanian tumblers, Russian guitarists, "gypsy" violinists—because it was cheap and sometimes, if Luigi himself had no bills to pay, they could eat even when they had no money. The successful ones, the rich ones, came there too sometimes because they remembered the little restaurant with gratitude from the days when they had not been successful, and sometimes they came simply to eat because in all Paris there was no spaghetti and ravioli and minestrone like that made by Luigi's wife, Maria, in the tiny kitchen at the back of the restaurant. Garlic and dried red peppers hung from the ceiling and when the door of the little kitchen opened, the breath of Italy itself came through the door into the restaurant—the breath of faintly resinous red wine and garlic and tomatoes, of olive trees and lemon flowers and sunlight, all compounded into one delicious nostalgic odor that was rich and bright, friendly and warm. It was worth coming a long way simply to sniff that perfume which flowed through the door from Madame Luigi's kitchen.

Madame Luigi, who had the simple name of Maria, was a small, birdlike, brisk woman with very black hair and eyes. Her husband was large and comfortable. Save on the bitterest days of winter, when the damp cold crept up trouser legs from the sidewalk, he never wore a coat but appeared only in trousers and shirt with bright-colored suspenders.

The restaurant itself was a small room with *banquettes* along the wall and iron tables with tops of worn and pitted white marble. On the floor there was freshly dampened sawdust and on the walls between the mirrors there were very bad paintings of scenes from Naples, Capri and Sorrento.

Luigi and Maria were Italian by every drop of blood but they were French citizens because one of them was born in Nice and the other in Ventimiglia just across the border from Italy on the French side of the town.

Roxie had said Luigi's to d'Abrizzi instead of Maxim's for two reasons. One was that Maxim's had seemed to her unthinkable with Germans and Fifth Columnists and rat Fascist French all about, and the other was that in the faraway rue Washington, the scent of Maria's kitchen was in her imagination. For three days, since the German army arrived and her own cook disappeared, she had been living upon pick-ups. She was a healthy woman who worked hard. She was hungry, but she was hungry not only for minestrone and ravioli but also for the warmth and friendliness of Luigi's hole-in-the-wall establishment.

She and d'Abrizzi took the Métro at the rue de Berri and changed at Concorde. She said to d'Abrizzi, "This is the first time I've been in the Métro for at least ten years."

He grinned. "Times change."

There were three German soldiers in the car with them and a sprinkling of French—small French, bookkeepers, and clerks and waitresses and a couple of workingmen in corduroy, the kind who had not run away because they had chosen to guard their few small possessions or because there was no way to get out of Paris or because in a kind of apathy it had seemed foolish for them to run away. It was their apathy which struck d'Abrizzi; it had the curious quality of the defeated who, without resentment or ambition, have accepted their tiny monotonous role in life. They

were little white-collar people—all but the two
workmen who seemed more tough; you could find
them the world over in any city, the dross, the
waste of cities and industrial life. They looked
undernourished and pallid and discouraged.

"It was the same kind in Germany," thought
d'Abrizzi with detachment, "who gave Hitler his
start. He made them believe there was a chance
for them. And he knew all the time there wasn't
a chance and when he got ready he double-crossed
them. He was one of them but he was smarter
than the others."

The three German soldiers seemed ill at ease.
One was tall and thin and red-haired and wore
gold-rimmed glasses through which he peered at a
guidebook. One was heavy and blond and stolid
and the third was the small scrawny type of German which no amount of beer and sausage will
ever feed into plumpness. Their gray uniforms,
bordered and tipped with green, fitted them badly
and although they were quite young, they were
misshapen and extraordinarily ugly.

"Cannon fodder," thought d'Abrizzi. "The
more intelligent ones they give better jobs."

One had the impression that the young Germans were quite bewildered by Métros, by Paris,
by the whole extraordinary chain of events which
had hurled them out of the villages and slums in

which they were born, through battle into the white beauty of this strange city which they could not understand because nothing of their blood had contributed to its creation, because it was so utterly, completely foreign. They seemed self-conscious and ill at ease, squirming a little on the hard seats, as if they suffered bad consciences.

"The Germans as a race," thought d'Abrizzi, relishing the satisfaction he got from the thought, "are an extremely ugly race. Very often they are grotesque. They are so often out of scale, out of proportion." In the pleasure of the moment his own grotesque ugliness did not occur to him, perhaps because long ago he had come to accept it.

He was aware of the glimmer of interest that lightened the resigned faces of the others in the car at the sight of his companion. Roxie was a beautiful woman, admirably dressed in expensive clothes. He knew what they were thinking—that of course Roxie must be his mistress, that of course he gave her a great deal of money because he himself was so ugly, and he felt a sudden gust of obscene and perverse pleasure partly because they were wrong and partly because their thoughts made him important in a new and different fashion.

Beside him Roxie looked at the newspaper he had bought her at the rue de Berri station, but her mind was not on what she read. Nothing in the paper seemed important. What was important, what claimed possession of her was the heavy sense of apathy and defeat in the car which carried them. *Parisiens*, even the dreary ones, were rarely like this. It was as if a light had gone out.

"No," she thought, "I can't bear it. I can't stay here. It's all over. There is nothing I can do to change it." And she felt a sickness deep inside her.

The train stopped at La Trinité and the three German soldiers got out. She watched them rise and shuffle toward the door, the one with the glasses still holding the guidebook, and she thought, like d'Abrizzi, "How ugly they are!" It was not like the ugliness of d'Abrizzi himself for that ugliness was illuminated by a kind of inward incandescence; it was ugliness which was alive. This shuffling unilluminated ugliness was heavy and loutish, the kind of ugliness one never found south of the Rhine. Yet as they disappeared, the door banging closed behind them, she was suddenly sorry for them. They seemed so young and lost and timid and stupid.

It struck her as odd that d'Abrizzi, with the champagne under his arm, did not talk at all. Usually he talked and talked. Now he only sat watching the others in the car.

In the Place Clichy it was very dark and for a moment they had to stand quite still until their eyes grew accustomed to the darkness and they regained their sense of direction. It was odd how in darkness you could lose yourself in a spot so familiar as the Place Clichy. She had crossed it many thousand times going to and from the theater. Instinctively she looked toward the Alhambra but it was dark like the rest of the square and the streets leading from it. There were no lights spelling out the words, *"Paris en Folie"* with her own name and the names of the other stars. *"Paris en Folie!"* The name echoed for a second in her brain as she stood there in the darkness. That was it! *"Paris en Folie!"* a bitter true ironical name now. That was it! She had never thought of it before. *"France en Folie!" "L'Europe en Folie!"* Folie in English meant not only folly but madness.

Then out of the darkness at her side came d'Abrizzi's velvety voice, *"Viens petite!"* and following him she walked toward the impasse where Luigi's hold in the wall hid away in the same blackness.

Just outside the door they very nearly collided with a big fat woman leading a little dog on a leash. The little dog yapped at them out of the darkness. Then she heard d'Abrizzi laugh and his voice saying, *"Ah, c'est toi, Filomena!"* and she knew that it was Luigi's older sister, a massive widow of fifty who helped in the kitchen.

"*Qu'est-ce que tu fais?*" Léon asked. And out of the darkness came Filomena's coarse hearty voice, "*Je fais pisser mon chien et je me cherche un Boche. On dit qu'ils aiment les gros types comme moi.*" Her hearty laugh filled the little street for a moment, almost shocking in the stillness, and a sad curious thought came to Roxie, "No, I can't leave it. I can't go where I will never again hear things like that."

But almost at once she thought too, "That's silly. The thing for me is to go."

Then Filomena, recognizing her, cried out with vast warmth, "*Ah, c'est toi, Mademoiselle! La Grande Vedette.*" Her French carried the rich Latin roll of the Côte d'Azur, which seems to echo back inside the mouth. "I thought you had run away. You—an American had no reason to stay."

"No," said Roxie, "I'm still here."

Curiously she could think of nothing more to say. It was as if Filomena had reproached her for the thoughts inside her head. The reproach was all the worse because Filomena had uttered it without meaning it as a reproach, honestly. It seemed to Filomena that to go away was the course dictated by common sense and therefore commendable.

The little dog began to bark again savagely into the darkness and Filomena, chortling, said, "*Voilà, mon Boche! Le petit veut que je me promène.*" In the darkness, she waved a big hand. Neither Léon nor Roxie saw it actually, but they knew she had waved to them with an expansive gesture. "*Bon appetit!*"

"*Merci.*"

Filomena in tow of the barking little dog vanished into the thick darkness and Léon opened the door of Luigi's.

Inside there was less light than usual but enough to distinguish the figures and faces of seven patrons. Four of them sat at one table, two at another and the seventh, a woman with a raddled face, a red wig beneath a hat covered with plumes and talon-like fingers covered with stage jewelry, sat alone in the corner. She was drinking Pernod and reading *Comœdia*. As Léon and Roxie came in the door, she looked up and Léon said, "*Bon soir*, Margot."

The painted lined face with the liquid powder congealed in the wrinkles, cracked into a grin of recognition. There was something curious in the grin—the reflection, the echo of some concealed, half-forgotten glory and magnificence. When she spoke her voice was like that of a bull frog on a warm spring night, hoarse but warm with vitality and ardor and sex. Long ago as a beauty, she was known as La Biche—the Doe—because of her great lustrous eyes. Léon could remember. His voice had turned kind. There was a warm beauty in it which, like his eyes, unexpectedly redeemed his ugliness.

She said, "*Bon soir . . . et vous, Mademoiselle.* Is the Alhambra going to reopen?"

"I don't know," said Léon. "That depends."

"And my job? I can still dance. I can still wear clothes and take them off too." She chortled wickedly, "*Nom de Dieu!* What has come into our world?"

"I'd take you on at once but for the jealousy of the other girls. It would make too much trouble for me."

She chuckled, aware dimly that this was a joke but aware too with a remote part of her befuddled intelligence that she was old and finished and raddled, that of everything there only remained an indestructible constitution and vitality.

She leaned toward them. "You know," she said, "a Boche made me a proposition." Then she winked. "The military governor himself, General Stulpnagel." She used the name, fresh out of the columns of *Comœdia.*

"I'd accept it," said Léon. "You're not as young as you once were."

Again she chortled. "You aren't any younger yourself, Léon. Look at that belly."

Then the door from the kitchen opened and

Luigi himself came into the restaurant, borne on a cloud of the heavenly odor that was the smell of Maria's tiny kitchen. He came toward Léon and Roxie, his broad face glowing with a kind of over-strained cordiality.

"I thought you had both gone away with the others," he said. "*Quel plaisir!*"

"No," said Léon. "We had business here."

"A lot of them did run away," said Luigi. "The faithful stayed."

He pulled back two chairs at a table between La Biche and the table with four people seated at it.

"I'm glad you stuck it," he said. And then he made a curious remark: "Those of us who remain give Paris dignity. All the politicians have scrammed except the traitors."

They sat down and Léon handed him the champagne. "It's champagne. Have you got any ice?"

"No ice, but Maria will make it cold as possible. You'll want Chianti with the dinner?"

"Yes," said Léon. "The champagne afterward."

At the next table the four occupants, three men and a tired untidy woman, were speaking a foreign tongue, strange to Roxie. She looked toward them and Léon said, "They are speaking Roumanian."

"Yes," said Luigi. "They are acrobats . . .

refugees without papers." Then he said, "I'll call Maria." And went to the door of the kitchen.

She came in, small, preoccupied, worried, wiping her hands on her apron. At sight of them a smile like a sunrise illumined the dark leathery face.

"What a surprise!" she said. "What a wonderful surprise! You stayed too . . . how wonderful, how dignified!"

Her reverberating accent was even stronger than that of her husband or Filomena. Roxie smiled, a smile which came from deep inside her, spontaneous and unsummoned. She felt a sudden unexpected pride at the praise of Maria. She had, it seemed, done the proper thing—staying behind when most of the others fled—without thinking very much about it.

"After the war," said Luigi, "there will be a society of us—the survivors, the *costauds*, the tough ones who stayed behind to face it."

"And what do you want to eat?" asked Maria.

"It is for Mademoiselle to decide," said Léon, looking at Roxie.

She planned the meal—antipasto, minestrone, ravioli with spinach and a salad of lettuce with bread crusts impregnated with garlic, a good rich full meal. She liked to eat well and plenty.

"That sounds good," said Léon. Then he looked

suddenly at the table where the two men were
seated. One of them was very Jewish in appearance. They were speaking German, the thick,
heavy German of Silesia. Léon beckoned for Luigi
to lean nearer to him. Then he asked, "What are
they?"

"Refugees," said Luigi. "No papers. One came
in two days ago from a camp in the south."

Léon studied them for a moment. Then he
turned to Luigi and, grinning, said, "What do you
run here—a concentration camp?"

Luigi grinned and shrugged his shoulders, "What
do *you* think? They came to France believing they
would be safe. We promised them that."

Roxie looked at him sharply, astonished by two
things—that Luigi who was not really French
should feel that France owed these shabby people
an obligation, the other that he should be so simple
and frank when such information could cause him
fine, imprisonment and perhaps worse. True, he
had known them both for a long time, for many
years. In that time he must have judged them and
decided that they were decent and all right. Again
the warm feeling of pride and satisfaction came
over her.

Then she heard Léon asking, "Those other people. Have they eaten well?"

"They've eaten, but not well."

"Ask them if they'd like the same as we're having?"

Luigi grinned because this was the kind of thing he liked. As he crossed to the table of the acrobats, Léon turned to the old woman with the red wig.

"Hey, Biche! What about eating?"

La Biche again turned on them the battered incandescence of her grin. "Sure," she said, "I can eat any hour of the day or night."

The acrobats and the two men at the other table were looking toward them now and Roxie noticed that the man who sat with the Jew had a deformed face. It was as if a part of his jaw had been broken and removed. He was smiling but one could only recognize the smile by the eyes. The effort only contorted the grotesquely shattered face, but the eyes gleamed with gratitude. It was the eyes of all of them that were remarkable. There was something soft in them and frightened and defeated, all save the untidy *"allay-oop"* woman on the team of acrobats. There was pride in her eyes and vengeance. She was perhaps thirty-five or six, handsome in the way of dark Slavs. Very likely she was much younger than she appeared to be.

In a low voice she said in bad French, "We thank you very much, Monsieur. We have eaten but we are hungry. When one has been hungry and afraid for a long time, it is like that. One stays hungry. One stokes up when one has the opportunity." She spoke simply with remarkable dignity. When she had spoken she returned at once to the intimacy of her own group.

Roxie said, "It's lucky we brought two bottles of champagne."

When the food came, La Biche did not attempt to force her company upon them. She pushed aside her newspaper and absinthe and began her second meal with enthusiasm.

The others ate hungrily. It was as the woman acrobat had said; when one is hungry for a long time, one stays hungry. There was too, said d'Abrizzi, watching them, the knowledge that this meal might have to last them a long time.

"I have been hungry myself," he said. "I have been hunted too . . . by the Turks in the old days. They killed my father and carried off my mother."

He spoke quite calmly between mouthfuls of ravioli and his very calmness made Roxie suddenly embarrassed. It was as if she felt the need of apologizing because, as an American, nothing very terrible had ever happened to her. She had been hungry sometimes. She had made compromises with men. Her stepfather had been cruel to her long ago in Indiana until she had run away; but these things were nothing. It was as if the dull misery of these others in the room was a reproach. It was a very long story—the misery of Europe, a long story always returning to the same theme, always astonishing her anew.

The ravioli was as good as it always was. The Chianti was just right, faintly resinous and slightly vinegary. For the first time in days, since the day the gray columns came up the Champs Elysées, she was feeling well again. The sensation of apathy began to leave her.

She laughed and said, "By the time we're through with the champagne we'll be a mass of acidity."

Luigi came and sat with them for a time talking about what was to come. No one knew anything. The English would give in. The English wouldn't give in. The Americans were going to help. The Americans were not going to help. Laval was up to dirty work. They had shot Daladier and Léon Blum. They had not shot Daladier and Léon Blum. The Germans were being very correct. The Germans had lined up and shot a lot of students.

In the end Luigi shrugged his shoulders and said, "What is one to believe?"

D'Abrizzi said, "Don't believe anything now. Wait."

La Biche in her corner began suddenly to sing and at the sound, one of the acrobats, a dark man with sad eyes and a mole on his chin, suddenly produced a concertina and feeling his way into the proper key began to accompany her. It was an old song, a very old song, she was singing in her cracked voice, "*Savez-vous planter les choux?*" She was suddenly quite drunk and sang in a croaking voice. At the encouraging sound of the concertina's approval, she began to sing with real gusto using the old-fashioned gestures of the music halls of fifty years earlier. The fake jewelry on her fingers sparkled and glittered. The Jew and his companion turned to listen, curiously but without mockery. The acrobats, being of the profession, understood that La Biche too was a professional. They did not laugh at her—at the glittering bogus jewelry, the raddled face, the nodding plumes of her battered hat. Luigi watched her, smiling with the peculiar paternal feeling which good Italians have for those who are "touched." It was as if he said, "There but for the grace of God go I."

D'Abrizzi leaned across toward the acrobats and said in a low voice, "You know, she was a famous performer once—a star. Her name was Yvette. They called her La Biche."

The performance of La Biche both fascinated and terrified Roxie. She thought, "She was like me once. What if that happens to me? I am almost thirty-three. I already have to think of my figure." And with a sudden start she realized that she had been thinking in French. To herself she was saying, *"Elle était comme moi dans le temps. Si cela m'arrive? J'ai déjà trente-trois ans. Déjà il faut que je me méfie de ma taille."* She was not only thinking in French, she was thinking in the French of the *coulisses*, of the Alhambra and the Place Clichy . . . as if this were her home, as if long ago Indiana and Broadway had faded out of her existence. And suddenly she thought, "But it is true. They have been good to me. All the success I've ever had is here. In a way it is my home."

"Savez-vous planter les choux?" came the hoarse voice of La Biche like a reproach, and then suddenly La Biche was out of breath. She pressed her dirty bejeweled hand against her enormous bosom and began to laugh wild, drunken hysterical laughter. The music of the concertina died away in a slow wheeze and La Biche said, "Ah, General Boulanger loved to hear me sing that. I was only seventeen." She hiccoughed and added soberly, "It was women who ruined General Boulanger but he was a very handsome man."

"Bring the champagne," said d'Abrizzi. And as Luigi rose, d'Abrizzi asked, "Where's Filomena? She must have found her Boche."

Luigi smiled mysteriously and said, "Filomena's doing patrol duty."

Maria came in from the kitchen and nervously

carried away the plates in a huge tray. Luigi returned with the two bottles and glasses for all and as he put the bottles on the table the street door opened, admitted Filomena and the little dog, and was closed immediately.

"They're coming," she said. And Luigi, whisking the extra glasses on to the shelf above their heads, said to the Jew and his companion and the acrobats, "Go into the kitchen. My wife will tell you where to go." They did not appear terrified. They rose with indifference, as if this sort of thing had long since become a habit, and filed out through the door into the kitchen. Quickly Luigi crossed to La Biche. "Don't say anything. *Compris?*"

She looked at him dully and then slowly the light of understanding came into her face. "You can count on me. I wouldn't help the bastards." With an effort she sat up and pulled her hat straight on her head. In some fantastic way by this single gesture she acquired grandeur.

To d'Abrizzi and Roxie he said, "Just answer what they ask you . . . only the others," he made a gesture in the direction of the kitchen door, "they weren't here. They don't exist. See?"

At the same moment the door opened and in the doorway appeared a German officer, a sergeant and a little French policeman. The policeman had dark hair, blue eyes and pink cheeks. The officer was very stiff and straight with an expressionless face. The sergeant was a heavy pink-faced man with hands like sausages. Beside them the little policeman seemed all grace and line like a dancer.

Luigi put down the champagne bottle and said, "Good evening, Messieurs." There was dignity in his manner and even a little condescension.

The little policeman was embarrassed and behaved like a bad actor. He was giving a performance because inside him there was a deep hurt and shame. He said that they had come to check the papers of the people in the place. They were making the rounds of all restaurants and cafés. There was such confusion the last few days with many dangerous characters at liberty. As he spoke he grew more and more miserable. The blue eyes said, "I don't want to do this, but what can I do?"

Luigi summoned Maria and Filomena and they came out of the kitchen leaving the door open to show there was no one there. The two Germans and the policeman turned first to La Biche. She had opened the enormous shabby handbag she carried and taken out her *carte d'identité*. As they came up to her she laid it on the table and pushed it toward them, withdrawing her hand in a dramatic and insulting gesture as if she wished to have no contact whatever with them. There was in the gesture a grotesque splendor, a travesty of the splendor of *Phèdre*.

The little policeman grinned and said, "She's all right. She's a character here. Everybody knows her." He made a brief gesture to indicate that she had wheels in her head.

This she took as a compliment and said, "Know La Biche? Of course everyone knows me."

The officer glanced at the identity card, clicked his heels, bowed and returned it to her. She did not touch it until he had turned away. Then with the tips of her fingers she picked it up and dropped it into the vast moth-eaten handbag as if in some way it had been contaminated.

Luigi, Maria and Filomena dutifully held out their cards. The policeman said, "These are good people. They are citizens."

The officer looked at the three of them and then back at the photographs on the cards. The gigantic Filomena, with a perfectly straight face, said, "Yes, Monsieur—the photograph is of me. I am, of course, much handsomer. The photographer caught none of my beauty!"

The officer looked at her as if he did not know whether or not she was mocking him. From her face it was impossible to tell. Then he turned to d'Abrizzi and Roxie and at sight of their special passes, his manner changed. He bowed more deeply and clicked his heels a little more loudly. His whole manner said, "Ah, these are different! They must be rich and important. At any rate they have some connection with the big bugs."

The little policeman echoed his thoughts in speech. He said, "These are important people. Monsieur d'Abrizzi is owner of the Alhambra Theatre and Mademoiselle is a famous actress. She is an American star."

"I see she is American. It says so on the card." Something seemed to puzzle the officer, perhaps that he should find important people in so small and humble a place. Things like that rarely happened in Germany.

D'Abrizzi said, "Mademoiselle has not had time to paste on her photograph. As you see the pass was only issued this afternoon."

The officer stared at her for a moment. Then he said, "Yes, I see. I am delighted to make your acquaintance, Mademoiselle. I have seen pictures of you in the German papers . . . many pictures. My compliments."

"*Merci*, Monsieur."

He did not go away at once. He gave back the passes and then stood awkwardly looking at Roxie with a kind of unashamed admiration. At last he said, "I hope I shall have the pleasure of seeing you perform."

It was d'Abrizzi who answered, "Yes, of course. She is opening soon in a new revue."

She smiled at the officer, why she did not know, except that it had long since become a kind of professional habit and because she felt d'Abrizzi's compulsion. It was as if he willed her to smile.

Then the officer clicked his heels once more and turning to Luigi he said, "Remember, everybody out and lights out at eleven. That is the Governor's order."

The three of them went out and Luigi followed, locking the door behind them. "They won't come back again," he said. And turning to Filomena added, "Bring the others up out of the coal cellar."

As she and Maria left the room, La Biche pulled herself together. "Shameful!" she said. "The dirty Boches!"

D'Abrizzi shrugged his shoulders. "It is only the beginning, honey. We'll have to put up with it; on the surface at least." Then a sudden rage appeared to seize him and he cried out savagely, "It stinks— it all stinks. To smell Germans in Paris—in Paris of all the cities in the world."

Filomena reappeared followed by the acrobats and the Jew and the man with the shattered jaw. At sight of them Luigi turned suddenly cheerful. "The pigs have gone," he said. "Now for the champagne."

He got down the glasses and filled them and then putting down the bottle he raised his glass and said, "To the day when no Boche will dare show his face in our beloved Paris!" He spoke wildly, nobly, with all the Italian flare for operatics, like Tamagno in a florid scene.

La Biche raised her glass. The old hands shook so that the champagne dripped on the untidy expanse of her vast bosom, "*A bas les Boches!*" she croaked.

The rue Washington is one of the few streets of Paris with little character; it is neither beautiful and splendid, nor narrow, nor dark and picturesque. It runs off the wide, now somewhat shabby splendor of the Champs Elysées in the very heart of Napoleon's Paris, only a little way from the Arc de Triomphe, a simple street of second-rate apartments with houses dating from the Second Empire squeezed between them, houses like the more important homes of a French village rather than Paris, which turn their backs upon the street and show the glories of their façades to the walled gardens beyond. The gardens are remarkable in the very heart of Paris, large gardens with terraces and chestnut trees and lilacs. From the street one is unaware of them; one sees only the façades of houses without character save for the large wooden doors which once swung open to admit carriages. It is a long time since carriages have passed through the great doors; the tenants use only the small doors set in the big ones; one has to step high over the threshold to enter.

It was one of these houses Roxie had rented from the Argentine. She took it not because it was charming or especially beautiful; its Second Empire charm and beauty had long since disappeared beneath the decorative efforts of a succession of rich foreigners and kept women, for it was an ideal hideaway. No one who was anyone ever lived in the rue Washington; it was a forgotten area in which even the police found nothing of interest. Roxie took it because it was cheap and convenient and comfortable in an over-luxurious fashion, and because of Nicky. Except for the weathered soot-covered house on the wrong side of the railway tracks in Evanston, Indiana, she had never had any home and she had no instinct for one. Home to her was any boardinghouse or hotel where she put down her trunk. In Paris she had lived nearly always at the Claridge. The rue Washington was only a little way off; she was not even forced to change the neighborhood. It was a neighborhood she liked with its cafés and tourists and foreigners and Fouquet's only a little way off with its good food and its changing spectacle of actresses and racing people, and kept women and bookmakers and expensive pimps. In the end it was Nicky who made the house in the rue Washington desirable. When she took up with Nicky a hotel was no longer desirable.

When they left Luigi's in time for the last Métro, big Filomena went out with them into the street and walked as far as the Place Clichy with the little dog. In the darkness figures passed them; they were all German soldiers, clumping along on their way back to quarters from cafés and cinemas. A warm, voluptuous fog had settled over the city and the Germans appeared out of it and disappeared into it like ghosts.

At the entrance to the Métro Filomena in her deep, rich voice said, "Good night and come back again soon." Then she turned to Roxie and said, "You will not go back to America."

"Yes," said Roxie, "I am tired. I mean to go back."

"No," said Filomena, "you will not go back."

She felt suddenly bored, too bored to argue with the big Italian woman. In any case it did not matter now, not with those gray ghosts coming out of the haze and pushing past her into the Métro.

They left Filomena and went down the stairs in silence. The train was filled with German soldiers, most of them like the three they had encountered earlier in the evening, dull, youngish, heavy. They stared dully, like cattle, at her and d'Abrizzi. There was a kind of hunger in their eyes. Watching them Roxie again felt a curious detached pity for them because they seemed so loutish and bewildered, so completely lost and homesick in Paris . . . where no one should ever be homesick. Once she turned toward d'Abrizzi to speak, but the sight of him checked her. He was sitting hunched up in his corner staring at the soldiers. In his ugliness he looked like a malignant spider. All kindness, all warmth had gone out of the pupilless black eyes; there was only hatred in them, so bitter, so hard that the eyes appeared to glitter. It was a d'Abrizzi she had never seen before. She had seen him angry and vengeful and jealous and full of contempt but never like this. There was something shocking in the spectacle.

She did not speak to him until they changed at Concorde for the Porte de Lilas line, and then only to ask, "Do you feel all right?"

"All right," he answered.

At the rue de Berri a sergeant accompanied by a policeman stepped out of the fog and asked them to show their papers. The policeman was apologetic like the little policeman at Luigi's and said to the sergeant, "It is all right. She is a well-known actress. Everybody knows her." The German stared at her and gave them back their papers. Roxie felt a sudden pleasure. It was nice to be so well known; it gave you a kind of protection wherever you went.

All the way along the Champs Elysées and into the rue Washington, d'Abrizzi was still silent. Once in the rue Washington he stopped and looked both directions in the dark street. She asked, "What's the matter?" to which he replied, "Nothing. I was just working out something." It was, she knew from long experience, no good trying to discover what was going on in Léon's head if he chose not to reveal it.

At the door she took the key out of her handbag and said, "You can't walk all the way home. I'll give you a pair of Nicky's pajamas."

"I don't need them," he said. "They wouldn't fit anyway."

They stepped inside and as she switched on the light in the big fake Venetian lantern, he said, "It's idiotic for you to stay in this house alone with all your jewelry and furs."

"I hadn't thought much about it. I've never been the scared kind. I keep a revolver under my pillow."

They went up the stairs and she asked, "Do you want more champagne or some *pâté*?"

"No. I overate at Luigi's."

She went into her room and brought out a dressing gown that belonged to Nicky. It was expensive and handsome, heavy black silk with red silk lapels and tassels, from Charvets. The touch of it made her feel suddenly cold and a little sick, because she did not know where Nicky was or even whether he was alive. He might never use it again.

As she gave it to Léon she said, "I sleep late. If you want coffee before I wake, knock on the door and I'll get up and make it."

"I'll want to sleep late myself," said d'Abrizzi. "I haven't slept much since that first day they came in."

She held open the door of a room that opened into the salon with the heavy curtains and the metallic gold cords. "I think there's everything you need. Good night, Léon."

He stopped in the doorway, started to speak and then checked himself.

"What were you going to say?" she asked.

"Nothing. It isn't ready to be said yet. It isn't born yet. In the morning perhaps."

"Okay. Try to sleep."

"Thanks. Same to you."

He spoke in an absent-minded fashion. The

thing was still going on in his brain. Suddenly she found herself making an extraordinary statement. "I don't think I've ever said it to you, Léon, but if anything should ever happen that we shouldn't see each other again, I want you to know I'm grateful for all you've done for me. Except for you, I'd still be just a lousy chorus girl. Just a punk!"

He looked at her with soft shyness in his eyes. "Thanks, honey. I get what you mean. You've always been on the level too."

"I guess it's because we know most of the answers."

He laughed, "I guess that's it." Then his voice changed a shade. "Maybe we'll need to know them more than ever now."

Then with Nicky's dressing gown over his arm, he went out of the room and closed the door, leaving her standing there, faintly bewildered and filled with affection and pity for his ugliness. No woman could ever love him. Whatever travesty of love he had known he had been forced to buy, one way or another. With her he had always been on the level. Never once in all their association had he ever bothered her, or so much as touched her.

Thoughtfully she put out the light and went into her own room. It had been the room of the Argentine's mistress and she had not troubled to change it, feeling that it was like any hotel bedroom. The bed was gilded with a canopy of peach-colored satin rising to a crown of gigantic white ostrich plumes. The furniture was all gilded and the curtains were of the same peach-colored satin as the canopy. One whole end of the room was mirrored. On the dressing table among the gold toilet articles stood the photograph of a man. He was very dark and handsome in a reckless, virile, half-savage fashion, with high cheekbones, intense dark eyes, a sensual mouth and a proud nose. Across the face of it was written in English "All my love forever to Roxie—Nicky." The inscription was a gay cynical denial of everything that was written in the face, for it was the face of a man who would never be able to give all his love to anyone or anything because there were too many things in the world to be loved.

She was aware now for the first time of weariness. It was as if the evening with Léon and the excursion to Luigi's had restored for a moment something of the old world that had been shattered by the confusion of that awful afternoon when she had seen the streets filled with trucks and gray-green uniforms that were an obscenity against the gray white of the Paris streets. The strain was gone now and with it the curious apathy which had alternated with fits of the only real fear she had ever experienced, a fear which was all the worse because it was formless and unanswerable.

She undressed slowly and when she had taken off all her clothing, she stood for a moment regarding her naked reflection in the mirror. As if she sought somehow to punish herself, she tried to find some flaw, some sign of fading or age; but there was none. Her body was firm and young, like the body of a young girl, a little more rounded perhaps but because of that all the more beautiful. God had given her beauty, a lavish beauty of body and face, and she was grateful to God for his favor to the daughter of a father she had never seen and a mother born in Poland. She had always been proud of that beauty in an odd fashion as if it did not really belong to her but was something which she should share, out of gratitude, as one might share the beauty of a work of art. And so she had never had any special modesty. When Léon, that night at the Ambassadeurs long ago, had offered to feature her as an American novelty—a fan dancer —she had no qualms. She accepted.

She was lucky, she knew. Her whole career had been built upon the beauty of this body and the shrewd exploitation of Léon. She was good as long as the body lasted. "A stripper," she thought, "is just as good as her figure. When it goes she goes with it." In Paris they had been very kind. They had never grown tired of her. On the contrary, they grew fond of her and faithful, loving her a little more each year so that she had become a fixture, a necessity at the Léon's Alhambra. Paris was like that, very different from New York where people grew tired of stars and forgot them easily.

Suddenly for the first time in her life she thought of the future. Until now it had never been necessary; it was as if things, mostly lucky things, had simply happened to her. . . . That dimly remembered elopement with a traveling salesman from Evanston, her first job in a night club, Old Stokes who had paid for her dancing lessons and wanted nothing of her but to be seen about with her, because he had once been a famous lady killer and wanted to keep the reputation of his prowess alive before the world; and then the chance to come to Paris with a troupe of Albertina Rasch girls and then the curious chance which made Léon pick her from sixteen girls dancing on the floor of the Ambassadeurs. And after that the fact that she had what Paris wanted, and last of all Nicky. And she did not know whether Nicky was good luck or bad. She only knew that he was the first and only man with whom she had ever been even remotely in love.

Before she switched off the lights and went to bed, she put her shining red-gold hair into *bigourdis* and took down from the empty book shelves a pile of magazines in French and English, devoted to astrology. For a long time she went through them, searching for something, some sign, some reassurance, regarding the future, exactly what she did not know. In the end she took from the drawer a chart made for her by Madame de Thonars in the square Chaussée D'Antin. Studying it she came again for the tenth time upon the prediction that the period into which she was entering would be one of change, excitement and probably suffering—all of which meant nothing to her. It might mean only the uncomfortable fact of the Germans' presence in Paris, the closing of the theater, the lack of all knowledge concerning Nicky, the desertion by the servants. Or it might mean something more terrible, something which she could escape by fleeing to America. But the chart said nothing whatever concerning any voyage, even a short one.

Despite the deep sense of weariness and nervous exhaustion, she was not able to sleep. In the darkness, faintly scented by the odor of expensive perfume, she lay awake, tormented and driven in a nightmare of emptiness, by a thousand thoughts, memories and fears.

The fear—that nameless inexplicable sense of contagious panic which had seized her when the first news came that France was falling and that the Germans were on their way to Paris was long since gone. For three days before they arrived, people had been quitting Paris—Jews, millionaires, concierges, shopkeepers, working men and their families. It was as if a plague of terror, horribly contagious, had swept over the whole city, picking its victims like the plague, at random, stealing away the sanity and common sense of people of every station in life. They had fled by train, by automobile, by delivery truck, by bicycle, on foot with children and household belongings pushed ahead in a perambulator. On the third day, as the city turned sad and empty and still like a body drained of all blood, the panic had finally seized her when she returned to the house to find that the cook and the chambermaid had both vanished with all their belongings. She had gone to their rooms to find them stripped and bare. In the kitchen a meal, half-prepared, cluttered the narrow tables. The sight of the bare rooms and the evidence of panic in the kitchen made her aware suddenly of her own *aloneness*, in the house, in Paris, in the whole world. Then there followed a strange inter-

lude of which, curiously, she could remember nothing at all. She only knew that she had awakened
from it by suddenly catching the reflection of her
own face in the mirror at the end of the room,
a face which so terrified her that the sight of it
shocked her into an awareness of her surroundings
and what she was doing.

There, on the bed beside her was a handbag already packed, beside it a jewel case and two coats,
one of mink and one of ermine. She had not considered how she would flee nor where. There had
been simply a moment of atavistic panic, compounded of many vague confused fears of fire and
rape and torture and death at the hands of invaders. When clarity returned she sat down, facing her reflection in the mirror, thinking, "You
are a fool! All you have in the world is here in
Paris! Nothing can happen to you! You are an
American with an American passport, born in
Evanston, Indiana! You have always taken care of
yourself since you were a child, because you had
to. Nothing can happen!"

Then quite calmly she had unpacked and putting
on a hat and jacket had gone out into the gray
empty streets to walk round the corner to the
Claridge. The hotel was empty. The concierge
remained and a man at the desk and four or five
men and two women who looked as if they had

been expecting the Germans all day long and were delighted that they were at last arriving. There had always been a great many Germans at the Claridge. Thyssen himself had always stayed there.

The man at the desk was glad to see her again. Oddly enough they never mentioned the approach of the Germans. She asked for a room on the Champs Elysées side and the concierge took her up to it. But never once did they speak of the Germans.

There in the window of the room she waited.

It was a gray afternoon with the sky overcast by clouds which shut out the sun and dimmed the gaiety of everything that was Paris. The long expanse of the Champs Elysées lay nearly empty, the shutters and doorways closed. Now and then someone passed on the sidewalk. The Métro no longer ran and no one entered or left the gaping station entrances. From her window she could see the decapitated turret of the Astoria Hotel and remembered the old story that the Astoria was built by German money with a turret and balcony overlooking the Arc de Triomphe from which the Kaiser had meant to review his troops as they marched beneath the arc. After *that* war they had cut down the turret and destroyed the balcony but that had not stopped the Germans from coming in twenty-five years later.

They would be coming now, at any moment, up the long vista from the Place de la Concorde to the Arc de Triomphe. She was here now alone —Roxie Dawn, born Irma Peters of Evanston, Indiana, in the embrasure of a high window in the Claridge Hotel waiting for the Germans to arrive. She was here because this was something one did not see every day—the death of Paris, the entry of a conquering army. She was dimly aware that this was one of the great occasions of history but she thought of it as a sight which she would be able to describe, a story which she would be able to tell for the rest of her life, as long as she lived. She could say, "I was there. I saw it. I did not run away." She could tell it if ever she went back to America.

In the soberness of the moment, all alone in the strange hotel room, thoughts occurred to her which had never occurred before in all her restless life, thoughts tinged by philosophical intimations, strange to her and born of the moment. How odd it was that she should be here alone at this moment, no longer afraid for herself but worried and afraid for a Russian whom she loved, whose life was even stranger and more disordered than her own. And this business of the stars and their effect upon her life; certainly there must be something in it, for whatever had happened to her throughout her whole life had been unplanned. It had happened, without reflection, without thought.

And then she heard music, distantly, from the far end of the great avenue, breaking obscenely the frightening unnatural stillness. There was no place for music in this empty gray city. Slowly the music took form as *"Deutschland, Deutschland, Über Alles"* and she felt suddenly sick and held more tightly to the brocade curtains. And after a little while she could, by leaning out, see the muzzle of the advancing column of mechanized troops coming slowly up the avenue between the chestnut and plane trees. Then a curious thing happened to her. She thought, "I don't want to see it. It is too awful—I cannot look!" And drawing the curtains across the window she went over to the bed and lay down.

But the curtains did not shut out the sounds. The music of the band died away and in its place came the throbbing, clanking sound of the trucks, and then just opposite the hotel the band blared out again, this time in the strains of the song written by the pimp Horst Wessell. She put her hands over her ears but the sound still came through the drawn curtains into the darkened room.

When it was over, she waited for a long time before going down to the street. It was nearly dark and there were already German officers in the great hall of the Claridge and German soldiers on the streets. Quickly with her hat pulled over her eyes, the collar of her jacket high up to hide her face, she made her way back to the rue Washington and the empty house of the Argentine. It was like the end of the world and she knew suddenly that she really loved Nicky who by now must be a prisoner or dead.

He had gone as a volunteer, since although he was born in Russian Georgia, he had no nationality whatever except that given him by the League of Nations passport. Once when she said to him, "Why do you go?" he said with sudden serious-ness, "When we were chased out of Russia, France took us in. Paris is the only home I've ever known since I was fourteen years old. I shouldn't want to see Germans in Paris . . . never Germans."

Now and then, rarely, he had turned serious and for a moment she would have a glimpse deep inside him, into another Nicky that was secret and hidden away. She had asked, "Why do you hate the Germans so much?" He looked at her sharply, "Because I have lived among them." Remember-ing the speech brought to mind the sudden furious hatred in the eyes of d'Abrizzi as he sat staring at the young German soldiers in the Métro. When she said, "Why are the Germans worse than other people?" Nicky had only laughed and said, "Because they just damned well are! They're dull and pompous and sentimental and muddled and brutal. And now let's forget it."

So he had gone to join a battalion of foreign volunteers—refugee Czechs and Poles, Jugoslavs and Jews and Spanish and whatnot. It wasn't a pleasant prospect. Such a battalion wasn't too well treated and was always under suspicion. When he came back on leave he said he did not mind because he had been through much worse experiences, which was probably true since his fourteenth birthday had found him an orphan, penniless, singing and dancing for his supper, in Stamboul with what was left of Wrangel's army. And after that he had wandered about Europe, sometimes with papers, sometimes without, through Roumania, Jugoslavia, Prague and Berlin and finally Paris where friends of his dead parents got him a passport. He had worked as bus boy and taxi driver, as dancing teacher and chauffeur and gigolo. He had been or done very nearly everything in life, and so he was tough. But nothing had ever quenched his vitality nor saddened his gaiety. She knew others like him who had never had any proper, decent life. If he had done odd, immoral, shady things, she could understand since she herself knew as a child what it was to be hungry. And he had known from the time he was a boy hunger and cold and death and worse things. She did not mind giving him money. Disordered and strange as her own life had been, she had been lucky, compared to Nicky.

And now she did not know where he was or whether he was dead or alive and she did know how much difference this made to her. She thought, "If he is still alive, if I ever see him again we will go to America and begin all over again. I will make him go."

It did not matter that he had never been there or that she herself had been away for so long that she would know no one there. They had both lived always, in a way, by their wits; they would be able to get on somehow. She did not attempt to deceive herself. She was thirty-two years old and all the success she had ever had was here in Paris. She was no longer a young girl who might love many times, carelessly because there was so much time still before her. She could not begin all over again as a chorus girl of eighteen.

In her sleeplessness, she thought suddenly of the radio, thinking "perhaps there will be something, some news." It was three in the morning. She was able to find only a foreign broadcast in a language which she decided must be Russian and a program of weird music which she discovered at length came from Casablanca . . . nothing else.

Then she switched it off and heard a knock,

very light, on her door. Switching on the light, she said, "Come in!"

The one who knocked was, as she expected, Léon. He wore Nicky's black and scarlet dressing gown. It was much too long for him and he had tied the scarlet cord tightly around his little belly and hitched the extra length up beneath the cord. His bristling black hair was rumpled and standing on end. He carried a half-smoked cigar in his hand. He was very awake, his black eyes glittering with the excitement of some idea which had taken possession of him.

"Did I waken you?" he said.

"No. I couldn't sleep. Come in."

"I can't sleep when I'm developing ideas . . . I was developing one all evening."

She laughed. "I knew that."

He crossed over to the bed and sat on the edge of it. "Do you mind the cigar?"

"No."

"Are you really awake—enough to talk?"

"Yes. What's the idea?"

He looked at the end of the cigar. "It's like this." Again he paused and at last he said without looking at her, "It is true that Nicky means something to you?"

"Yes . . . a great deal."

"And it is true that you don't want to go to America till you know what has become of him?"

"Yes."

"It might be that if he was a prisoner you could help him."

"How? How with Germans?"

He grinned. "You are handsome. I might even say beautiful. You are a famous star. All Germans, even the most sophisticated, are like country bumpkins just come to the city."

"So I am to play Tosca now?"

"Maybe."

"It's very melodramatic."

He looked at her sharply. "And what do you think we have been living in for twenty years . . . ever since the last war. What have we been living in but melodrama? What is Hitler but melodrama and Mussolini and Daladier and Reynaud and their girl friends? What is Stalin but melodrama, and Carol and Lupescu? What was Rasputin and the Czarina? What is more melodramatic than Schuschnigg and his mistress and Fifth Columnists and poor Dollfuss? And Stavisky and Thyssen? And Chamberlain with his umbrella as the comedy country bumpkin? It's all rotten melodrama; the kind you couldn't play on the stage because it will stink. We've been living it in Europe for twenty years."

She sat up in bed suddenly fascinated by the

passion of the ugly little man. She had never thought about it before but what he said brought back a rush of memories. Paris itself, always on the edge of tragedy and disaster, had been bad melodrama.

"It could be done," he said. "You might be able to help Nicky if he is alive. You are not stupid."

"Thanks."

"You could possibly find out a great many other things from the Boches."

"Am I to be Mata Hari as well as Tosca?"

His swarthy face was suddenly contorted in an expression of annoyance. "This is serious," he said. "It is not funny." His cigar had gone out and he put it aside and lighted another. "You don't think *Parisiens* are going to take this lying down. You don't think Paris is going on like this . . . beaten, without spirit. It's apathetic now, but it will change and then our time will come."

"*Our* time?"

"Yes, our time. There is a job to be done. We can make Paris so uncomfortable for the Boches, they'll be glad to go home. They're homesick already after three days. No German is ever really at home in Paris. To him its always a wicked, immoral place where everyone's wits are sharper than his own where he understands nothing."

"You *do* hate them, don't you?"

"Yes, I've always hated them wherever they've turned up—in Alexandretta, in Athens, in Milano, but most of all in Paris. They never belong anywhere but in Germany."

"I don't hate them. I haven't any feeling at all except that they don't belong in Paris."

"Have you ever known Germans?"

"No . . . not really."

"Some day you will know what I mean."

"So what do you want me to do?"

"You heard what Filomena said tonight?"

"You mean that I wasn't going back to America? That is silly."

"Maybe, but I think not. I want you to stay here until you know what has become of Nicky. I want you to be in the show when I reopen it. They'll come to you like flies to honey—the Boche officers. Because you're American you'll have a special *chic*, more than the *Parisiennes* themselves. Because you're American, they won't be suspicious of you."

"If you mean that I'm to two-time Nicky for the cause, the answer is no."

"That is up to you . . . how well you manage the game. I'll do my part. Some of the girls will play. They'll play to the limit. I'll be very important to the Boche."

"As a procurer?"

He shrugged his shoulders. "Call it anything you like, diplomacy, spying, sabotage, pimping . . . it's all the same to me under the circumstances. It's been all the same in Europe for twenty-five years. The war isn't over. France is not defeated forever. One day there won't be a German left in Paris because it won't be safe even for a German traveling salesman. One day you'll see them hanging from lampposts alongside our friend Laval and the others who invited them in."

"I don't know. It's all too fantastic. I can't tell you now."

And then the sound of footsteps in the hallway came to them faintly. D'Abrizzi heard the sound first and sat up very straight. Then Roxie heard the sound too and quickly took the revolver from under her pillow. They both looked toward the door. In the hallway someone turned on a light which showed beneath the door. D'Abrizzi quickly took the revolver.

The door opened and in the doorway stood Nicky.

He was dressed in a fantastic suit of large checks and wore a bowler hat. The suit was too small for his big frame. It was the kind of suit one saw on bookmakers at Auteuil and Longchamps in the enclosures frequented by the concierges.

His face wore an expression of utter astonishment. Then he grinned, "*En bien! Enfin je suis devenu cocu!*"

Léon stood up, uncertain whether or not Nicky was serious. Roxie threw back the bed covering and climbing out of bed crossed the room. She said, "Nicky!" and that was all she was able to say for she began to cry. The tears were tears of happiness, of relief, of utter relaxation. She would have fallen on the floor but for Nicky's arms. He held her for a moment, kissing the top of her head and grinning sheepishly at d'Abrizzi. He said, "And so I enlist and then another fellow tries to make my girl." Then d'Abrizzi knew that he had not been serious even in the beginning, and he felt an odd hurt strike at his heart . . . that no man ever considered him a rival because he was so small and ugly. To be like this scamp of a Nicky he would have given all his money, his theaters, everything he possessed. To be tall and handsome and always certain that when you came into a room every woman turned to look at you, and most of them found you desirable on sight.

Nicky began to laugh, "It was like a scene in one of your own shows," he said, "you sitting on the end of Roxie's bed in my dressing gown with a gat in your hand."

D'Abrizzi threw the gun on the bed. It was a curious anti-climatic gesture, as grotesque and comical as his own short thick figure in Nicky's dressing gown. It had always been like this for him, as far back as he could remember. He moved to the door and before he went out, he said, "You needn't worry about me. I'll get some coffee around the corner."

They did not answer him. They were scarcely aware that he had gone out of the room for in all the world, in the midst of defeat and confusion and death, there were only the two of them.

Afterward, when everything was still again and peaceful in the awful peach and gold bedroom, he told her as nearly as he could what had happened to him.

He could not tell her much that had happened to him during those last days because he had been unconscious most of the time. The first thing he remembered had happened a week ago when he awakened, aware that he was in a strange place he had never seen before and that he had come out of a nightmare through a tunnel of darkness. The room in which he found himself, with a bandaged head, lying in bed, was small and dun-colored, with faded wallpaper in an ugly design of stripes interspersed with liver-colored roses. There was at the far end a washstand with a cheap pitcher and a bowl of the sort one sees outside bazaars with the packing straw still sticking to them, and there were two chairs, one large and upholstered in olive-colored plush, the other black, stiff and forbidding as a puritanical priest. The bed in which he lay was of some dark and heavy wood and above it hung a cheap crucifix with the body of Christ done in vulgar polychrome. The curtains at the window were of cheap lace, white and stiff with starch, hanging behind over-curtains of heavy dark-brown plush ornamented with ball fringe.

Slowly he understood from the room itself that he was in a humble house in some provincial town. And then slowly, fragment by fragment, like the shattered colors of a kaleidoscope which in the end resolve themselves into a pattern, odd fragments and pieces of events returned to him and took form.

He remembered the flight along the roads and through shattered villages with the planes swooping down, bombing and machine-gunning soldiers and old men and women and children alike. He remembered seeing one old woman and a fair-haired little girl fall dead beside the road, their bodies riddled by the bullets of some young German in the plane overhead. He remembered shaking his fist and cursing with an anger so violent and impotent that afterward he vomited in the ditch where he had taken refuge. He remembered too the curious wild sense of panic and rage at the suspicion and finally the certainty that he and the other men in his regiment had been betrayed by someone, somewhere in the government or in the army itself. And he remembered at the same time thinking of these people, a few of them friends, many of them acquaintances, out of the bright life of Paris, who had talked of the Nazis with indifference or sympathy; the Nazis were not so bad, they said; the Nazis stood for order and decent government; they would protect the people with money. And even as he thought of these people he knew that these were the ones who had betrayed him and his friends in the regiment.

And there was that last memory of fighting from behind a low wall in a trampled garden, and the fury which had flowed in his veins like fire, above all that last wild reckless fury when he fired his rifle, first at the planes overhead and then at the Germans coming across an open field, again and again until the barrel of the gun burned his skin.

There had been only one thought in his mind. These louts, these monsters must never reach Paris. They had no right there, even as tourists. They were brutes who could not possibly understand all that Paris was. Delicacy, beauty, gaiety, wit, were all things beyond the comprehension of Germans. In that moment, while he stood there fighting without concern as to whether he lived or died, he remembered all the things which had always been distasteful to him in Germans wherever he had met them . . . in Paris, in the Alps, in Istanbul, in the Tyrol, at home on their own ground. As he fired at each gray figure coming out of the forest, he found himself making a game, savage and bitter, out of the killing. "That one," he would say, "is for your muddled thinking! That one for your sloppy sentimentality! That one for your self-deception! That one for your devastating national sense of inferiority! That one for your cruelty! That one for your revolting emotionalism! That one for your lack of good taste—for the architecture of Berlin, for the way your women dress and the way you furnish your houses! That one for your bad food and gross appetites!"

Lying in bed he remembered it all very clearly. Beside him almost shoulder to shoulder had fought a little dark man with blue eyes called Chico who had been a garage mechanic in Montparnasse. Chico kept muttering and firing and swearing. And every now and then he'd yell, "You'll never get to Paris . . . you fat, dumb, swine! You'll never get to Paris!" And then suddenly he didn't hear Chico's voice any more and turning to see what had become of him, he found Chico lying dead on his face, his tough muscular arm hugging his rifle close to him.

Then he had gone on firing, cursing the gray figures, filled always with the obsession that the ugly, clumsy, gray figures must never pass him and get to Paris. That was all that mattered in that moment; the rest—the doubts, the betrayals, the confusion—was forgotten, save that now and then in some remote part of his brain a voice kept saying, "When it's over we'll get those who betrayed us! We'll hang them to every lamppost up and down the Champs Elysées."

The odd thing was that he thought and acted like a Frenchman although he possessed not a square meter of French soil nor a drop of French blood but was a foreigner born in the wild remote mountains fifty miles from Tiflis.

When the tanks came out of the forest, plunging and tossing as they came, like elephants of steel, he kept on firing, now at the tanks, but nothing happened. The steel elephants simply came on and on toward the neat village gardens. He remembered thinking what a pity it was that they should crush the carefully tended rows of lettuce and young onions and cabbage and green peas. And suddenly he saw the gardens in a new fashion. He had never before thought of them in that way —each small square of garden as a tiny work of art, created by the carpenter, the little shopkeeper, the plumber, the clerk at the *Mairie*. Into each small plot a man or perhaps a woman had poured something of his serene and orderly spirit. They were there, each little garden neat and ordered and beautiful because some Frenchman loved the earth, because he loved to eat well, because he had for nature itself, whether it manifested itself in the pollen carried from flower to flower by the bees or in making love to his own wife or mistress, a kind of mystical devotion. It was not the drum-beating Wagnerian emotionalism that found its expression in Wotan and Fricka and Thor and Freia, but something clearer and more beautiful, filled with order and reason. It all became clear to him suddenly as he fired across the crumbling wall at the tanks moving forward to smash the little gardens. He knew why it was that the Germans and the Frenchmen were so far apart, so remote from each other that understanding was very nearly beyond hope. It came to him, out of the spectacle of the tanks and the gardens, suddenly in a burst of understanding.

One of the tanks was quite near now. It veered suddenly and as it passed in front of him, its machine gun sent a stream of bullets rattling against the wall which sheltered him. That was the last thing he remembered.

And then he had wakened in the dull, ugly little room, knowing nothing of what had happened since the moment the tank had spit its bullets at him. He did not even know whether the steel treads of the tanks had ripped up the pretty gardens and smashed the wall. He did not know how long he had been unconscious nor where he was, nor what had happened in the world outside, nor whether those clumsy, ugly, gray figures had ever reached Paris. What troubled him most was the fact that he did not know what had become of Roxie. When he had gone away to the regiment the idea that the Germans would ever reach Paris was fantastic and impossible.

It troubled him because he was aware vaguely that, unlike any other woman he had ever known, she was in some curious way a part of his existence, a part indeed of himself. He had not thought of it before; in his reckless fashion he had accepted her as he had accepted many women. Perhaps she had gone back to that odd country America from which she had come. There was no reason why she should stay behind when she had only to board a train to leave for her own country where she would be safe and warm and comfortable and well fed.

Certainly he was not without experience of women. He had loved a great many women in various shades and degrees, but this one was different. For him she had something the others had not possessed. With his tired mind he attempted, wearily, because his bandaged head ached and he felt weak, to analyze what it was that made Roxie different. There was her singular beauty, her beautiful long legs and her feet and ankles, the beautiful hands, which seemed to be a special gift of nature to American women. But it was more than that which made him love her; it was, perhaps her quality of honesty and warmth, even her disillusionment, her lack of all sentimentality. Beauty could fade; you could grow sated with beauty or become weary of it. Beauty of body and face alone was not enough. It was more than that—much more. It was something deep and hidden which neither of them ever spoke of. He could not, in his weariness, quite define it.

He tried to remember her, dancing at the Alhambra or at home, or at Maxim's, or in the country at St. Jean-Aux-Bois, in the cheap little villa by the river. Sometimes he succeeded, sometimes he failed. Sometimes the memory of her returned only dimly in a kind of haze. "That," he thought, "is because there is something the matter with my head."

He felt presently an immense weariness. His eyes closed of themselves and presently he was asleep.

When he wakened there was a small dumpy woman in a black dress with graying hair strained back from her plump sallow face standing beside the bed looking at him. As he opened his eyes, she smiled and said, "Good morning, I see you are much better." She had a bowl of broth on a tray with two rolls lying beside it.

He said good morning and then asked, "Where am I and what has happened?"

She put down the tray and asked, "Do you feel well enough to sit up?" She put one strong arm behind his shoulders and pulled up the pillows.

"Yes, I feel quite well."

"When you have the broth you will feel better."

She placed the tray on his knees and started to feed him the broth from a spoon but he protested, "I can feed myself." It was extraordinarily good broth, savory and pungent. "Just tell me what happened . . . what has happened to Paris?"

She looked away from him out of the window and said in a low voice, "Paris has fallen!"

It was a simple speech and she endowed it with an extraordinary quality of bitter tragedy. She was a commonplace, plain little woman, dressed in dowdy black. There were millions of others like her in France. He knew well enough what her life was. She had a husband and one or two children, and the husband had a little shop and she kept this dull little house for him and managed his book-keeping as well. At holiday times she would work in the shop. And they had a small garden like the ones he had seen menaced by the tanks, where they worked side by side in long summer evenings and on Sundays after all the family, dressed in their best black clothes, had come home from mass.

He knew her well. In her small way she was France. She had never wanted war. All she had asked was to live her small, quiet, self-contained existence. She was dull and unpretentious and conventional and thrifty.

She was all the things which to him as far back as he could remember had been tiresome and boring, all the things he himself was not. Yet now in that modest dreary room he felt very near to her, and he was aware of the curious profound dignity of the woman as she said, "Paris has fallen!" and turned away, her black eyes wet and glistening. He felt near to her, he thought, because they felt the same about Paris. Her Paris and his were quite different cities—hers a great and beautiful city which she visited perhaps three times a year to shop at the Galeries Lafayette or the Bazaar de l'Hôtel de Ville and eat her lunch in a cheap restaurant and then shop again and then hurry to catch the suburban train to be home in time to cook supper for her husband and her children. His Paris was a city of lights and gaiety and champagne, of Maxim's and the Ritz and the races—a city of gaiety and brilliance no other city ever attained.

But there was another Paris which belonged to them both as it belonged to Chico, the little garage mechanic, who had fallen beside him there at the garden wall. This was the Paris which belonged to all of France, to the great and the simple, the rich and the poor, the clever and the stupid, because all of them through centuries had created it— the Paris which was the blossoming of all that was French. It was a generous Paris, and in a way it was a symbol; in a way it had been given to the world. It had taken fugitives and the unfortunate and people like himself who had no country, and it had given great treasures lavishly to the rest of the world—treasures of thought, of reason, of art, of beauty.

So he understood the dignity and the beauty of the dumpy little woman in black when she said, "Paris has fallen!"

It had happened two days earlier, she told him. For a long time there had been no news and only confusion and rumor with German tanks and armored cars and infantry passing through the streets of the half-wrecked village. And then a neighbor who had run away returned on a bicycle to say that the Germans were in Paris.

She herself had not run away when the others

had gone. With three or four old men and women and three neighbors she had gone to hide in the crypt of the church. They had been ordered like all the others to leave the village, but she and the others had remained behind because it had seemed safer than to run away. For two days before the Germans came they had seen others who had fled, pouring through the village streets. They had heard their stories of the panic, the slaughter by German planes along the road. One woman carried her dead child; they could not make her leave it. On the top of a wagon in the straw in the midst of piled up furniture lay a grandmother, the poor old body riddled by machine-gun bullets. There was a little girl with her arm shattered. . . .

So they had decided to remain behind rather than join the long line of refugees. In any case, the woman said quite simply, this village was their home; if they were to die it was better to die here than among strangers on some lonely crowded road.

In the crypt they had been safe enough, and when the Germans had gone they had come out and gone to their houses. Some of the houses had been bombed. Luckily her own house was untouched save for a shattered window or two. Her husband and two sons were in the army. She did not know where they were nor whether they were alive or dead.

Tears filled her eyes again as she said, "In the last war I lost two brothers and my husband was wounded. It is too much to ask . . . two wars in a lifetime."

As if her emotions had exhausted her, she sat down on the ugly plush chair and took a handkerchief out of her plump bosom and blew her nose.

"When I came back to the house," she said, "I found you by the garden wall. There was another soldier dead beside you. The pharmacist helped me carry you into the house. We buried the dead one in the little garden on the other side of the wall."

Then, noticing that he had finished the broth, she rose briskly and came over and took away the tray. "The pharmacist says you were very lucky. He says that you might have been killed but all you had was a bad concussion. The bullet pierced your helmet and glanced off your head." She smiled weakly. "You must have a hard head. You'll be all right in a few more days . . . but you must lie still and be very quiet." Then quite formally she said, "My name is Madame Dupuy, Madame Jacques Dupuy. My husband is a contractor here in Béthisy."

Quite formally he answered her, "My name is Nicholas Stejadze. I am a *Parisien*."

"I know your name. I found it on the plaque. It

is an odd name for a *Parisien*." Then as if unable
to support her curiosity she asked, "Are you in
business, too?"

He grinned. Now he was going to be exposed
to her disapproval. "No," he said, "I'm not in business."

"Ah, a professor or a *fonctionnaire*?"

"No, Madame, I'm afraid I do nothing at all but
enjoy myself."

"How old are you?" she asked bluntly.

"Thirty-three." As if in apology he added, "I
was born in Russia . . . in Georgia. I was an orphan. I had no education."

She shook her head and made a clucking sound
of disapproval, but almost immediately a sudden
light came into her eyes and she said, "Well, I suppose all of us would live like that if we could afford
it. There is so much to be enjoyed in the world. I
can never understand people who say they do not
know what they would do with themselves if they
did not have to work."

That was a very French remark and also a very
polite and thoughtful one.

"Perhaps you are an *amateur*? Perhaps you collect something?"

He smiled again, "No, madame, I am afraid I
do not even collect anything." He thought, "I
might have said I collected women." But that, he

knew, would shock her. In all the world there was nothing so respectable as this *petite bourgeoise.*

Suddenly while she was speaking to him she walked to the window. So he only added, "I'm afraid I am a useless person . . . one of those for whom there will be no more place in the world when this is finished."

Her answer was muffled by a sigh, "If it is ever finished. . . ."

She fussed with the curtains. "You must not go to the window," she said. "They might see you."

"Are there many quartered in the village?"

"No. It is a very small place. There is only a corporal and four soldiers, but if they found you they would ship you off to a prison camp. No one in the village but the pharmacist knows you are here." As an afterthought, she said, "And it would be very hard on me. They are very severe to people caught sheltering soldiers."

"I will be careful. I will go away tomorrow."

"No. You won't be strong enough."

"Well . . . as soon as I can."

"Then you must go south below the Loire."

"No. I mean to go to Paris."

Her face crinkled with alarm. "That is very dangerous for any soldier, but especially for a foreigner like yourself. . . ."

"There is someone there I must see. Would it

be too much trouble to ask for a pencil and a bit of paper?"

"Of course not."

"And I would like to shave. I must look very savage."

"No. Your beard gives you a romantic look. I can remember when a great many soldiers had beards." She smiled in a nostalgic way. "I always liked beards. I was sorry to see them go out of fashion."

She went away and in a little while returned with paper, a corroded inkwell and a frightful needle-pointed pen. On a second trip she fetched hot water, a bowl and her husband's extra razor—a huge old-fashioned elegant affair with a tortoise-shell handle. Clearly it was his best razor left at home and reserved only for special occasions. Before she left, she turned in the doorway.

"Do you think that in the end they'll be driven out of Paris?" she asked.

"Of course. We shall drive them out somehow."

"It seems so awful," she said. "Like having pigs in the salon."

If the remark had not been made with such seriousness he would have laughed. Again the air of tragic dignity invested the small dumpy figure. She felt as he felt . . . the Germans must be driven out because they did not belong there. It was a situation which was insupportable, like a violation of nature. It could not endure.

Her sallow face still pinched with worry, she closed the door and went away.

When she had gone he got weakly out of bed and went to the mirror to look at himself. The reflection made him laugh. The beard and the bandage were grotesque enough but Madame Dupuy and the pharmacist had put him into one of Monsieur Dupuy's nightshirts, a cotton affair embroidered in a design of red thread, which reached only to his knees. He thought, "If Roxie could see me now, she would certainly laugh."

When he had shaved, he sat down and pushing aside the wash bowl he wrote a letter with the horrible pen. It read:

"Darling: I am in a little place called Béthisy somewhere near Compiègne. I was wounded, very slightly and am coming to Paris in a day or two. If this reaches you it's just to tell you I'll turn up. Don't think I'm dead. Alive or dead I'll haunt you always. Nicky."

When he asked Madame Dupuy if there was some way of sending the note to Roxie's house in the rue Washington she was pessimistic. There was, she said, no post, no telephone, no telegraph. One could only enter or leave Paris if one had special papers. However, she would do her best.

Suddenly, while she was speaking to him, she walked to the window and drew the heavy plush curtains.

"It is the patrol," she said.

He heard the sound of heavy boots . . . the four German soldiers and the corporal . . . on the cobblestones outside the window. Then he heard the hoarse voice of the corporal shouting, "*Halt!*"

While he dressed two of them guarded him. The corporal and the other two took dumpy, sallow little Madame Dupuy away to the *Mairie*. He protested but there was nothing to do. The corporal said in German that she was a dangerous person, that people like her shot good German soldiers from ambush. When the corporal returned, he would not say what had become of her, and when he looked at Nicky's papers he said, "Ugh! A Russian pig! A Slav!" The corporal was a dumpy little man, clearly a nobody, now swollen with his importance as the *Gauleiter* of Béthisy.

They took him to the local prison, a single dark little room with barred windows, and later at sundown he was placed in a truck in charge of a squad of soldiers, and driven away through the blue dusk of summer evening in Northern France. It was lovely country, with the river wandering through flat green pastures, with lines of poplars against the sky. The men in the truck revealed that they had been ordered to treat refugee volunteers with special severity. They tried to discover why he had run away from Russia, and when he told them his story of the escape with the last remnants of Wrangel's shattered army, their faces went blank and stupid. They were too young to remember anything of the Revolution or the last war, and it was clear that they had been taught nothing save that the Germans were the master race and that their Führer was a miracle. They could not understand that he was a refugee from the last war and not the political oppression which preceded this one. They could not understand that he believed himself, if not actually French, at least *Parisien*. Why, they asked, if he was Russian, had he troubled to fight for a degenerate, weak people like the French?

After a little time he did not attempt to argue or explain; it was like trying to have an intelligent conversation with a troup of baboons. Their very training had made intelligent conversation impossible.

It was long after dark when they arrived at a concentration camp set up on the edge of what had been an air field. He knew vaguely where he was

—probably in the Department of the Oise, but he was unable to interpret even the landmarks or the road signs which still remained. His head hurt him and the growing darkness made everything confused.

That first night he lay down almost at once on the pile of straw that was pointed out to him in the barracks, and fell asleep. In the morning he felt better and strong enough to look about him and talk to the others in the camp. They were an odd mixture, mostly foreigners like himself, some of them Jews, of all ages and nationalities—many of them refugees from Austria and Czechoslovakia and Germany. There were a few soldiers from the volunteer refugee battalion. Most of the older men and some of the younger ones were frightened. It was clear that all of them had been herded together here as foreigners who had found sanctuary in France or who loved France enough to fight for it. Some of them had been sent out from Paris after the Germans had entered the city and their patrols had begun picking up people. It was clear too that they had been herded together because some special punishment had been reserved for them. One of the older men, an Austrian Jew, told him that this was a camp reserved for Jews and communists —a label which always included anyone whom the Germans wished to liquidate.

When he had had a breakfast of coffee and bread, he tried to discover what had become of his papers, but the corporal to whom he addressed the inquiry only spat at him and said, "Nobody knows and anyway it doesn't matter because you won't need any papers from now on."

After that he returned to the barracks and sat down and tried to think; everything in him of the scamp, the rogue, of the fugitive, of the gentleman who lived by his wits, came suddenly to life. He thought, "They can't keep me shut up here—not these stupid Germans! I've got to get out of here. I've got to get back to Paris. I can still fight them from there, no matter if there isn't any French army left, no matter if in France there isn't any more war." And what he meant always was, "I must get back to Paris. I must fight for my beloved Paris, to make her free again." For Paris was the only home he had ever known. Paris had been kind to him.

He was filled suddenly with a great contempt for everything German. It was a profound contempt, for not only the *Parisien* spoke out but the poetic Slav and the Asiatic, who was older even than Paris.

He went out of the barracks quietly, he engaged a rich Austrian refugee in conversation and picked his pocket of two packages of cigarettes. Money he did not want or need; he had never had any money and despite that fact he had always managed to live very well.

Then in a leisurely, casual way he made a circuit of the barbed-wire enclosure. It was not the first wire which had shut him in. He had been in camps like this in Bucharest, in Budapest, in Germany. None of them had ever held him. This one, he knew after the tour, could not hold him. It was hurriedly constructed, a makeshift affair in which to corral the victims the German army was gathering in wholesale day by day. Any of the prisoners could escape if they had the courage and the initiative; the only risk was the chance of a shot from a sentry. But most of the prisoners were too frightened. Some of the more wretched seemed to have been paralyzed by a kind of animal fear. They lay face down on their straw, or they sat holding their heads in despair. One old Jew leaned against the side of the barracks and wailed as if he were in Jerusalem instead of the open country north of Paris.

In himself there was no fear. There was only hatred of his captors and contempt and defiance and a kind of excitement and pleasure at the challenge to escape. He forgot the dull pain inside his bandaged head and grew impatient for the sun to go down.

It was easier than he had imagined. He had only to go to the latrine and wait until the sentry outside the wire had passed on his round. It was too easy; he would have enjoyed it more if there had been searchlights and machine guns and sentries every few yards. This was nothing. He had only to wait until the single loutish sentry had passed. Then quickly he slipped through the wire and vanished in the darkness that closed down around the whole camp.

All night he walked, following roads which, by the stars, led southward. Sometimes they ran through forests which he fancied he recognized, and sometimes they ran between open fields. He passed through three tiny villages whose names meant nothing to him as he ran his finger over the signs and read them in the darkness by sense of touch. They were called St. Pierre-sous-bois, Anglet and Pontavec. Three or four times he was forced by weakness to rest and three or four times, when the dimmed lights of a motor appeared on the road, he slipped into the ditch and lay there until the gray cars had disappeared into the darkness.

The dawn came up slowly as it does in northern France, in a warm blue haze which blurred the outlines of farms and poplar trees. The road turned a deep gray and then a paler gray and at last it lay white between the thick forests on either side. On the one side there was a high ivy-covered wall that ran as far as the next turn in the road, one of those walls which guarded a great property. This he followed for nearly half a mile when it was broken suddenly by an opening more than a hundred feet wide. There through the opening appeared a wide vista cut through the forest. Below, surrounded by water and a vast expanse of green lawn there rose out of the morning mists a great false Renaissance château which seemed to float in the waters of the wide moat. Halfway down the vista in an open space stood the statue of a man on a horse. In the mist rising from the moat both horse and rider appeared like ghosts.

And then he knew suddenly where he was. This was the Château de Chantilly and the ghostly rider was the Grand Condé.

He had had great luck for in Chantilly he was certain to find people who would help him. Chantilly was filled with stables and horse trainers and jockeys and people like himself of uncertain nationality. That he had no papers would be less troublesome here than in some provincial village. Making his way along the wall he passed the old houses on the outskirts of the village and once he had crossed the bridges over the Duc d'Aumale's canals he knew where he was. He had been here many times to the races. He knew the stables. He might even have the luck to fall upon a trainer or a jockey whom he knew.

The streets were empty, perhaps because of the early hour, perhaps because of the German patrol which twice he sighted in the distance.

Once inside the town he took the narrow back streets. Here and there a bomb had fallen, shattering a house or a stable. In one place a high wall had been tumbled across the narrow street, leaving the house inside the wrecked garden naked with all its insides obscenely exposed. The bombing must have been done simply from a wanton sense of destruction for there was nothing in Chantilly —only the château and the summer villas and the horses and the race course. Again he cursed the Germans.

A moment later he passed an open gateway and through it he saw a red-haired woman building a fire in the big courtyard. Opposite the gateway was a simple stucco-covered house and on either side of the courtyard were empty stables, their doors open, the horses gone. Quickly he entered the gateway, closing the big gates behind him. As the gates creaked on their hinges, the woman looked toward them and, seeing him, screamed.

While he lay telling the story, Roxie listened without once speaking. She watched the dark intelligent face, speculating with some detachment as to what went on behind it, deep inside him, in that part of him which she had never been able to reach. All she had known of him was the surface, attractive, amusing, tender, fickle, charming, ardent. What lay beneath all that—the thing he really was, the soul, what he believed and *was*, she had never touched. And now even while she listened she understood that the fault was not altogether his. She herself had a surface at times very nearly as shiny and attractive as that which concealed Nicky. She was aware presently that both of them had constructed over years this glittering hard surface as a kind of protection against the softness inside which was themselves. It was a process which happened in the world in which they had both lived for so long. There was pride which must be protected from hurt by the built-up scales of cynicism and mockery, and affections which must not be hurt in a world where lasting affection and loyalty and even love were not common. One had, sometimes, she knew, to be a scamp, to be hard, to be deceitful merely to keep a roof over one's head and fend off starvation. Anyone would have said that Nicky, without background, without home, without nationality, was also without loyalty to anyone or anything; yet she knew that was not true. There was something there deep inside him which was warm and gay and kindly and perhaps even loyal. Only there was no way of getting to it. It was there, she knew, else he could not have made so great a difference in her life.

She could, of course, have said to him, "Come now, my friend, let's chuck all the wisecracks and the laughs and be ourselves. Let's tear off all these protective scales and come to really know each other. It will be much better that way. What we have now is wonderful, but it is shallow and cannot last. We must somehow know each other, know what we *are* and why we love each other."

But that too she could not do, because the process, even if it were possible, would be so painful that it might be a cure that killed. She understood that he, like herself, had been hurt and disillusioned so many times that the very tissue of the scars themselves protected them. If ever it happened, if ever she got through to him, it must come about through some catastrophe, some tragedy of such violence that they would be revealed to each other in the end, naked and stripped of all but the very essence.

It had all begun casually because they found each other attractive and amusing and sympathetic, but it had become much more than that. The knowledge alarmed her because there was always the doubt that after all her instinct might be wrong. It might be that Nicky was only charm and good looks and cynicism. Underneath the protection there might be nothing at all.

"And maybe," she thought, "I am just being a fool again." Only this time there was pleasure in being a fool.

Then suddenly she heard him talking about the red-haired woman building the fire and for the first time she spoke to interrupt him. She asked, "Was she good-looking?"

He laughed and taking his arms from under his head, lay on his side with his head supported by one arm. He touched her and asked, "What's the matter? Are you jealous?" And she thought, "There it is again . . . the shell, the professional manner." There was a cheapness about the speech which struck back into his shady, disordered past. And she answered, "No, I just asked out of curiosity."

"Well, to tell the truth, she wasn't either young or pretty. She had nice red hair but she was freckled and middle-aged and fat." But even as he spoke she did not believe him.

"Not that she wouldn't have given in," he added. "She didn't have the opportunity."

He said that at first the woman was frightened. She was building the fire outside to make coffee because the gasworks had been bombed and her stove burned only gas. When she heard his story, she wasn't any longer frightened—at least not by his appearance. On the contrary she turned rather coy and said, "All right, you can hide here but come inside. Someone might come in the gates or look over the walls."

She had run away with most of the rest of the town but had turned back because she remembered the horses and could not bear the idea of leaving them without food or water. Her husband was in the army and the stable boys had gone away. There were twelve horses. But when she returned the Germans were already there and the stables empty. She was half-French and half-Irish, the daughter of a trainer who had come to France from Ireland.

And Nicky, going on with the story, looked at Roxie suddenly grinning and said, "She liked me very much. She fell for me at once." To which Roxie answered, "Yes, I take all that for granted.

I've seen women look at you. I know just how they look at you—the damned fools. It makes me ashamed of being a woman. Get on with the story."

There wasn't much more to tell. He had a bath and shaved with the razor of another husband and the woman gave him the suit with the loud checks which fitted so badly, and a bowler hat which did fit fairly well, and when darkness fell he set out for Paris following the tracks of the Chemin de Fer du Nord which seemed the shortest way and the way least likely to bring him into trouble.

There hadn't been any trouble. In fact the whole trip had been remarkably easy, especially since the engineer and fireman of a stray engine had given him a lift, almost to the Gare du Nord. They didn't care for the Germans any more than he did and could not support the idea of Germans in Paris. A little way outside the Gare du Nord they slowed down the engine and let him off.

"And so," he concluded, "I came straight here to discover you and Léon in a compromising situation."

"Oh, lay off that," she said. "And what are you going to do now?"

He shrugged his shoulders, "Who knows? Who knows anything these days?"

"I want to go to America and I want you to go with me."

He did not answer but sat up suddenly resting his chin on his knees. "America," he said presently. "That's a great idea. I'd like to see New York . . . to see if it's as wonderful as all Americans say. But not now. Now isn't the time."

"Even if I went?"

"You don't want to go . . . not really. Not now. Anyone would be a fool to leave Paris now. The fun has only begun."

"What do you mean?"

"There's a job to be done here. There's a lot of excitement. I want to be in on it."

"And what are you supposed to be? What are you going to do about papers?"

He laughed. "Léon can fix that up. He's smart enough and corrupt enough. He knows all the inside tricks. He's helped me out before. I might have gone to jail with some of the Stavisky boys but for Léon." He looked at her suddenly. "I've known Léon for a long time . . . in a way I've known him always. We're both part Asiatic. I think we'll be able to handle the Germans."

She remained thoughtful for a long time and presently said, "Léon is going to reopen the Al-hambra."

"That's an excellent idea."

"And he wants me to stay with the show."

"There's nothing wrong with that."

"He has some other ideas too. He wants me to do the Mata Hari stuff."

He looked at her sharply, and after a moment said, "Do you think you have brains enough?"

"Do you?"

"Yes."

"Then you don't object?"

The dark face grew serious and for a moment she thought, "Maybe now I am going to get through the shell. Maybe now I'll know what he is, what he feels." Her heart began to beat so violently that beneath her breast she felt pain.

But he only said, "I couldn't answer that now. It's something that would need thought. But you certainly could be useful."

She said quietly, "You wouldn't mind my going the whole hog?"

"What do you mean?"

"Doing everything a female spy is supposed to do."

The color came suddenly into his face and the black eyes grew brilliant. "If ever I caught you two-timing me I'd beat the hell out of you." And suddenly she felt wildly happy. America did not matter now. Nothing mattered because for a moment she had seen inside him.

She said, "I'll go and wake Léon and make some coffee."

Major Freiherr Kurt von Fabrizius von Wessellhoft was the son of Herr and Frau Doktor Freiherr Oberregierungsrath Frederick von Fabrizius von Wessellhoft. He was eight years old two days before the signing of the Armistice of November 11th, 1918. At that time he was a blond, straightbacked little boy living in a great white house in Silesia with his mother, his older sister, a young nurse schoolteacher from Swabia called Lisa Dinkel and four or five old servants. They were safe in the remote huge old house on the edge of the dark forest and had plenty to eat because there was a large farm and no matter how severe the restrictions nor the levies made by government law there were always ways of hiding away plenty of food. And the government agents of the district did not trouble too much if Frau Doktor Freiherr Oberregierungsrath Frederick von Fabrizius von Wessellhoft failed to turn in as much as such a rich estate should contribute. She was the widow of a great judge and of a very old family descended remotely from the Elector of Brandenburg, and in any case, no one in their part of Germany went hungry except the workers in the mines and the small factories so it did not seem to matter.

Small Kurt and his sister were having supper with their mother and Lisa in the little room off the great hall when the old forester Herman brought in the news. The mother was a straight, thin woman, handsome in a provincial fashion which had nothing to do with clothes or styles. She had rather cold blue eyes, a noble profile and a severe manner. She wore her hair in braids drawn and pinned so tightly about her head that the skin seemed drawn back from the high cheekbones. Lisa, the governess, was only twenty-three, slim and ivory-skinned with red-gold hair which she wore cut short. There was a softness about her that was nowhere evident in the thin stiff Lutheran figure of Frau von Wessellhoft. Lisa came from the south, from Swabia. There was in her both the blood of Austrians and Slavs. When she moved it was with the grace of a swan. Her voice was soft and she laughed easily.

When the old forester came in he stood holding his hat in his hand respectfully, for this part of the world was still dimly feudal. One's relationships, one's dignity, one's respect, were less determined by what one was than by what one's ancestors had been. The forester was an old man, too old for any service, with a broad, weatherbeaten face, a beard and very bright blue eyes. When he addressed Frau von Wessellhoft, it was with her full title Frau Doktor Oberregierungsrath.

He said, "Frau Doktor Oberregierungsrath, I have bad news. Our army has stopped fighting. There is an Armistice!"

The great blue eyes of the Swabian governess grew darker suddenly and tears began to stream down her face. Frau von Wessellhoft's narrow handsome face seemed to grow even narrower and more Gothic. The lines about the mouth hardened and the nose seemed to grow sharper. She sat a little more erect. For a long time she sat staring into nothingness, while the forester waited.

At last she said, "It is indeed bad news, Herr Forester. Now only God knows what will happen to us."

Lisa, weeping, said, "It has all been for nothing . . . for nothing." And the older ones knew that she was thinking not like Frau von Wessellhoft of wounded pride and ravished glory but of her own fiancé and her brother.

The forester asked, "Shall I tell the others, Frau Doktor Oberregierungsrath?" And Frau Wessellhoft said, "No, that is my duty. Go back to your own wife and house. I will tell the others." She rose and turned to the governess. "Weeping does no good, Lisa. Tears will not help us now. It has to begin over again. That is the only way."

She went out followed by the forester, and when she had gone the boy and his sister got down from their chairs and went over to Lisa, leaning against her, rubbing their small faces like little animals against her breasts. This was something they were never allowed to do in the presence of their mother. The girl kissed the tops of their heads to comfort them but the tears would not stop flowing. Presently when she was able to speak, she said, "Come we'll go up to the nursery and play a game of Ludo before you go to bed."

The two children understood nothing, but the boy said, "It doesn't mean that you'll leave us, does it, Lisa?"

"No. You mustn't think about it at all." And then the boy said, "Can we all sleep together, all of us in the big bed tonight, Lisa?"

She looked at him, smiling, "If your respected mother gives permission."

"Please," the child said, "I am frightened."

"What is there to be frightened of?"

He did not answer her because he could not describe what it was that he was frightened of, for it was a strange phantasmagoria of fears in which the ghosts of slaughtered boar and deer, of cannon and flags, of dead men, and strange nightmare figures half-men and half-beast seemed to come toward him screaming and crying out words which he could not understand. Sometimes the nightmare came to him in the dark hours of the night, sometimes in daylight, as it had come on him now at the sight of Lisa's tears and his unbending mother's pride. It was like the old picture that hung in the dark back stairway, moldy and forgotten. Whenever he had to pass the picture he ran very fast. Once when he was seven years old, he fell on the stairs and broke off a tooth. Sometimes in the nightmare his grandfather, the general, was there and his dead father who had become a bitter judge instead of a soldier because he was born lame. They were the most frightening of all.

So to Lisa he said, "I don't know."

"Never mind," she said and pressed him close to her side. She loved him very much and there were times when she felt a wild desire to take him in her arms and flee with him away from the dark forests of the north to the pleasant valleys, the gay music, the dancing, the bright clothes of her own Swabian country in the south. There, she was sure, the nightmare, would disappear.

Twenty-two years after the night the forester

had come to tell the news of Germany's defeat, Freiherr Kurt von Fabrizius von Wessellhoft rode into Paris in the gray and green uniform of a major in a great gray Mercedes armored car. He sat beside the General who had been appointed military Governor of Paris, a paunchy man with gray eyes from which the heavy lower lids sagged away, leaving a faint rim of red beneath their gray coldness.

The General, twenty-four years earlier, had seen the Eiffel Tower and domes of the Sacré-Coeur shining in the misty sunlight twenty miles away, but neither he nor any of the German army had come any nearer. For four years they fought and in the end they lost and now they were here at last entering Paris on the road by which all invaders had entered the city since the beginning—the famous Route de Flandres which led down from the north through the fertile fields of Picardy and the Valois. Many times invaders had entered the city by this road and many times they had gone away and never had Paris suffered any change.

The column in which the General and his aide now rode passed through Le Bourget, past the great flying field, past the factories of Aubervilliers, past the nearly demolished fortifications which had held the Germans back for so long in another earlier war which France had lost.

It was not a triumphant entry. The day was gray

and the streets were empty. Most of the houses were shuttered and here and there, like lost forgotten people, there appeared on the narrow sidewalks beneath the trees the figure of an old woman or a pair of men in workingmen's corduroys and neck cloths. There were no flags and no cheers, but only silent stares. There was an air of defeat, of deadness, but no cheering nor even any curiosity. The General sourly thought, "We will find no welcome here in the workingmen's quarter. We will find friends only in the middle of the city— among the rich and the powerful, who invited us in . . . the rich and powerful who are fools, the ones we will pick fast, as clean dry bones." For the General was old, older than his years and wily and wise and without illusions. He knew the game the Party played and he knew exactly the part he played in the scheme of things.

He did not like any of it very much. He was much more concerned with the disease of his kidneys which caused the great dark pouches beneath his red-rimmed eyes. He did not like rich men, he did not like industrialists, he did not care for bankers. They were vulgar. The Party could pilfer all of them so far as he was concerned, and more luck to the process. He was an army man and his father had been and his father's father before him, back to Frederick the Great. He had been sent to

Paris because he was no longer young and was shrewd and had the reputation of being a good administrator. There would be a lot of tiresome meetings and negotiations with the slippery, quick-witted French and no pleasure at all in the job. He did not even find any satisfaction in this "triumphant" entry. If it had come twenty-four years ago at the time when from Meaux you could see the domes of the Sacré-Coeur shining in the morning sun, there would have been some feeling of pride and triumph. But for him it had come too late. He was too old and too bored. Slyly he glanced at the young officer beside him—Major Freiherr von Fabrizius von Wessellhoft, a fellow who came of good enough Prussian stock. A Wessellhoft had been a marshal under Frederick the Great. The young fellow should be all right, but somehow he was not, perhaps because he belonged to the Party. A lot of the younger men were like that. It did something to them: it made them shifty and divided and uneasy, as if they found it impossible to serve two masters competently. It made them both vulgar and dishonorable.

He had not asked for the Major as one of his aides. The Major had been imposed upon him from above, by what means he was unable to discover, but he suspected that he had been assigned to spy and report back not to the army but to the Party.

The column had come to a temporary halt and the General sighed heavily and looked about him. A motorcyclist shot past and the band in the lead of the column began to play the "Horst Wessell" song. At the sound of the music the young Major at his side sat up a little straighter, his small blue eyes grew bright. But the General only grunted. The sound he made might have meant anything at all. In fact it was a grunt of contempt for the song and the pimp for whom it was named. A fine sort the Party had been in the beginning—pimps and gangsters, homosexuals, neurotics, small crooks and paperhangers and shopkeepers! A fine lot! Well, they would come and go, murdering, torturing, killing each other off, but the German army went on and on. It would survive them all.

The motorcyclist shot back past them and the column started to move again. They were now actually entering the gates of Paris.

Beside the General, the young Major was suddenly alive with satisfaction in the moment. This was a supreme moment of triumph, of revenge, of glory. It was a moment which in some way struck far back into the past to that night when the old forester had come into the small room and said,

"Frau Doktor Oberregierungsrath, I have bad news," and Lisa, lovely kind Lisa, had burst into tears and Mama had risen and gone out with the frightening, hard look of suffering in her blue eyes.

Now, long afterward, he recognized that moment as the beginning of it all. A little while afterward the big white house on the edge of the forest was sold and they had all gone to live in Berlin where they sometimes went hungry and in winter they always were cold because, Mama said, the money they had got for the big white house wasn't worth anything. It took ninety million marks to buy a newspaper and Mama had only been paid two million marks for all the good farm land and the big house on the edge of the forest—not enough to buy a newspaper. And he and his sister had been forced to go to a common school where other children, who his mother told him contemptuously were communists and liberals, had teased his sister and himself. For most of his childhood he had not really had enough to eat and he had been humiliated and scarred by wounds which his mother tried to heal with words of pride and glory. And then a miraculous man who called himself Der Führer had changed all that, and when he was eighteen he joined with other young men like himself who suffered from humiliation and hurt pride in a great army of young men who learned that his country, like himself, had been tricked and swindled, humiliated and treated with contempt.

Now at last, he would have revenge for the humiliations which he had known as far back as he could remember. He would be revenged on those people who laughed when one uttered the word "German," on all those who laughed at the sight of German tourists, fat, bespectacled, staring while they munched sausages before the wonders of Paris and Vienna and Rome. He would be revenged on those who in drawing rooms in London or salons in Paris had turned away coldly when they heard his very German name. He would be avenged upon all the world which thought Germans crude and brutal and uncivilized and politically undeveloped. All his life, whenever he had gone outside his own country, he had been aware of the words "German" or "*Deutscher*" or "*Allemand*" as something which aroused varying shades of mockery or hatred or scorn or ridicule. He was not the only one who experienced these emotions, but all those who like himself had grown up from childhood humiliated and disinherited by the whole world outside Germany—disinherited, even scorned for a time by great masses of their own people.

It was a long account to settle. One by one, the items of the account would be settled in every country in the world until at last all of them grov-

eled before the word "German." The account was
already settled with weak, soft Austria, with sturdy
Czechoslovakia, with Poland, stiff and proud in her
contempt for everything German, with Norway
and Holland and Belgium and the other soft de-
mocracies which did not understand true nobility,
true civilization, true beauty—all those countries
which stubbornly resisted the imposition or even
the influence of true Kultur. They had all been
betrayed by the very civilizations which resisted
Germany—by their very gaiety and freedom and
softness and good living, by all the things which
had always been absent from the world he had
known since the very beginning.

The excitement raced through his body like fire,
an excitement greater than he had ever felt before
even in the arms of a woman. It was a physical
thing, almost choking in violence. No longer
would Germans need to ask, almost with a whimper
in their voice, "Why do you not like us? Why do
you refuse to be our friends?" Now the others
would have no choice. Now it did not matter
whether Germans were liked or hated. Nothing
mattered so long as they were feared.

Once he turned to the General and said, indicat-
ing a little group of French workingmen beneath
the chestnut trees, "See how feeble they are! How
small! How degenerate!"

The General did not answer him. He only turned his head phlegmatically as if the effort hurt him and then looked straight ahead once more at the thick muscular neck of the Silesian driver.

It was a pity, thought young Major von Wessellhoft, that cities could no longer be sacked as the Huns had sacked Rome. Alas! The orders were that the invading army was to be "correct . . . very correct." By being "correct" the theory was that they would soon win over these feeble French, and then they would be able to attack the enemy they hated most of all—the English—those *verdammte* English, so rich, so powerful, so arrogant, who even while they smiled and shook your hand made you feel inferior and awkward and crude. No, there were still the English and after that their mongrel cousins, the Americans, who in their way were worse since they did not even seem to care what you were. The Americans, a debased people incapable ever of understanding culture.

No, there was a long account to settle. Fate had been very good to him, sending him here as aide to the Military Governor, to witness the humiliation of the degenerate French.

Yet there was a sense of uneasiness and dissatisfaction even now as he rode at the head of the column occupying Paris. It was not as he had imagined it. This was scarcely a triumphant entry with the city empty and only a handful of workingmen and their women—all of them doubtless *verdammte* communists—watching the long gray column with apathy. It was too much like the way Englishmen and Viennese and Dutch and even Americans had behaved in the past when he came into a room— as if an outsider, an outcast had suddenly come through the door.

Ach! They would find out! They would be taught manners if they had none! They would be made to love the Germans and grovel before them! To the Major it did not occur that one could not love and grovel at the same time. It was one of the many things which had never occurred to him in all his thirty years.

Then suddenly the long steel-gray cavalcade came into a great white square, ordered and beautiful in line and scale and proportion and beyond it a wide avenue rising up and up to the final triumph of a great arch. It was like the singing beauty of a great symphony rising to a climax. The square and the great avenue were empty, but their emptiness only made them seem the more splendorous and magnificent, symbols of something which had never touched him nor his father nor his father's father, something which had never been in the loins or heart of any German. Swiftly Major von Wessell- hoft experienced again the sickening feeling of inferiority which had poisoned all his existence since the beginning.

The band ahead in the heavy trucks blared "*Deutschland, Über Alles*" with all the strength of brass horns and leather lungs, but the brazen music only echoed in mockery across the great empty space. Rage took possession of him. The cold handsome face grew red like the face of a drunken man, and a curious thought was born somewhere in the remote regions of his baffled regimented mind, "Only when all this is utterly destroyed, only when everything which is not German has been smashed from the face of the earth will Germans be given the honor and respect they deserve!"

At that very moment the big gray Mercedes passed the Hotel Claridge where an American showgirl lay on a bed with curtains drawn, her hands over her ears because the sound of "*Deutschland, Über Alles*" in the streets of Paris was unendurable.

There was for d'Abrizzi no question of simply putting on the new revue he had planned for the stage of the Alhambra. Its very title was impossible. It had been called "*A Nous la Victoire*" and now there was no victory but only defeat and the title on the placards before the Alhambra and on buildings and walls and wooden fences all over Paris made reading which the ordinary citizen found unendurable. One by one they were ripped down or defaced, not because of any hatred for d'Abrizzi or the Alhambra, but because with the gray-green uniforms everywhere it was impossible to have cried at you from walls and houses—"*A Nous la Victoire!* A revue in five acts with Roxana Dawn, Pernod, Sally d'Arville, Constanza, Lilli de Perche, Les Tiller Girls and eighty beautiful models—eighty!" So the placards came down.

It was clearly not possible to stage skits which depicted Hitler as a light-witted house painter, and Goering as a eunuch guarding a harem, and Goebbels in the costume and make-up of a rat. And there were the tableaux depicting the triumphs of Napoleon with the uniforms of the German armies filled by the overplump bodies of somewhat elderly chorus girls.

When d'Abrizzi sat down with Nicky and Roxie, he was forced to check off nearly all the revue as a loss. A new one had to be written and staged in which every speech, every scene would be subject to the censorship of the Germans.

"It will," he said, "be a frightful headache."

"And the others . . ." asked Nicky, "are they all coming back?"

"They are all coming back but Lilli de Perche. She is a Jewess. She has gone to Nice with everything she possessed."

"You can't blame her," said Nicky.

When Nicky had gone to the cellar to fetch wine, Roxie looked at Léon and said, "What about his papers? If they can't be fixed up, I'll force him out of the country with me."

"Don't worry about the papers. By tonight he'll be a French citizen with a French passport and all the necessary papers. He will be Pierre Chastel, born in Cairo in 1904, the son of the French vice-consul."

"You might have asked him what he wanted to be," said Roxie.

"There wasn't any question. That is who he had to be."

"He can't stay forever in this house. I'm afraid he'll get bored and go out and get picked up. They might treat him as a spy."

D'Abrizzi chuckled, "He's a brigand. That's what he really is, born in the wrong century and wrong place."

Then Nicky returned with the bottles and they no longer talked of him. Only Roxie went on watching him slyly and thinking about him, thinking that he could charm the birds off the trees.

When Nicky had opened the wine, he said to

Léon, "You know that this reopening business is going to make you and Roxie damned unpopular with decent French people? It's going to look as if you approved of the Germans and believed in collaboration."

Léon laughed, "I'm prepared for that. When it's all over, people will understand. I wouldn't ask Roxie to go back in the show if it wasn't like that."

"All the same, it's going to be unpleasant," said Nicky.

"It's not worth doing at all if people don't believe we're friendly toward the Boches. That's what lets us get away with the rest of it."

The wine made him suddenly gay. Nothing could dampen the natural spirits of Nicky but Roxie didn't feel anything at all. She wasn't enthusiastic about the idea of sabotage. She still liked none of the plan. She didn't feel anything at all, only a sort of blankness tinged with dread. She had no feeling of the Germans being awful. She couldn't even hate them. She didn't know anything about them. They were simply shadowy figures in gray-green who seemed rather dreary. They were certainly very strange and foreign in Paris, stranger even than the Algerian rug merchants who sold dope.

Léon gathered up the papers he had spread on the table. They included an outline of the new revue, a list of the cast and a list of questions. Slipping them into his dispatch case, he said, "And now for the lion's mouth."

"And when do I get out?" asked Nicky.

"Tonight or tomorrow. Don't be a damned fool! You'll have plenty of excitement later." Then he kissed the top of Roxie's head and was forced to stand on tiptoe to do it.

For the first time, she laughed. "*Vraiment, Léon,*" she said, "*tu es formidable!*"

"*Toi aussi,*" he replied. "Once in rehearsal you'll cheer up."

"I can never be any good as Mata Hari."

When he reached the street, he crossed to the opposite side and looked back carefully at the house. Certainly it had possibilities—with its dreary, inconspicuous façade, and the curious ancient cellar beneath. And the rue Washington itself. Looking at it, no one would believe that anything could happen in so commonplace a street —anything but bourgeois domesticity and boredom.

At the corner he had the luck to pick up a horse-drawn fiacre. He directed the driver to go to the Ritz and settled back into the tempo of the days of carriages. There were still very few French people on the wide sidewalks. The cafés were doing business but the tables on the sidewalks were surrounded by German officers. He passed the Traveler's Club and thought, "That is where La Païva lived. It must have been odd in her day when the Champs Elysées was still a magnificent street and there were no picture houses and automobile agencies." Now it was very little better than the Boulevard des Italiens. La Païva was the last of the real demimondaines; now all women seemed alike. At Maxim's it was impossible to tell tarts from ladies. Look at Roxie. Once a girl with her beauty and wits would have had a palace and jewels and the richest, most elegant motor in town. All Roxie wanted was a taxi, a bedroom, sitting room and Nicky.

Against the clop-clop of the horse's hooves, he sighed heavily. Paris had changed . . . even within his memory it had changed. How much would the Germans change it? From somewhere in the back of his mind the answer came quickly—"Not at all. Six weeks after the Germans have gone, you won't know they've ever been here. Life will be just the same." It was probably the same two thousand years ago when Julius Caesar wrote of it as his "dear Lutetia." You couldn't change Paris because it was an idea, a point of view, a way of living, a philosophy. It was indestructible.

Clop! Clop! went the hooves of the horse on the warm asphalt. By fiacre it was a long trip from the rue Washington to the Place Vendôme; in the same time you could go from one end of Paris to the other by taxi.

His mind fell into a groove, slipping along in a chorus of names: La Païva, Cléo de Merode, Miss Howard, La Castiglione, Cora Pearl . . . the names strung together were like a wreath of jewels or of flowers . . . all the luxurious trollops of the past. They belonged to Paris, growing out of the earth of Paris itself, with their grace and wit and beauty. Each name opened up a vista of gaiety and charm which enchanted the Byzantine mind of the ugly little man, dulling the edge of the frantic boredom born of the slowness of the fiacre. The Place de la Concorde swept past him in a kind of dream. He did not fully wake from it until the fiacre turned into the rue Castiglione and entered the ordered spaces of the Place Vendôme.

.

The Ritz was not Léon's dish. It had always lain outside the circle of his Paris, a world which to him was too rich, too exaggerated, too pompous. He preferred Fouquet's to the Ritz bar. In Fouquet's you might find pimps and bookmakers and kept women and swindlers, but there was a kind of reality, even an earthiness about them; in the Ritz bar you saw kept men and lecherous middle-aged women and over-rich Americans and tramps in sequins. The difference was, d'Abrizzi sometimes reflected, that in the world of Fouquet's people worked at what they did; the world of the Ritz was full of phonies. And d'Abrizzi liked people who worked; the others made him uneasy.

So when he paid off the driver of the fiacre and turned toward the door of the Ritz, the old uneasiness smote him although the Ritz was now a German hotel and the kept men and lecherous old women had fled Paris.

There were Germans everywhere, in the entry, in the main hall, with a sprinkling of men who were there like himself, on business, and two or three women who by their clothes and figures, he judged to be the wives of Boche officers and officials, in Paris to clean up now that they could order anything they wanted and pay for it on their own terms. Watching them, d'Abrizzi speculated that not all the jewels and French clothes in the world could make much difference in their appearance. They possessed a kind of destructive magic, even the dozen or so German girls who had worked for him in his revues. They could ruin an expensive costume merely by putting it on.

He sighed and entered the lift, aware that the two tall officers inside looked at him with distaste and even hostility. He knew they were thinking, "Another Jew!" although he hadn't any Jewish blood except for some remote strain which somehow got into the blood of every Levantine. He stepped aside for one of them to leave the lift, and suddenly experienced a wild desire to jump up and down on the feet of the man. When the moment had passed he was frightened at how nearly he had come to doing it. It was not the arrogance of the fellow which annoyed him nor even the single glance of contempt, but the fury which he felt deep inside himself, the sudden fury of a quick-witted intuitive man for stupidity. The blank stare from the Teutonic blue eyes had been one of utter fathomless stupidity, the stare of a man without intuition. The pride was born of stupidity which could not see there were other people in the world more acute, more clever, who would always defeat him in the end.

Then the lift stopped at his floor and he got out and walked along the corridor to the suite of Major Kurt von Wessellhoft.

An orderly opened the door of the sitting room which was like any Ritz sitting room in the world —red and gold—except that this was a very large room and a large table had been placed in one end of it, a table filled with papers, neatly deposed in orderly piles. In German he explained to the young lieutenant who sat at the table what he had come for and when the lieutenant had gone into the next room, Léon sat down on one of the gilt chairs, his dispatch case on his knees against his paunch, his small feet swinging clear of the red carpet.

Then the door opened and he bounced off the chair. In the doorway stood Wessellhoft, and in his blue eyes was the same opaque stare of the man in the lift. Again d'Abrizzi felt the wave of fury sweep up the back of his neck. One could not talk to eyes like that; nothing happened behind them; they understood nothing. Their only virtue was that you could deceive them, because they saw nothing but that which had a material and a literal existence, things like tables and chairs.

Major von Wessellhoft bowed and sat down behind the table. Without being bidden d'Abrizzi drew up a chair on the opposite side of the table and opened his dispatch case.

"I have brought everything for the censorship," he said, "Some of the acts are ready to begin rehearsals."

"Rehearsals?" asked von Wessellhoft, sitting up straight.

"Yes, it must be a whole new show."

"Why?"

Léon thought, "Here it is again!" Then he said, "As you must understand, the original revue was a patriotic affair. There were many things in it that would not be . . . " He searched for the word and found it, "appropriate now."

"Yes, I suppose so."

"We are calling it *'Paris! Toujours Paris!'*!"

The German Major was thoughtful for a moment. At last he said, "Yes, that's good. That is what we want. We do not want to change Paris. We want it always to be Paris. We want only that it should understand us and the New Order."

D'Abrizzi's face did not change its expression, but behind it his mind was working rapidly. He thought, "So far! So good! He does not comprehend what such a title means!"

From there they went on to one point after another. The Major showed a surprising interest in the theater and an astonishing amateur knowledge of odd technical things which a layman could not have known.

"I compliment you, Major," said d'Abrizzi, laying it on rather thick, but with Levantine skill "on your knowledge. You talk like a professional." The Major smiled. "I have always had a great love of the theater, and a knowledge too. That is one of the reasons why I was assigned this post."

To d'Abrizzi's astonishment he spoke almost

with humbleness. He was being polite, far more polite than Léon had expected. The little man had come with his dispatch case, prepared for insults, prepared even to cringe if necessary to achieve this greater thing that was in his heart and mind. And now this Major was being humble before the theater. There was something naïve about it, like the attitude of a villager in Paris for the first time. It was, he supposed, the German attitude toward Kultur—that it was something to be worked at, with great concentration, awe and laboriousness.

"And the cast . . . it will be first class? It will be the same?" asked the Major.

"All the principals have agreed to come back . . . all save Lilli de Perche."

"That's a pity! I remember her. She was a very fine low *comédienne*."

"She ran away to Nice. She is a Jewess."

"Perhaps that was wise," said the Major. He piled the manuscript of the revue neatly together and at the same moment the door was opened by the orderly. Behind him was a waiter carrying a tray. At sight of him the Major pushed aside the manuscript and said to the waiter, "Put it down here before me.' His French, Léon noticed, was idiomatic, correct but spoken with a thick accent.

The waiter was a middle-aged man, rather anemic, half-bald, with black eyes and an appear-

ance of insignificance. He approached the Major
and then did a curious thing for a waiter at the
Ritz Hotel to do; he put the tray on the wrong
side of the Major.

The act caused a sudden explosion. The face
of the Major grew red and he shouted. "Pick up
the tray and put it down on the other side! I insist
upon being served properly!"

The waiter apologized rapidly in French, bowed,
picked up the tray and put it down properly on
the other side of the young Major. Then he drew
aside the napkin and stood waiting as the Major
surveyed it. There was a chicken sandwich, a small
bottle of wine and coffee. After the first glance
his temper flared.

"I asked for the coffee to be brought up *after*
I had eaten, when I sent for it. Take it away and
bring it back again *hot*!"

The waiter again bowed and apologized. He had,
he said, only obeyed the instructions given him.

"I am not interested in your instructions. I want
what I order."

The waiter took away the coffee and bowed
backward out of the room. D'Abrizzi turned to
watch him and a second before the waiter closed
the door he glanced at d'Abrizzi and Léon understood.

The Major was saying, "I can't understand it

. . . in a hotel like the Ritz. Everything is always wrong. We wouldn't tolerate such service at the Adlon."

But d'Abrizzi understood, *Paris! Toujours Paris!*

"We'll read through the manuscripts and send you word if there is anything unsuitable. You will have them back in twenty-four hours. We are very anxious that the revue should reopen quickly. We want life in Paris to go on just as before."

He rang the bell and the lieutenant reappeared. He was a rather soft pink plump young man who looked as if he had no beard.

"There is one more thing," said d'Abrizzi, "the question of passes and identification papers for the cast."

"We are changing theater hours so that the theaters will be closed at ten o'clock."

"That gives the performer a very small margin and it will be difficult during rehearsal time."

The Major looked at him sharply. "You can vouch for every member of the cast?"

"As much as I can vouch for anyone. All are actors and actors are international-minded. They are rarely interested in politics. Otherwise they would not be willing to reopen."

"Have you a list of the names?"

"Yes." D'Abrizzi fumbled again in the dispatch case and brought out a neatly typed list of names.

It had almost an official look, for d'Abrizzi had had it attested by a notary and there was a seal and ribbon attached.

The Major glanced over it and then looked up, "Roxana Dawn. She is still here?"

"Yes."

"But she is American."

"Yes. But she has lived here for fourteen years. It is like home to her. She is a great favorite in Paris."

"Yes, I have seen her. Four or five years ago when I was attached to the Embassy here." Slowly he folded the paper, laid it with the manuscripts and looked away from d'Abrizzi. "She is a very beautiful woman—very like a woman I know." Then he said, "You will reserve a box for me on the opening night."

"That has already been arranged, Major," said d'Abrizzi. It had not been until this second.

The Major rose as a sign that he was to leave. "I will send an officer to the theater tomorrow at five. Make certain all the cast is there. He will check on their identification papers and stamp the passes. That will put everything in order."

D'Abrizzi stood up. "Thank you, Major, for your co-operation."

"It is nothing at all. I have a great love for the theater. The theater has always been one of the finest things in our German Kultur."

D'Abrizzi went out, thinking, "It is going to be easier than I had hoped." He was thankful suddenly, instead of being annoyed, at the opaqueness of the blue eyes. A Latin would have been intuitive, and therefore suspicious.

When the ugly dark little man had gone, the German Major turned his attention to the sandwich, but although he had had nothing since his second breakfast and was hungry, he found no satisfaction in it. The behavior of the waiter had upset him, profoundly, not simply because the man had put down the tray on the wrong side and brought the coffee against orders, but because these two derelictions were only a part of a long succession of similar annoyances. Things like that were always happening; the lift stopped for him at the wrong floor, people on the street turned to look into a window or crossed to the other side when he approached; the sheets on the bed were pulled too far down by the chambermaid so that it was impossible to draw them much above his waist; the operator of the switchboard was forever ringing the wrong number. Many of these things, he conceded, could be attributed to the natural inefficiency and sloppiness of an inferior undisciplined people, but many of them seemed to him deliberate. Even the French could not be so hopelessly inadequate in their functioning.

These things were superficial but he was aware that beneath them lay a contempt infinitely more profound, so profound that at times he wished ardently that he was with a regiment in the line rather than here in the Ritz in Paris. All the excitement of the first news of his appointment as aide to the Military Governor of Paris had long since vanished and in its place there was only a sense of dullness, irritation and boredom. Nothing was as he had expected. It was all like the "triumphant" entry into Paris which had been as dull and uninspiring as it was possible to be, with even the sun hidden behind gray clouds. The Ritz was not like the Ritz as he had known it before, filled with gaudy people coming and going, the center of an excitement which he had always viewed from the outside with scorn but also with enjoyment. The memories of the bar were not pleasant ones—they were memories of people bowing coldly or turning away from him because he was German—but they were better than the dullness which now infested the place. The bar, the whole of Paris, was like a beautiful animal which, in danger, feigned death. The shell was there but in it were only the invading soldiers wandering everywhere with guide-books and instructions, studying Notre Dame, the

Invalides, the Louvre, the banks of the Seine—all the wonders and beauties which somehow seemed only to dissipate the satisfaction of victory and weigh upon the invaders by the very essence of all they represented.

In the back of the Major's mind there was a curious image. He never saw it quite clearly but it was forever there, stealing into his consciousness each time he passed a group of German soldiers with open guidebooks staring, with craned necks, at the white façade of some superb monument. It was the image, imprinted in his memory since childhood, of a yellowed engraving which hung in his childhood on the gloomy back stairway of the big house in Silesia—the stairway where the monsters of the German forest and German mythology had swarmed about him. The engraving was called the "Sack of Rome" and in it the Goths and Vandals, clad in the skins of wild beasts, stood in the Great Forum staring like savages at the half-ruined wonders of the city.

Major von Wessellhoft had always hated the picture. He hated it now more than ever and each time the memory of it emerged from the back of his mind he thrust it back again with a fierce conscious effort of will.

The waiter reappeared presently with the coffee, placed it with elaborate politeness on the table before the Major. When the Major lifted the pot and poured it, he discovered that it was not hot as he liked it. It was not lukewarm either; it was simply wrong but "good enough" as the waiter belowstairs had remarked "for any Boche." At the discovery a wild rage swept over him and then vanished suddenly, leaving him empty and weary, without the force to send the coffee back again. He could insist that the waiter be discharged and un-doubtedly his orders would be followed, but he knew that even this would do no good. Undoubt-edly the waiter did not care much whether or not he was sent away. And doubtless he would only be given another place where he would not be in evi-dence.

Wearily the Major pushed the coffee aside and took up the papers d'Abrizzi had left on the desk. It was odd how defeated he felt; he had accepted eagerly the post of aide so that he might be in Paris to witness the triumph, and now there was no triumph but only a feeling of deadness. The vic-tory seemed to crumble the moment you touched it.

But this fellow d'Abrizzi! He rather liked him. Like most people in the theater he seemed to have very little nationality. Like most Levantines he was always with the winning side. Very likely he had no loyalty to anyone or anything. One day

they would all be like that, like the Levantines—
Americans, Norwegians, Jugoslavs, English, loyal
to nothing but one idea, the New Order, the glori-
ous new Germany which could impose loyalty by
force. No, this d'Abrizzi was all right. You could
do business with him. If only the others were one-
half as reasonable.

The Major set to work on the papers d'Abrizzi
had left. The sun had gone down and it was already
growing a little dark in the room. He rang for the
orderly to turn on the lights.

Deep in her heart, hidden away even beneath
the level of her own consciousness, Roxie had a
sense of awe about life. This was partly because
although she had never planned anything further
ahead than where she would go for her next meal,
fortunate things had happened to her, almost as if
she had worked out step by step a calculated career.
The unhappiness, the hunger, even the cruelty she
had known, faded out of her existence so that they
had no very lasting reality; this was perhaps because she was a natural, healthy animal, or perhaps
because having come out of nothing at all, she expected very little and the good things which oc-

curred to her always astonished her and were remembered.

The first escape from a squalid home in the slums of a factory town had ended in misery, but it was the escape she remembered and not the unhappiness of betrayal by a cheap and bragging traveling salesman. The freedom that came of the escape was worth more than all the misery which had been the price. When she got her first job in the floor show of a cabaret, it was by accident and not because she had planned it, but she took advantage of the accident and worked hard and so she was picked with fifteen other girls by a Broadway agent to go to Paris to the Café des Ambassadeurs. She knew vaguely that Paris was the capital of France but she had heard nothing of the Café des Ambassadeurs.

It was in the years when the Ambassadeurs was like the last evil flower blooming upon a plant that was already rotten and dying, when it was a brilliant and dazzling interlude in the melodrama of Europe called "The Long Armistice." While she danced, the scene all about her had no significance beyond the fact that it was more flamboyant than anything she had ever seen or imagined. She did not see that among the cabinet ministers and millionaire speculators, the kept women and the actresses, the rich tourists, the ambassadors and the beauties, the jewels and the flowers and the lights, lay the seeds of a corruption and decay which were to bear fungoid flowers of evil and tragedy. To Roxie it was all "simply wonderful" and most wonderful of all was the moment when a card was handed to her by one of the waiters as she stood with the other girls at the edge of the floor waiting for the star turn to finish.

The card, the other girls told her while they changed from costumes to street clothes, was from one of the great theatrical producers of Paris. It was unlikely, they said, that he was on the make for her; a man in his position could have as many girls as he liked. It must be, the other girls suggested enviously, that he wanted to offer her a job.

And so she had gone out into the restaurant itself to be led by the headwaiter with great ceremony to a table where a little dark, ugly man sat alone with a bottle of champagne. It was her first sight of Léon.

He rose and said in thickly accented English, "I am Léon d'Abrizzi. I put on shows in Paris. Will you have some supper with me?"

They sat down and she allowed him to order her supper because she was still a little dazzled and made shy by the spectacle all about her. It was late and the spectacle was beginning to break up. The ambassadors, the kept women, the actresses, the speculators were beginning to drift away. The little dark man, so small that he seemed almost deformed, was watching them. He said, "Take a good look at this. It is the orgy before the end of the world. When the end comes, no matter who wins, it will be terrible, like the fall of Rome."

The speech puzzled her and she did not try to understand it, for not even remotely did she have the knowledge and background and understanding of the little man. She simply put it down as "highfalutin" talk and let it pass.

What he said next interested her more. He said, "I would like to offer you a place in my new revue."

While they ate, and she ate heavily because she was eighteen and healthy and dancing was hard work, he explained to her what he wanted. He had heard of something called "fan dancers" in America. It was a new idea, a new way of exploiting naked female beauty, which would, he thought, be very successful in Paris—not for the French as much as for all the foreigners who came to Paris because it was gay and wicked. He laughed and said, "It is not the French who make Paris weecked —it is the foreigners. The French are a drearily respectable people."

The "fan dancer," he said, must be American. That would make the act all the more exotic and effective. Europe, just then, was mad for everything American . . . cigarettes, jazz, girls, automobiles, everything. He would like to know if she would do the act for him.

She asked, "Why did you pick me?" and he laughed. "That is why I am a successful manager. I am a good picker. You are young. You are beautiful. You are graceful. You have a body so beautiful that even naked there is nothing indecent or immodest about it. And besides you have a face like a virgin." He lighted a huge cigar and said, "I do not say this to flatter you or to seduce you. I am stating facts. I am very professional."

Then he asked her name and she was still so bedazzled that she answered "Irma Peters." He looked at her in sudden astonishment and asked, "That is not your professional name?"

"No. I was born Irma Peters. My professional name is Roxana Dawn."

He considered this for a moment with his head a little on one side, looking like a swarthy turtle. Then he said, "Dawn. . . . Dawn . . . *ça veut dire l'aube*. Not bad. A little silly but it will do."

It was as simple as that. When the new d'Abrizzi revue opened it was called "*Paris en Splendeur*" and in it was a "sensational American fan dancer" called Roxana Dawn who appeared for her number as the favorite Peri in a magnificent tableau called "*Le Rêve de Paradis*." The number was a spectacu-

lar success and after that Roxana Dawn appeared
year after year in the revues at the Alhambra. Paris
was faithful. And so she had never gone back to
America. She sang French like a French woman.
She spoke it, even the "argot," like a Parisian, but
she found nothing remarkable in this. It seemed
only natural that you should learn the language in
which you worked. It was almost as if she had
never had any other life.

She was grateful to d'Abrizzi. For fourteen years
they had been friends who treated each other decently in a dying world where betrayal and thiev-
ery were the code of behavior. This too seemed
to her a reason for wonder.

So it was with the feeling she had about Nicky.
It was something that had come to her unsought,
which she had accepted as she had accepted all else
that had ever happened to her. She hoped for a
little happiness, and what she found was something
she had never suspected—that there could be an
existence without loneliness in which everything
was shared with another person. For that was
what it meant to her. It was an awesome experience
which her instinct told her to mistrust. It made her
afraid, and so on the afternoon Léon went to the
Ritz, she said to Nicky, "I am going out for a little
time."

"I shall go with you."

"No. You must not until Léon has your pass."

"It is safe enough."

"Wait till he gets your special pass. Then no one will question you."

"Where are you going?"

"To Madame de Thonars."

"Who's she?"

"An astrologer."

He laughed. "Why? Are you afraid of something?"

She did not answer at once. "No. Only I want to know something."

"What? Maybe I can tell you."

"No you couldn't."

"It's all rubbish."

"Maybe. I don't know. Neither do you." She turned toward him. "There must be something in it . . . something in the stars. Otherwise things could not happen to me as they have."

He placed both hands on her shoulders. "Are you going because you want to find out what is to happen to us?"

"No . . . and in a way, yes."

He still kept his hands on her shoulders looking at her. But something happened in his eyes. It was almost as if they changed color or a light appeared behind them.

"I'll tell you something, honey. I'm satisfied if you are, for good . . . for always."

She thought, "Now I am going to hear it. Now I am going to get inside." But he did not go on. He turned away from her and went to the window. "I've never had any home or any education except what I picked up by my wits. I'm really only a savage, but if you can take it that way I'm yours for good. You don't have to go to an astrologer to find that out."

"I can take it," she said.

He turned toward her with a smile which seemed to envelop her in warmth. "All right. Go along to your fortuneteller. I'll be a good boy and stay in the house till Léon comes with the pass. I've a lot of things to think over. I feel as if I were coming to life again—the way I used to be. I see prospects."

She did not ask him what he meant for fear of destroying the mood between them or driving him back again inside the shell of mockery. Suddenly she felt much older than Nicky, and much wiser, but at the same time there was in her heart a little pang of sadness and envy.

Madame de Thonars lived in a large house in the

Square Chauseé d'Antin. On one side was a famous and elegant brothel and on the other an apartment house. The Square itself was old but nondescript and unpicturesque and across it from time to time had come prime ministers, kings, actresses, dressmakers, ambassadors and American millionaires— all people who were afraid, seeking from Madame de Thonars some hint or assurance about the future which weighed upon them. Nearly all of them came out of fear although a few came seeking excitement and a few because they were quite mad. Madame de Thonars was both fashionable and famous because three times at least she had foreseen great historical events—the assassination of the Archduke Ferdinand at Serajevo, the assassination of King Peter of Serbia and Barthou at Marseilles and the rise of Adolf Hitler. Her great success she herself attributed partly to her study of the stars, partly to her knowledge of European history, and partly to the fact that she was a clever old woman and made shrewd and daring guesses.

She had not fled Paris when the Germans came because the stars told her it would be safe to remain, because she was old and fat and liked luxury and because she enjoyed good food and was greedy. A refugee on the road did not eat well, sometimes did not eat at all. So she stayed, in the house in the Square Chauseé d'Antin behind locked and bolted doors.

Here Roxie found her in the room on the ground floor where she received her clients. It was a small dark room hung with commonplace *tapisserie de verdure* which had slowly accumulated the dust of twenty years. Even on a sunny day the room was so dark that artificial light was necessary. This was supplied by a bare electric bulb hung by a wire from the ceiling.

When Roxie was brought in by the chambermaid, she was seated at a large table covered with papers spread in disorder beneath the naked light bulb. The light fell downward on the wide flat, sallow face and the enormous bosoms. She was dressed like the cashier of a cheap restaurant, tightly in a dress of shiny black material with a high collar. As Roxie came through the door she looked up and took off the heavy gold pince-nez which she wore attached to a heavy black ribbon.

She said, "*Bon jour*, Mademoiselle!" And Roxie seated herself in the chair on the opposite side of the table where she had sat so many times before.

When they had made a little talk about the Germans, the weather, the reopening of the revue, Madame de Thonars said, "I knew you would not go away. It is in the horoscope that you will stay here . . . for a long time—to the very end."

"To the very end," asked Roxie, "of what?"

"Until there isn't a Boche left in Paris."

"They will be driven out?"

"They will go away. They will run away of their own accord when everything about them collapses."

"And when is that?"

"It may be a long time."

Madame de Thonars swung around in her chair to a fireproof steel filing case such as you would find in a lawyer's office. Pulling open a drawer she fingered through a number of folders, choosing one at length, drawing it out and placing it on the table before her.

"You have not been here for a long time," she said.

"No. Everything was going very well."

"And now?" The seeress looked over the top of her pince-nez at Roxie.

"Now . . . I don't know. Everything is mixed up."

Madame de Thonars opened the folder before her. "Well, we shall see."

Roxie lighted a cigarette and for a long time Madame de Thonars worked with pencil and charts. Then she pushed away the folder and the charts, took off her pince-nez, closed her eyes and pressed her hands against them. She remained thus for five minutes. Then a shudder passed through her fat, elderly body. (This was a part of the performance and not essential.) After a time she opened her eyes and began to speak.

"Something has happened to you. Something to do with a man. It has never happened to you before. It is a good thing. Stick by it. Go where he goes. Do what he does, because nothing like it will ever happen to you again. I cannot predict what the end of it will be, but the thing itself is good, even if it ends badly. You are planning a new venture, probably in the theater. This will begin a success and end abruptly. I cannot tell you the reason. You will be entering on a new phase of life at about the same time, some kind of work you never did before. On the whole, everything is good."

Then she opened her eyes and in a businesslike fashion replaced the pince-nez and closed the folder before her.

A thousand questions rushed through Roxie's brain but there was, she knew, no use in asking them. Madame de Thonars had spoken. She had replaced her pince-nez and that meant that the séance was over. After that gesture she never answered questions.

So Roxie only said, "Thank you. I believe I understand what you mean." But she did not under-

stand. The whole thing left her confused. Usually
the seeress was more exact, she gave more precise
clues.

"You must understand," Madame de Thonars
was saying, "that this is a difficult moment in the
world. Too much is happening. The stars themselves are confused."

Roxie crushed out the end of her cigarette and
stood up. And then Madame de Thonars did an
unusual thing. She got heavily out of her chair and
walked with her as far as the doorway. As Roxie
went out the seeress patted her shoulder, "*Au revoir*," she said, "and good luck. There is much
trouble and suffering ahead, but we shall come
through it as we always have."

In the hallway Roxie slipped five hundred francs
into the hand of the chambermaid who held the
door open. Madame de Thonars was very delicate
about money. Outside in the square stood a gray
German car. Roxie turned to the chambermaid and
asked, "What is that?"

The chambermaid smiled, pleased. "It is from the
German governor. He has sent his car for
Madame." Then her face grew serious, "But you
must tell no one."

As she crossed the Square, Roxie thought, "He
too is afraid." Only people who were afraid or a
little mad consulted Madame de Thonars.

All the way back to the rue Washington she was thoughtful and puzzled a little by Madame de Thonars' behavior. For once the seeress had failed her. What she had said was vague and unsatisfactory and scarcely worth the fee of five hundred francs; certainly it had brought her no peace and done nothing to stifle or give form to the vague sense of confusion which troubled her. She thought, "Probably the whole thing, as Nicky says, is rubbish. Probably I wouldn't be impressed by her if I had been decently educated. That's the trouble with both Nicky and me. We really don't know anything. We were really never taught even how to behave. We aren't very civilized." But she could not escape the feeling that Madame de Thonars had suppressed something she had found in the charts, something which had led the old woman to walk with her as far as the door to pat her shoulder and say, "Good luck!"

She went home by way of the rue Boissy d'Anglas and the rue Faubourg St. Honoré. It was a bright afternoon and hot and Paris seemed more like itself. Little shops were opening up again and there were more people in the streets and the sight of them cheered her. It meant that many of those who had run away were returning. One saw again the ubiquitous delivery boys and concierges walking dogs and women with string bags and long loaves of bread under their arms.

At the rue Washington she unlocked the small door in the great gate through which carriages had once passed and went up the stairs. The salon was empty. She went from room to room calling Nicky's name but there was no sign of him, nor any response. She thought wildly, "He has gone out! He may never come back!"

The drawer in the boule table gave her the clue. It was open and the keys to the cellar were gone.

Quickly she went to the hall and through the doorway down the worn stone stairs. There in the great vaulted cellar she found him, rummaging about among the pieces of old cast-off furniture. At sight of her he looked up, grinning.

She tried not to show any anxiety but said, "I thought you had gone out."

"No. I was trying to amuse myself. I couldn't sit up there doing nothing all the afternoon."

"What did you find?"

"Nothing. It's all a lot of rubbish. But I did get a couple of ideas." He looked about him at the ancient cellar. "It's a wonderful hideaway. You could get away with anything here."

Upstairs in the salon, she asked suddenly, "What do you mean—the place is a wonderful hideaway?"

"No. I can't tell you. The idea is not yet ripe." His eyes were brilliant with excitement. It was a Nicky she had never seen before. He was imitating Léon in his behavior.

"You are not going to do anything foolish?"

"No."

She moved nearer to him, her body filled with foreboding, anguish and desire. "Listen to me, Nicky. I have said I'd stay here with you. We could both go to America where it is safe but you refused that. This is war. They shoot people in war. Promise me that you won't behave like a fool."

He laughed at her. "Twice in Roumania I was taken out of prison to be shot. I was only sixteen years old. It didn't happen. No, it's not in the stars that I end like that."

He had meant to say more, but she clapped her hand over his mouth and said, "Don't talk like that!"

He pulled away her hand and said, "All right! Whatever you like."

"Listen to me, Nicky. This has nothing to do with us. You're a Russian, I'm American. None of this has anything to do with us."

The mockery went out of him suddenly and quite soberly he said, "It has to do with all of us, with you and me and Léon and Luigi. It has to do with everybody—with everybody in the world. Léon knows that."

"Léon knows nothing at all."

"He's smarter than hell."

She looked directly at him. "There are some things Léon doesn't know. He doesn't know what a woman feels who loves someone."

He laughed, "Who . . . me?" And she knew that he had slipped away from her once more. Then ashamed of his mockery, he kissed her, but it was no good. She wanted suddenly to cry, but she only said, "You are a son of a bitch! At heart you're a cheap *maquereau*."

"What do you expect? It's only luck that I can read and write my own name."

"I'm not going to quarrel. Nothing can make me."

The light footsteps of Léon interrupted them. He came up the stairs into the salon, carrying his dispatch case and hat. As he came in, Nicky said, "Well?"

"It went off very well . . . better than I had hoped it could possibly go. I've got papers for everyone." He grinned toward Roxie. "Even for Mata Hari."

"Don't, Léon . . . It isn't funny." She forced herself to speak in order not to cry. It was over and gone again and her instinct told her that there

was something, some secret between the two men,
which she was not permitted to share.

Then slowly the new revue began to take form.
It was made of bits and pieces, mostly old-fashioned spectacle and low comedy jokes turning upon
the triangle. There was no satire since it was not
possible to risk offending the Germans. Very often
they would take home to themselves satire not
aimed in their direction. That, said Léon, was because of their vast sense of inferiority and the over-
sensibility which accompanied it. They were, he
said, a whole nation of people living perpetually
in the expectation of being mocked or insulted.

Léon had most of the work. He took Nicky
as one of his secretaries but Nicky was very rarely
in the theater and the work was done by the same
grim-faced Polish woman who had done it for
twenty years. Where he spent his time was clear
not even to Roxie. He said that it was safer that
he come to the theater only often enough to justify
the appearance of being employed by Léon. A
good many people knew him as Nicky and not
as the Pierre Chastel recorded on his papers and
on Léon's list of employees.

The grim-faced secretary was the daughter of a

circus clown who had been trained when a child as a wire walker but tuberculosis of the hip had put an end to that career and at twenty Léon had given her a job. She was very thin and walked with a limp, dressed always in black, and wore her graying hair drawn back from the thin bitter face. For twenty years she had satisfied her hunger for tents and journeys and lights by holding Léon's small black notebook and watching others perform. She was called Wanda Beck. She remembered everything, from the lines of the skits, to the smallest button or feather on the costumes of "Les Girls." Only Léon knew where she lived, and he knew nothing of her life, whether or not she was married or had a lover, or whether even she had friends. For at least ten years he had seen no sign of any emotion in her impassive face until the day when a German sergeant came into his office bringing a message from Major Kurt von Wessellhoft.

She was standing by Léon's desk when the door opened and the German, without knocking, opened the door. At sight of the gray-green uniform her dark face turned a deep red color and before Léon could speak she said in German, "One knocks before entering the office of a gentleman."

The sergeant stared at her stupidly for a moment and then something, perhaps the intensity of her fury more than her words, made an impression. He took off his cap, and awkwardly like a lout, stood there holding it in his hands, "Pardon," he said, "pardon," pronouncing the word thickly as "*pardone*."

When he had left the message and gone away, closing the door with awed gentleness, Léon turned toward her and saw that she had broken the fountain pen she held in her hand. The hand was bleeding and the blood mingled with the ink. She seemed unaware that she had injured herself. Then suddenly the pen fell from her hand to the floor. She began to sob, pressing her hands against her face so that it too was stained with ink and blood.

Awkwardly Léon tried to calm her but there was nothing to be done. She kept crying out, "*Les cochons!* What have they done to Poland! *Les cochons!*"

At length her fury wore itself out and, ashamed, she said, "I beg your pardon, Monsieur," and limped away toward the washroom. When she had gone Léon went back to his work, thinking, "I can trust her. There is no doubt of that!"

One more recruit.

At Luigi's little restaurant where Léon and

Roxie and sometimes Nicky ate nearly every evening because it was friendly and only a little way from the theater, there were three more recruits—Luigi himself and his wife Maria and his sister, the big Filomena. La Biche with her dusty plumed hat and stage jewelry was always there because she had long since become a pensioner, and now was a pensioner most of the time on credit, for all her *clientèle*, the rich foreigners and a few Parisians who once had slipped her banknotes as she made her begging rounds of theaters and night club doorways, were gone. Now there were only poor people and German soldiers who chased you to cover at ten o'clock in the evening. La Biche had eaten her meals at Luigi's for thirty years. It was not possible now, said Luigi, to turn her away when she had no money.

Night after night Filomena walked her yapping little dog up and down the sidewalk outside the small restaurant, her eyes and ears and nose alert in the darkness for the sight or smell or sound of a German soldier, ready to pass casually by the darkened door and give three quick warning raps on the glass. At the sound of the three raps, all those inside who had no papers disappeared through Maria's trap door into the coal cellar.

There were more of them lately for the Germans had begun to run to cover Czechs and Dutch, Belgians and Austrian Poles and Jews and Slovenians who long ago had fled to Paris because Paris offered refuge and freedom. Some had not been able to escape and others had remained because Paris seemed a better hiding place than a concentration camp or a small town. Paris for centuries had hidden refugees in her bosom. There were hiding places in Paris which no one could discover, especially when you had help from honest citizens and sometimes from the authorities themselves.

They made an odd lot; among them were lawyers and acrobats, doctors and printers, dancers and scientists, even a former cabinet minister and a chief of police. By day they had no life for it was not possible to risk being picked up on the open street. By day they hid away in the dingy flats where someone had given them refuge, in cellars and attics, in garages and dark alleys. Only at night in the darkness could they come out into the air and find their way to Luigi's. Some of them had money and some had none. When they could pay, they paid, when they could not Luigi fed them on vast pots of spaghetti and macaroni and polenta. It was not easy because prices rose, but Luigi dipped into his savings and there was help from another source. One night Léon led him into the kitchen and said, "Who is paying for all this?"

Luigi shrugged his shoulders. "Sometimes they

pay. Sometimes I pay. What does it matter? Prices are going up. Money is going down. In a little while there will only be pieces of paper which you will have to take because the Germans hold a pistol to your head and say, 'Take the paper. It is worth ten marks.' *Que voulez-vous?*"

"All the same," said Léon. And after that Léon left money from time to time with Maria. He had plenty of money hidden away; he was not for nothing a Levantine. No one could trace the thousand-franc notes that you took from under the floor.

There were times in the evening when a kind of sad gaiety crept into the café, as on the evening when the acrobat had taken up his concertina to accompany plaintively La Biche's rendition of *"Savez-vous planter les choux?"* and her memories of General Boulanger. There were times when there was good talk, sometimes in many languages, sometimes in awkward French. Sometimes there was talk between professors and journalists, doctors and scientists, which was as brilliant as any talk had been in the old days at great dinners.

All this Roxie watched, for it was a world that was new and strange to her, a world whose suffering was outside the realm of any personal suffering she had ever known or touched. And the talk made her ashamed because she was so ignorant of the things they talked about. She herself had known what it was to be poor but these people about her were at once poorer and richer than any poverty or wealth she had ever known. There was in their dark eyes a kind of sadness which she had never before encountered—the sadness of a lost people, not only without a home or a nationality but without hope. There were times when a light came into their eyes, the light of a hope which perhaps would never concern or touch them, who were lost already, but a hope which was that of others outside the walls of this narrow, tortured world in which they were trapped. And there was fire too in their dark eyes in the moments when they talked of things beyond the understanding or experience of Roxie herself, making her feel small and empty and insignificant. She would listen to the talk, understanding little of it but impressed, knowing that the things of which they spoke were beyond the bounds of things material or real, yet possessed of a reality greater than any of the shabby things upon which her whole life was founded.

Nicky, beside her, would listen too and sometimes Léon who, with his Levantine shrewdness, understood far more than themselves. But Nicky was more impatient, more childish than she or Léon, and after a time he would grow restless and try to draw their attention away from the talk by some joke or piece of mockery back into the shallow trivial world in which he himself felt secure and at home. Watching him, Roxie felt a sudden, blind pity for him, thinking, "If he had had a chance, he could have been *someone*. He is clever. He is good at heart. Because he never had a chance, he is a tramp." And she would know suddenly, with a quick contraction of the heart, that it was pity which lay at the very foundation of her strange feeling for him. He was like a child. In spite of all the evil he had known, in spite of all the shamelessness of his life, he was innocent.

Once while the three of them were listening to the good talk, she found herself watching his dark face, the eyes bright with a kind of hunger to understand what it was not possible for him to understand because he was half a savage, and as she watched she felt other eyes upon herself and turning she found ugly Léon's face, smiling a little, the hard intelligent black eyes soft with that look of kindness which so rarely illuminated them. He grinned and without saying anything filled his glass with Chianti, then, raising it, he said, "To you both, *mes enfants!*" By that gesture she knew that, having caught her unawares, he had discovered not only the fact that she loved Nicky, but the depth of that love which Nicky himself did not understand. Only once again did Léon even speak of it or show any sign of what he had discovered and that was long after there had ceased to be a Luigi's. In that curious hard and lonely world in which the three of them had lived since they were born, there was no place for what he had seen. It was as if what he had discovered were so precious that in their perverse and shameless world, one needed to be ashamed, as savages are ashamed before the shrine of an unseen God. But the knowledge in some hidden way brought herself and Léon nearer to each other, nearer than they had ever been in all the years of their friendship and their trust in each other. And there was in the black eyes of the little man who was so ugly that no woman had ever loved him, a look of envy and longing.

There was among the motley group of refugees an old Jewish professor whose story had come out bit by bit as he talked in bad French. He was Austrian by nationality with a long thin face, gentle eyes and white hair. First they had taken his son, a doctor, off to Dachau. For a long time they had heard nothing of him and then one day came a simple notice that the son was dead, how or why they were never told. A daughter with her husband and family had been deported to Poland. A second daughter who was a violinist had been made to scrub the pavement before the Hotel Bristol in

Vienna, day after day while she wore across her back a placard reading, "I am a Jew and a communist. I do this as penance." One night she was found dead in a cupboard where she had hanged herself. Then the professor and his wife had tried to escape by way of the Tyrol, crossing the frontier near St. Anton at night by way of mountain paths. They succeeded but the old lady died in Switzerland partly of exposure and hardship, partly because she no longer had any will to live. After that the old man made his way alone somehow to Paris, because Paris was kind to refugees and in Paris there were many men like himself, distinguished and intellectual men, who would help him. And they had helped him, hiding him away even after the Germans came, passing him from house to house when danger threatened. It was a hard life for a man who had been used all his life to comfort, to having his own books and his own study. He never told the whole story, perhaps because it would have been impossible for him to have talked of his suffering. It came to them in bits and pieces from the other refugees, from Luigi, from the old man himself. All of them at Luigi's grew very fond of him because of his gentleness and patience.

And then one night when Léon and Nicky and Roxie came in after rehearsals, Luigi came to them quietly and said, "Do not ask for the professor. He is dead."

The old man had written a note of apology to the family of the house where he was hiding saying that he meant to join his wife, his son and his daughter since he was too old and too sad to continue living. He advised them when they found his body to take it after dark into the street and leave it there. Then no one would ever know who he was or who had befriended him and hidden him. And that was what they had done.

No one ever spoke of the professor again. He was not the first who had disappeared from among those who came to Luigi's after dark. Sometimes it was suicide, sometimes it happened that they were picked up by the Germans. One did not gossip about things like that. They were too terrible and too near to everyone in the little room.

Always each night, at a different hour, there would come suddenly Filomena's three sharp raps on the glass and Luigi would go quickly from table to table saying, "*A la cuisine!*" and those who had no papers would disappear through Maria's trap door into the coal cellar. And every evening at that time Nicky's dark eyes would grow black with hatred and contempt. And at last before they slipped away into the darkness, one by one, La

Biche would raise her glass of absinthe and say drunkenly and solemnly *"A bas les Boches!"*

"A bas les Boches!"

The toast of La Biche Roxie heard again and again from one end of the city to the other. One heard it whispered. One read it in the eyes of passers-by on the street, one heard it cried out in secret places like Luigi's. The apathy of the captured city did not disappear; rather it changed its form and degree of intensity. Sullenness took its place and now and then violence broke out suddenly like flames from a smoldering heap of wood. A German officer was shot outside a Montparnasse garage; another was stabbed not far from Luigi's in Clichy. A sergeant was beaten at the Porte de Lilas. German posters threatening punishment were destroyed and torn from walls or covered with scrawled obscenities. And La Biche's toast appeared everywhere on walls and boardings. *"A bas les Boches!"* Big Filomena while walking her dog always carried a piece of chalk. Her Rabelaisian nature made her very good at thinking up obscene insults.

Each time she heard of some new violence, the shadow of fear crept over Roxie, not for herself or even for the future, but only for Nicky, for she knew that somehow in some way he had to do with these things. It was not that he said anything. He was secretive when she tried to discover where he had been during the day. He only laughed and said, "The usual places," and mentioned a list of bars and restaurants and "clubs."

And then suddenly one night, he said, "Tomorrow there will be some furniture delivered here. Don't be surprised. The men who deliver it will know where to put it. Just let them in when they come."

"Furniture?"

He grinned, "Yes. There is all that empty space in the cellar for storing things. I had a friend who had no place to put his furniture. He didn't want the Boches to steal it."

She looked at him directly and said, "You're lying, Nicky. It's not furniture."

Laughing, he said, "No. It isn't."

"What is it then? I don't mind what you and Léon do, only I want to be in on it. Tell me. What is it?" He didn't answer her and she said, "Are you afraid I'll betray you? Do you think that little of me?"

Again he grinned, "No. Of course not. It's only that we didn't want to alarm you. And what you don't know you can't reveal. What Léon and I are doing is not in your blood. You aren't made for guerrilla warfare. You don't hate enough. To be a good guerrilla you have to hate enough not to care what happens to you so long as you accomplish what you set out to do. I learned to be a guerrilla before I was fifteen years old."

"I do hate the Germans. I hate every one of them in Paris."

He took her hands and spoke very earnestly, "Hate is more than that. A lot more. It's something deep inside you and it's there all the time. Gnawing at you. It is not a pleasant thing. It doesn't just come and go when you are angry about something. It's always there!"

She listened, thinking, "It's true. I don't really hate. How do you hate? And why?" Perhaps it was not in her. Perhaps she could never hate the Germans as Léon and Nicky and Luigi hated them, as an inferior race of savages. It was extraordinary that Léon and Nicky and Luigi with all their shadiness and their humble stations in life should feel that even a German general was contemptible. Yet it was true and she understood the hatred without being able herself to feel it.

"No," Nicky was saying, "you've never really known any Germans." Then his mood became more serious and he said, "I'll tell you about the furniture. I have become a newspaper proprietor, financed by Léon. This 'furniture' is not furniture at all. It is a printing press and type and all the things that are needed—and it's guns too and grenades and stuff needed for making bombs. And the cellar is to be the newspaper office. The paper is called, '*La France Eternelle*' which nothing can destroy!"

She was thoughtful for a moment. Then she said, "You might have told me. After all, it is *my* house."

He laughed, "You are not going to be mean about it. You're not going to refuse two old friends like Léon and me?"

"Sometimes I think I am being used by both you and Léon. Sometimes I think I'm just being a damned fool!"

"No, my dear. You were never a damned fool. You're too smart. But sometimes you are being used by Léon and me. This house is very convenient . . . the last place in the world one would look for trouble. It's so dull and undistinguished. And you're American and an actress. And there is plenty of room in your cellar."

He went on listing the advantages of the house. "Best of all," he said, "it is in the heart of Paris where the Germans have set themselves up and taken over."

"All the same, I don't like it."

"You aren't being jealous of my seditious activities?"

She felt a desire to slap him but it passed quickly. She said, "There is really nothing I can do." After a silence she said, "For the last time, Nicky, will you go to America with me?"

It was a simple question but she was aware of how important the answer was to both of them. Whatever happened to them for the rest of their lives would depend upon the answer. It came quickly.

"The answer is no. I have a job to do here. What should I do in America but go back to rotting away, slowly. I've got something here. I'm alive again the way I used to be. Even if you went, I would not follow you much as I love you. That, my dear, is the bad luck of being loved by a guerrilla. Bandits expect their women to follow *them* wherever they go. For a thousand years, the women of my family have followed their men. Some of them were killed in battle. Some of them starved to death. My father was born in a forest on the edge of a battlefield while his father was fighting the Czar in rebellion. Does that make you understand a little?"

"Yes."

He suddenly put his arm about her and said gently, "You Americans, like a lot of Europeans, have been too lucky. You have grown soft, thinking that automobiles and water closets are the beginning and end of life. You've lost or forgotten the savage pleasures of heroism and hate and sacrifice."

She was aware suddenly that the revelation was once more very near. This voice was Nicky speaking, out of the very depths of himself, the Nicky who was bad and sometimes evil because life had been too soft and savorless. It was not the boy ashamed because he had never learned to be civilized, for whom she felt pity, but a hard man, perhaps a savage one.

"Do you love me very much?" she heard him asking.

Quietly she said, "Yes, very, very much." It was the first time in all her life she had ever spoken those words with feeling and suddenly she was ashamed.

"Will you go to America or will you follow me?"

She smiled, "There isn't any choice in the matter for me." And she heard the self-hypnotized voice of Madame de Thonars saying, "Go where he goes. Do what he does. What has happened to you will never happen again."

In the morning, after Nicky had gone out, a great furniture van appeared before the door. The great doors which once had admitted carriages were swung open on stiff creaky hinges which had been undisturbed for years and four men carried in several large crates marked "Furniture. Fragile. Handle with Care." Roxie directed them to the great cellar and when they had deposited the crates among the accumulated rubbish of years they went away again. They were workingmen, three of them over sixty, for the young men were the prisoners of the Germans or dead. One of them grinned quite openly at Roxie but the others gave no sign of understanding that she knew what the furniture was.

When they had gone away, closing the great door again, leaving the exterior of the house blind and undistinguished, she went back to her room, and for the first time in her life she was really afraid. It was not the sudden hysteria, the panic which attacked her when all the others were fleeing Paris. This fear was a thing with deep roots, extending into the past, flowering perhaps evilly in the future, mingled with dread and foreboding. Somehow, without seeking it, she had drifted into a situation which could only end in violence and calamity. For the first time in her life she was not going it alone. She was entangled with other people, with Léon and Nicky and, she suspected, Luigi and Filomena, and the man who had carried in the "furniture." What happened to her touched them all; what touched any of them touched her. A moment of panic swept over her, and she thought again of Madame de Thonars and the stars. It was an odd destiny for a girl born on the wrong side of the tracks in Evanston.

A little later in the day Nicky returned and with him were a man and woman, each carrying a valise.

"These are the new servants," said Nicky. "They will take care of the house and in their spare time they will clean up the cellar." He introduced them as "Monsieur Chabetz—Henri" and "Madame Blanc—Josephine." By their manner, Roxie saw they really were servants. Like the furniture movers they gave no sign of understanding what lay beneath the surface.

"Josephine," said Nicky, "is an excellent cook. We shan't any longer have to live on sandwiches."

But to Roxie, their presence meant only one thing. Here were two more people whose lives were entangled with her own. Their safety was her safety. Their peril was hers. To her this seemed a terrifying thing.

And the same night Nicky said, "I am going away for two or three days. Don't worry about me."

"Where are you going?"

His face grew serious. "That I can't tell you. It is one of the rules. I'll tell you when I return." Then, he smiled, "You're not going to be jealous, are you? It has nothing to do with women."

"No, I'm not jealous. I'm only worried."

"There's nothing to worry about. I'm awfully good at such things. I've spent most of my life going places, across frontiers and through cities without any papers. I know all the rules. And this time I have papers . . . the most beautiful set of papers."

"The show will open while you're away. I wanted you to be there." She was aware that she was not behaving as a trouper, or even a sensible woman, but like a clinging suburban housewife. She was ashamed but she could not help herself.

"What difference would that make? You've opened shows before now. I've seen you a hundred times."

"But it's different this time." Again she was ashamed and hated herself.

"You're behaving like an ingénue."

"Perhaps."

It was a strange opening, different from any other she had ever known. There was no enthusiasm among the principals or the chorus people. There was not even any excitement. Sometimes, during rehearsals, there had been a laugh which, isolated, died quickly away. And now on the evening the Alhambra was lighted again after so many weeks, there was none of the atmosphere of an opening night.

In her dressing room, Roxie put on her make-up and put the flowers which Léon had found somewhere into a vase. It was not only that Nicky's absence worried her. She already hated the audience which began to assemble nearly an hour before curtain time, like country yokels fearful of being late. Twice she went to the peephole in the curtain to look over the house and each time what she saw left her depressed and troubled. One by one the rows began to fill with gray-green uniforms. Here and there she discovered a single man or a little group of people in civilian clothes. Who were they? Why were they there? Would they hiss and boo because the actors on the stage had consented to carry on and entertain their enemies? They could not know why d'Abrizzi had consented to reopen, why she and all the others, most of them linked to her now in a common plot, had returned. They could not know and no one could ever tell them until it was all over and there were no more Germans in Paris.

And the Germans themselves, sitting there in the gaudy theater, soberly, row after row of them like correct well-behaved gray ghosts. How would they behave at a revue of which they could scarcely understand a word?

As the time drew near, the sense of dread and panic increased. She took off her dressing gown and stood naked while her elderly maid glued and stitched and taped the few gilded feathers which were her costume for the first spectacular scene. Her skin was cold and her hands trembled so that the maid looked up at her suddenly, saying, *"Mais, vous êtes souffrante, Mademoiselle? Qu'est-ce qu'il y a?"*

"There's nothing the matter with me."

Distantly the music came from the orchestra out front, through the sets, through the door itself, but this time it brought no excitement, nor any gaiety. For weeks now she had accepted the presence of the Germans in Paris; apathetically she had grown used to them. But this was different. She felt with horror a new sense of their reality, hating them fiercely, as a kind of formless and menacing mass, and she was glad, for she wanted to hate as Léon and Nicky hated. But she remembered what Nicky had said—real hate was something inside you that did not come and go merely when you were angry or frightened. It was always there, feeding your strength and your courage.

Then the call boy knocked his double knock and called out, "*Deux minutes*, Mees Dawn."

She had heard the call a thousand times before but it had never sounded like this, as if you were being warned that in two minutes you would be taken out and shot. She stood up, still feeling chilled, although the room was hot. She thought, "I must go through with it . . . now! There is no time to escape. I have to go through with it." And then from somewhere inside her a voice asked, "Oh, why didn't you go home? Why didn't you go away before Nicky came back?"

The door opened suddenly and the call boy was standing there. He was red-faced and excited, "*Venez! Venez! Mademoiselle! On vous attend!*"

Following him she managed somehow to cross through the darkness to the foot of the ladder which led up to the great flight of stairs sweeping down from the top of the theater to the lights and the audience. Dizziness seized her. Climbing the ladder was no easy thing with the great headdress of gilded feathers that was very nearly her only costume. The feeling of dread and betrayal returned to her. She remembered as she climbed what Léon had said, "You needn't be afraid. The Boches will think that you are meant to be the

German eagle and think that you are paying them a compliment, but all the time you will be the Eagle of Napoleon which was always gold. The German eagles are black."

At last she reached the top of the ladder, realizing that for the first time in all her career she was late and the orchestra was repeating the last six bars to give her time. Then as she stepped from the ladder into the spotlight at the top of the stairs she heard the voice of the *compère* calling out triumphantly, *"L'Aigle d'or! La Reine des Oiseaux!"*

Still giddy, she extended her golden wings and her slippered feet felt their way downward from step to step into the blaze of lights from below. Her nakedness did not trouble her. She had no consciousness of it. She waited as she moved down the steps for the jeers of those loyal French who would believe she was betraying them.

Step by step she descended to the blare of the music. There were no jeers and no boos, no whistling, and as she reached the bottom of the steps, a wild, warm roar of applause came to her across the rosy glow of footlights and the old sense of arrogant confidence in the perfection of her own body returned to her.

Carefully, to the beat of the music, her naked body undulating in response to the applause, *la Reine des Oiseaux* moved forward to the footlights to take her place in the center of the line of girls each dressed in a few feathers to represent a bird. She stood between a blonde girl who represented a heron and a girl with red hair who was a falcon.

Now on the edge of the footlights she could see into the darkness of the big theater and discern row after row of gray uniforms, interrupted here and there by the civilians in black clothes. The German soldiers were applauding wildly. The faces in the rows near to the stage had a tense excited hungry look—the look of starved soldiers at the sight of so much naked female flesh.

Then as she paraded slowly to one end of the great stage, there emerged out of the yellow darkness the faces of four German officers in a box. Two of them were applauding, one of them laughing loudly. The aspect of the fourth was quite different from the others; he sat very stiff and upright, his arms folded across his chest. He was handsome in a cold gray, blond fashion. She might have passed by him forgetting his existence and his indifference but for the peculiar burning look in the gray-blue eyes. He was looking directly at her—there could be no mistake about it—with a look in his eyes so concentrated and intense that she felt a sudden moment of unaccustomed shame at her nakedness.

As she passed the box a second time, she meant

not to look in his direction but it was as if she had no power over her own movement. It was as if the intensity of the look in the burning eyes forced her to turn her head. When she looked at the box he was still watching her, seated stiffly upright, his arms folded. And now after many years, she was aware, horribly, like a well-brought-up young virgin, that she was naked. It was the first time it had ever happened to her.

The curtain descended and rose again, not once but four times in response to the applause and cheers of the hungry soldiers. Each time the eyes were there in the hazy golden darkness, burning, in the frame of the harsh handsome young face.

Twice during the course of the evening d'Abrizzi came into her dressing room. Carefully he closed and locked the door behind him and spoke in a whisper.

"It is going well," he said. "It is terrific!"

For the first time a little of the old excitement gave an edge to his voice.

"Yes."

She was troubled by the figure in the box but said nothing of it to d'Abrizzi. He would only think it, after all her years of experience, silly to be disturbed by the stares of a lecherous spectator. She could not explain to him that this one was different, that the mad intensity of his eyes had made her feel ashamed.

"Two more of the girls," he said, "have joined us."

"Are you sure of them?"

"They are old friends—Alice and Odette. One of them has worked for me for fourteen years. She has a son of twelve. They can be trusted."

"And Nicky?"

"I've heard nothing from him. There's nothing to worry about. He's smart and he's afraid of nothing."

It was right then, she told herself, what she had said weeks ago—that Nicky was born out of his time, that he belonged in the Balkans or in some remote period of the past when there were bandits.

After the final curtain, d'Abrizzi came in again, his black eyes glittering. He was jubilant.

"The cheese has caught a mouse," he said.

"What kind of a mouse?"

"An aide to the Military Governor . . . von Wessellhoft himself."

"Oh!"

"The one with whom we had all our dealings. He wants an introduction. He wants to take you out to supper."

"What am I to do?"

"Accept. We can't turn down so big a rat."

"And Nicky?"

"I wouldn't worry about him. He can trust you." He looked at her sharply, "Can't he?"

She looked at him with sudden anger. "What do *you* think?"

He shrugged his shoulders, "Okay, honey." And then went on to the point. "We may need this Major some day. If you handle him properly, we may be able to use him. What do you think?"

"I have very little experience as a spy."

"It does not matter. Please him, charm him. It will help keep them off us."

She was troubled again by the burning look in the eyes of the man in the box, for she was certain now that he and Major von Wessellhoft were the same. She had had plenty of experience in handling men. Always she had been successful, but she did not like drunken men or mad men, because they were unpredictable. The look in the man's eyes had certainly been a look of madness.

She was nearly dressed now and d'Abrizzi said, "May I bring him in?"

For a moment she hesitated, still troubled by a curious sense of foreboding, as if in some part of her brain a voice was warning her.

Then she said, "Yes," and rising, turned away from the mirror.

D'Abrizzi opened the door and groveling a little, falsely and almost too much she thought, said, "*Entrez!*"

He came through the door and she saw at once that he was the man from the box.

D'Abrizzi said, "Mademoiselle Roxana Dawn," and the German made a jerky bow. His face was pale but the same burning look was still in the eyes. Quite naturally she held out her hand to be kissed, and then in French, with a strong guttural accent, he said, "It is a pleasure. They tell me you are American."

"Yes. Thank you."

"May I compliment you on your superb performance?"

"*Merci encore.*"

The idea that she gave a superb performance filled her with an hysterical desire to laugh. God and Nature had given her a superb figure, developed by climbing trees and swimming in Evanston, Indiana. She had no illusions about her success, her art or her morals. They were all simple and natural endowments, very slightly increased or embellished by conscious effort. Her success had come because Frenchwomen, even those who exposed themselves in music halls, had figures which by comparison with her own, were wretched. Vócally she had a strong, sonorous, untrained natural mezzo-soprano and God had given her a primitive sense of rhythm denied to the more civilized and sophisticated French. The rest of her success came from a lack of shame about displaying the magnificence of her body. For her that was no trouble at all. Now the compliment made her want to laugh. Performance?

At the same time she was appraising the German's face and figure. There was something splendid about the perfection of the shoulders and hips and carriage and the face had a brutal sharp sort of beauty. It was a male beauty, yet the effect was not male. Out of experience and instinct her whole body, whose dictates she trusted far more than the dictates of her untutored uncertain reason, was filled with distrust. This was not the direct maleness of a man like Nicky; there was something wrong about the German's good looks, like a projected figure slightly out of scale.

"I would be honored, Mademoiselle, if you would have supper with me."

Her instinct told her to refuse, to make excuses, to save herself before it was too late, from what she did not know; but behind the Major's back, d'Abrizzi's black eyes were speaking to her eloquently, urging her on, repeating now all the things both he and Nicky had said before.

"We will go where you like," he said. "To some correct place."

The word "correct" struck her as absurd. The Germans were obsessed with the word. Everyone, everything must be correct. Was it because they were unsure of themselves, not quite civilized? Was that why the idea of formality and correctness was so important to them?

She obeyed the counsel of d'Abrizzi's eyes. "Yes," she said, "we can go to Maxim's if you like."

A bright look came into his face, "Good! It is a gala night there. The Field Marshal is going there. I arranged for his special protection. It will be very gay and official and correct." He stepped forward and took from her the mink coat she had picked up from the chair.

"*Permettez*," he said and put it round her shoulders. Then he clicked his heels together and bowed. "Shall we go?"

At the door of Maxim's she felt a sudden wild desire to leave him and return home. She had not been seen in a great restaurant since the Germans had come to Paris. She knew what she would find inside—only Germans and a few of the French who had sold out or compromised with their enemies. She had no desire to be counted among them, but she knew that she could be useful only if the Germans accepted her. Her conscience troubled her too because until now she had been so useless. Nicky and d'Abrizzi had done everything, all the plotting and organizing and recruiting. They had taken her house as a kind of headquarters and she had accepted the risk of discovery, but beyond that she had done nothing.

In any case it was too late now and too awkward to turn away and leave. The revolving door was turning against the blackness of the curtains inside. There was nothing to do but to step forward into the darkness.

She pushed aside the curtain and suddenly she was in the midst of all the familiar red plush and gold. There was the same music and the same barman and the same *grues* sitting on their stools by the bar. But the men were different, all but one or two in the uniforms of the German army. There was a sickening sense of wrongness about the figures reflected in the long mirrors. Maxim's for fifty years had been the heart of Paris, a kind of symbol with the bar and the music, the red plush and gilt and the girls at the bar.

Then two of the girls looked toward her and smiled. They were the smiles of prostitutes filled with admiration for one of their number who had become a great star and wore sables and diamonds and came in with a high-ranking officer. Yet there were other things in the smiles—recognition, understanding perhaps, and something secret too as if they were saying, "We too are putting up with them but in the end we shall drive them out."

She thought suddenly, "Perhaps they help to distribute Léon's and Nicky's paper. Perhaps they are recruits like myself."

Then her old friend, Albert, the *maître d'hôtel* was standing there before her smiling and bowing.

He was delighted to see her again. He had heard that she had stayed behind in Paris and was troubled because he had not seen her. The restaurant was carrying on. It seemed the best thing to do. There was the same good food, the same good wines. But all the time he spoke, so professionally, so glibly, his pale blue eyes were a negation of the words he spoke. There was, behind the smile, a curious secret look of hurt and shame and hatred.

Then to the Major, he said, "I beg your pardon, sir. There will be a table in a moment. There is a couple leaving." He smiled quickly, almost secretly at Roxie and again she thought, "Does he know? Is he one of us?"

The Major was standing beside her, very stiff and upright and unseeing, as if he did not want to recognize the other soldiers in the place. Then a couple came out of the square room—a wine merchant and his American wife. Roxie frowned and looked away. She knew them. They were a pair who were on the other side, they were among the traitors, the sellers-out. They had welcomed the Germans to Paris. There were others like them who had been willing to sell out friends, country, their own mothers in exchange for what they believed and hoped was protection of their property and privileges. She looked away, thinking, "The girls at the bar are worth fifty of them."

Albert was leading them now toward a table for two—the only table in the room that was free, save for a large empty table on the opposite side set with a dozen places. That, she divined, would be the table of the Field Marshal.

Albert drew back the table and summoned a waiter. "Change this for the gentleman," he said. Then he bowed and went away as Roxie and the Major seated themselves on the *banquette*. The waiter pushed back the table, and then an astonishing thing happened. He lifted the cloth to replace it with a fresh one and there beneath the cloth just in front of Major von Wessellhoft lay a copy of a newspaper. She saw first the black headlines in bold type.

"L'EUNUQUE ARRIVE À PARIS! LE MARÉCHAL, SYMBOLE D'UNE CIVILIZATION STÉRILE!"

That was all she saw. For a second she thought wildly, "They know! They have planned this!"

And then almost at once she saw that this was not true. The strange, stiff Major did not know. He stared for a moment at the newspaper as if fascinated, as if a snake instead of a newspaper had appeared from beneath the cloth. The waiter regarded him in terror, still holding the cloth in his trembling hands.

She was aware that all three—the Major, the waiter and herself were the victims of a kind of suspended animation. The waiter broke the enchantment. He said passionately, "Monsieur, I know nothing about it! I did not know it was there! I swear it!"

Then Major von Wessellhoft did a strange thing. He picked up the paper, folded it carefully and put it into his pocket. To the waiter he said, "I believe you. Go on with your work."

To Roxie he said, "Have you seen that paper before?"

She spoke quickly, her heart still pounding, "No. I know nothing about it."

"It is a pity. We are trying to be so correct. We want all Frenchmen to understand that we are to be their friends, to save them from their corrupt democracy. This sort of thing does no good."

Only then came to her the realization that as her companion had folded the paper, she had seen its name, its title printed above the headlines. The printed title remained before her eyes, imprinted against the mirror and the figures opposite. *"La France Eternelle!"* It was Léon's and Nicky's paper. It had been printed in the cellar of her own house! They had indeed worked quickly.

Almost at once she was aware of an excitement and confusion all about her, of German officers standing and the two or three French people who were perhaps traitors or were, like herself, fighting on the other side. That was something you could never really know until it was finished. The band began to play *"Deutschland! Deutschland!"* She turned toward the door as the Field Marshal came in.

She had seen many photographs of him in newspapers and always he had seemed monstrous and unnatural, gross and false, jovial and sinister. Now the reality surpassed anything she had imagined.

He stood for a moment in the doorway, surrounded by seven or eight young men, most of them blond, like a bad, elderly actress making an entrance. His immense grotesque body was covered by a uniform of pale canary yellow. The great rubbery chest, with breasts like those of Erda, was ornamented by dozens of decorations. As he stood there, he raised one pudgy hand to his throat to adjust the decoration that hung there, and she saw that the fingers were covered with rings, diamonds and emeralds and rubies.

Then he moved forward as Albert, walking backward, bowed him toward the empty table. Albert, like Léon, rather overdid the bowing so that the whole scene seemed to go out of focus slightly and slipped over the border into burlesque and mockery. Roxie felt a wild hysterical desire to laugh.

As the Field Marshal moved forward the troupe of young officers followed. They were good-looking and healthy and straight, yet there was in their arrogant carriage a curious nervous self-consciousness. They were clearly unhappy young men save for one with a boldly made-up face who seemed brazen and gay.

In the midst of the scene she was aware suddenly of the tenseness of the Major, standing there stiffly beside her. She turned toward him and saw that his face was a deep, angry red. He had taken a fork from the table and bent it double with the fingers of one hand. She thought, "How extraordinary! He hates him!"

Then still watching the Field Marshal as he carefully placed the young men at the table as an old dowager might have done it, she said softly, "*Mais, c'est formidable!*" and with equal quietness her companion answered her in a strangled half-voice. "Yes, it is true. He cannot make love himself. He surrounds himself with those who can. *C'est un voyeur.*" And she was aware again that her companion hated the Field Marshal with a cold passionate hatred. She thought, "So it is like that! It is possible that among themselves they hate each other more than they hate us."

Then the Field Marshal seated himself heavily on the red plush *banquette*, his thinning, dyed, blond hair reflected in the mirror behind him, and all the others in the restaurant seated themselves again. Fascinated, she watched him as he asked Albert to pour the champagne and Albert took the Jeroboam from the ice and in turn filled the glasses, beginning first with a few drops in the glass of the Field Marshal. Albert performed the operation with the same exaggerated air of ceremony with which he had bowed in the Great One. The filling of each glass before each young man became a delicate mockery, too subtle for any German ever to understand. Albert, the most experienced and impeccable of waiters, gave the performance of a vulgar *bistro garçon*, groveling before royalty. But the Germans liked it. It was obviously their idea of how a waiter should perform his duties.

All at once she was aware with a kind of horror that the Field Marshal was looking directly at her. She turned away but without seeing him knew that he was still watching her and she still saw the smile with the wet unnaturally red lips, the puffy cheeks and the cold blue eyes, opaque with madness. The Major was saying something in a low voice. She did not hear all of it, only that he said, "Pretend not to notice." And she experienced for the first time a feeling of friendliness for him.

She occupied herself with the menu card, but in a moment she was aware of someone standing by the table speaking to the Major in German. Without looking up she heard him reply coldly in French as if to reproach the newcomer, "Very well, then." And turning toward her he said, "I would like to present Lieutenant Hessell."

Looking up she discovered one of the young men from the Field Marshal's table—the bold, frivolous one who had made so gay an entrance. He pulled out the table with an air of arrogance. The Major said, almost with an air of apology, "We shall have to go over to him."

Aware that everyone in the room was staring at

herself and the Major, she crossed the room, her knees trembling. As they reached the table, all the good-looking young men rose but the Field Marshal remained seated. She saw, looking at him with fascination and repulsion, that he was made up like a *cocotte*, heavily, even to the green-tinted shadows on the eyelids. She thought, "He is exactly like a Madame—a wicked old Madame, the kind who would beat the girls and steal from them." She was aware of all the other cold blue eyes, that they did not look at her with flattery and admiration as other men looked at her, but nakedly and coldly without warmth or gallantry.

Aware deep inside her of the cold sexual hatred of a woman for a perverse impotent man, she thought, "I will force him to kiss my hand." And instead of bowing, she held her hand toward him across the table. He understood the gesture and a glint of humor came into the eyes. Bending a little, painfully, for he was tightly corseted, he put his lips to her hand. As she withdrew it, she was aware that its whiteness had been stained by the red of lipstick.

He said, in thick heavy French, "I am enchanted to make your acquaintance, Mademoiselle." And to the Major, "You are very fortunate to have found so charming a companion." Then in German he said something more. The Major did not reply in German but in French. He said, "I beg you, Monsieur le Maréchal, to wait for another time. It would be embarrassing and not very correct. In any case Mademoiselle is an American."

For a second the eyes of the Field Marshal turned cold and he said, "You are quite right, Major. I beg your pardon." The frivolous young lieutenant tittered boldly, and the Field Marshal said, "Well, on some other occasion." And turned to speak to the young man on his right.

"*Venez,*" said the Major quickly, and bowing again they left the table.

The Major's face had taken on again the unnatural red color. As they sat down he said, "He asked us to sit at his table. What he wanted of us was unspeakable." He took up the menu card, placed a monocle in his eye and said, "I should avoid all of them. They are not healthy."

Then Nicky was with her, very near he seemed and astonishingly real. There was gaiety in him and abandon and tenderness. In these others there was something dark and twisted and complex. The awareness of them, the awareness of a concentrated, intricate lechery, became overwhelming. It was as if the room were filled with a nauseous fog. She thought, "Nicky! Oh, Nicky!"

The rest of the evening held for her the quality of a nightmare.

She had come, hoping to find a little of the old gaiety. She loved the old Maxim's. She had been happy there and gay, in the fantastic years between wars. She had loved the luxury, the good food, the brilliance of a spectacle made up of senators and their aging mistresses, courtesans, millionaires, dressmakers, ambassadors, actresses. There were times when the ostentation seemed vulgar and melodramatic, when the luxury cloyed. There had been a strange kind of insanity about it, as of people feasting in the crater of a volcano. But it had never been like this.

A sense of doom, of complicated Gothic perversion, a curious blend of animal vigor and utter decadence filled the mirrored room. It was as if the tables were peopled by characters out of Felicien Rops, as if they were caricatures with heads of animals. Opposite her the Field Marshal was a caricature with the head of a pig, rouged and made up, even to shadows beneath the puffy eyes. The long table was like a caricature, laden with lobster and pheasant and magnums of champagne. Why was it, she thought, that Germans always seemed to be caricatures of themselves? She remembered them all, the fat tourist families in Cannes, the sweating youth groups with knapsacks on their backs in the Salzkammergut who should have been beautiful but were not, the pompous generals with scarred faces and monocles in the Walterspiele in Munich, little ratlike Goebbels and the Führer himself. All, all were caricatures, even the man beside her for all his cold good looks. He was a caricature of a young Prussian officer.

She saw that the young men at the table opposite were conscious of her beauty and kept watching her. Even the Field Marshal himself leered at Major von Wessellhoft as if to congratulate him on his conquest, and she remembered what the Major had said, *"C'es un voyeur!"* And the revelation of the newspaper with its streamer, *"L'Eunuque Arrive à Paris."* And then out of the past there came the memory of a joke about the birth of the Field Marshal's child, brought back long ago by d'Abrizzi from Berlin before there was a war. . . . "If it is a boy, there will be a twenty-one gun salute—if a girl, eighteen. If nothing at all, they'll shoot the adjutant."

All the while the Major was being "correct." He ordered partridge and champagne and salad and *pâté de fois gras*. And as she ate, she thought of the millions of people in Europe who had not enough to eat, of children starving and old people dying of exposure, of the frightened dark eyes of the refugees fed by Luigi, because of the men in this room. And as she hungrily ate the pale pink *pâté de fois gras*, watching the grotesque table on the opposite side of the room, she thought that she was beginning to understand something of the hatred that drove Nicky and the little swarthy Levantine, d'Abrizzi.

The Major conducted the conversation rather in the manner of a cross examination, asking her about New York in which he seemed to have a great interest, and what it was like to live in a country where there was no real law and citizens lived at the mercy of gangsters.

All the while she kept watching him, speculating as to what sort of man he was, for she had never encountered any man like him. Out of experience she knew from his manner that he found her attractive and even desirable, yet the adventure of the evening was passing without any advances from him, save for the burning, mad look in the blue eyes. She might as well be having supper with an elderly virgin governess.

Presently she began to feel both bored and tired. It would, she decided, have been more interesting if he had made violent and annoying love to her. It was after one o'clock when at last she said that she must go home. The party of the Field Marshal was becoming riotous and the feeling of uneasiness and the sense of the sinister grew more oppressive. She felt that if she did not escape she must scream.

The Major quietly paid the check and, rising, pushed back the table. She knew that all the eyes in the room were again directed toward them. In those eyes her companion had achieved what none of the others had accomplished; he had made a great conquest in the midst of the sullen resentful city.

He went with her back to the rue Washington in the gray bulletproof car driven by an orderly. He still spoke to her in French. He didn't attempt to touch her but he said presently, "You know, you are very beautiful."

"Thank you."

He went on: "I have enjoyed myself very much this evening. I hope you have enjoyed yourself."

She answered politely, "Very much."

"I hope it is the first of many evenings like this. I hope you feel the same way."

"Yes, of course."

She saw that they were taking a wrong turning and told him to correct the driver. The rue Washington was neither a fashionable nor a notorious street, only dull and obscure and difficult to find if you did not know Paris.

They arrived presently, under her guidance, at the big door of the house. He got down with her and said surprisingly, "Is it too late for me to come in and have a glass of wine?" The "correctness" made her want to laugh again. She was praying in her heart that Nicky had returned and was waiting for her. So she said quickly, "It is very late. Besides, it will be difficult with my servants. They are French. They might not understand my bringing you, a German officer, into the house. I cannot blame them. They have been with me for a long time."

Gravely he said, "I understand." Then he brought his heels together bowed, kissed her hand and said, "You will not be offended if I come to the theater tomorrow evening?"

"No."

She put the key into the lock and pushed open the door.

"Good night."

"Good night."

As she closed the door she heard the big gray car with bulletproof glass roar away down the empty silent street.

Then as she locked the inner door someone switched on a light and her heart stopped beating. From the hallway above Nicky appeared in pajamas and the red dressing gown, coming down the steps three at a time. When he took her in his arms she began to cry and suddenly he held her at arm's length saying, "What is it? What happened? Who brought you home in a car?"

Upstairs, over a bottle of champagne, she told

him the whole story of the evening, crying now and then from weariness and nerves. He listened, sometimes laughing at her description of the behavior of her admirer and the account of the rouged Field Marshal and his party at Maxim's.

"It was not funny," she said gravely. "It was like going into hell. I'll never again go back to Maxim's until there isn't a German in Paris."

Again he took her into his arms and kissed her, and she thought how different he was from the strange man with whom she had spent the evening. Nicky was excited, tender, warm, humorous, lovable. She had never loved him so much.

Excitedly, while she undressed, he told her of all he had been doing. He had been to Toulouse and Marseilles. He had been led across the border of the occupied region through copses and forests by a peasant. Returning he had been hidden in a cart of hay. The trip had been successful. He had acquired twenty recruits for the program of sabotage.

When he had made love to her, she said in the darkness, "I am afraid."

"Of what?" he asked.

"I don't know. Don't think I'm silly but I never met men like these Germans."

"They are animals . . . very sad, depressing animals," he said.

In the darkness she wondered again about the

question of hate and dismissed it. She could not feel hate but only disgust. Then suddenly she said, "Do you think d'Abrizzi is right in asking me to be agreeable to them?"

He was silent for a moment. Then he said in a very reasonable voice. "Yes. You may learn things from this sad Major, and if any of us should be arrested you might be able to help us if you are clever enough."

"I am not very clever."

He laughed. "I think d'Abrizzi is right, so long as you don't fall a victim to your correct admirer."

"It is nothing to laugh about," she said gravely. "I will be faithful to you long after you have forgotten me."

"Oh, no. That never!"

Then she asked, "Do you think that business of finding the *France Eternelle* under the tablecloth meant anything? Do you think it was arranged by them as a trap?"

"No. It was put there by one of us . . . a waiter or perhaps a scrubwoman. There are many of us."

When Major von Wessellhoft left her he went back to his apartment in the Ritz. He undressed and went to bed but there was no sleep in him. He lay awake, tormented, until the gray light came in between the brocade curtains.

Because a strange thing had happened to him. For the first time in all his existence a woman had become important to him and it was the wrong kind of woman. It had happened quickly, coming upon him without warning, as if all the pent-up, congested, unsatisfied desire had suddenly flowered in this one evening. Somewhere in the dark reaches of his tight, regimented mind, old shadows had risen out of the remote past to confuse him. Among them was the figure of the Swabian girl by the name of Lisa who had taught him as a child of five to read and write. For a long time, unconsciously, he had judged all women by Lisa. Because she had always come between him and any woman he had ever known, there was something twisted and thwarted in his soul.

And then as he sat in the box at the Alhambra, Lisa had suddenly appeared again, coming down a light high flight of stairs, naked save for the gilded feathers of the eagle . . . the eagle . . . the eagle. The Eagle was there too among the worshiped images of his spirit—the eagle—symbol of pride and arrogance and conquest and victory, of all that he had been taught since childhood. Now Lisa had come back into his life as an eagle. It was like a wild dream in which symbols fell into place to make a pattern of fantasy. *La Reine des Oiseaux* had Lisa's skin, her white ivory body, her dark hair, her clear blue eyes, her soft voice. But this woman who looked like Lisa was everything he had been trained to deny . . . she was American, of a mongrel race. She was an actress, possibly a harlot, at least a courtesan. It was evil of Lisa to return thus, as if she were having her revenge for the humilities she had borne as a Swabian in a Prussian family. Toward morning, sleepless, he had begun to hate rather than love her. But there was no escaping her.

In the morning after Nicky had gone away she lay in bed with the pink satin curtains still drawn across the windows, for a long time, thinking. In the darkness, alone, things seemed cleared to her, but more vivid too and more frightening. She had a great need for clarity because her life had become confused and full of dread.

Lying there, she thought first of all, "It is because I don't know where I am going. It is because I have never before been attached really to anyone or anything. I am afraid now because in spite of anything I can do I am entangled with other people and cannot escape and because I am in love with

Nicky. Always before I have been free to do what I wanted, to quit and run away if I grew tired or bored or afraid. Now I cannot run away."

All that was changed now, and gone, vanished as if it had never existed. In her house, only a little way from her in the vaulted cellar, people to whom she was tied by the terrible bonds of conspiracy were at work printing the paper she had seen for an instant last night on the table at Maxim's.

The first knowledge had come to her suddenly in the gray hours before dawn after Nicky, with the simplicity of an animal, had fallen asleep. She was aware dimly of a kind of wonder at what was happening to her, what indeed had already happened to her. It was as if she were suddenly growing a soul, a new kind of awareness, of many things she had never understood nor even known. For one, the curious warm loyalty of Luigi and his family to the frightened, despairing refugees abandoned by those who had promised them sanctuary. She had discovered Léon's bitter, stubborn determination of which she had never before had any suspicion, and the change in Nicky, as if all his evil traits in the past had been born of restlessness and despair and were now dissipated because he had a purpose. She saw very clearly that what Léon had said was true—Nicky was meant to be a bandit not a gigolo.

She was astonished too by the Major and the young officers in Maxim's, not because she was innocent and inexperienced—in her world all sorts of strange vices and perversion were common enough—but because the quality of all these men was inhuman and alarming. She had met few Germans in her life and no Prussians at all.

She felt a desire to talk with someone of all these things but she did not know how to talk of them and could think of no one with whom she might talk. Nicky would only dismiss them impatiently because he lived by action and not by thought, and Léon would only say, "What did I tell you?" And she was not at all certain that she could talk of them because she was accustomed to talk in slang only of trivial things or the things associated directly with her own ego and her own career. She felt ignorant and very humble before these revelations, as if until now she had never really understood anything, even the simplest things.

The sudden growth of soul, of depth, of understanding is not a simple, easy thing. It comes sometimes to people late in life, and the later it comes the more painful and bewildering the experience can be. It was happening now to Roxie. It had been happening since the moment when she had turned away from the window in Claridge's because she could not look at the spectacle of German soldiers coming up the Champs Elysées. She was growing a soul and the process bewildered and hurt her, because never before had anything ever touched her, even in her relations to other people. Something was happening even to the quality of her feeling for Nicky, which made all that happened before seem trivial and fleshly and shaming.

A little before noon, she rang for coffee and it was brought after a very long time by the man Nicky had provided as *maître d'hôtel*. He came in dressed in a striped waistcoat and shirtsleeves as if he had been doing the house when she rang. He showed no sign of being anything but a servant. He performed his duties to perfection with an air of experience and detachment.

He asked her if everything was as she liked it and instead of answering him she looked at him directly and said, "I understand. You do not need to pretend."

He looked at her with a perfectly empty expression in his black eyes. "Pretend what, Madame?" he asked.

"We are all together," she said. "You do not have to pretend to be a *maître d'hôtel*."

"But I am a *maître d'hôtel*, Madame," he said. "Monsieur d'Abrizzi engaged me." Then he smiled a little and added, "But we *are* all together, Madame. We are all citizens or friends of the Republic."

She felt a sudden affection for the little man. It was extraordinary how intelligent the French always were, even the little people like this man. For her it was not a new thought and yet it was always new, and a little astonishing.

"You are right, my friend," she said, and found that, without any conscious sense of will, she had held out her hand to him. He took it without hesitation as if the situation in which they found themselves wiped out all differences between them. It was a curious, simple gesture direct and friendly, and for her it had a profound meaning. It was as if she had become one of them, *really*, for the first time, as if she had accepted at least in a small way the entanglement which she could not escape.

When he had gone away, she experienced a curious feeling of completeness and satisfaction as if she had come suddenly to life, as if the numbness of mind and spirit were gone. She was no longer alone as she had been all her life.

When she had dressed she went down into the big lower hallway and turned the latch of the door leading into the cellar. The latch moved but the door did not open and she thought, indignant, "After all it is *my* house." Then she knocked twice, and three times, each time a little harder. After the third knock a voice asked, "Who is it?"

"It is Mademoiselle Dawn. I want to come down."

She heard the sound of bars being lifted and in a moment the door opened and the *maître d'hôtel* stood there, "I'm sorry, Mademoiselle. It was Monsieur d'Abrizzi's orders to keep the door bolted while we were working."

"Of course."

He stood aside while she descended the worn stone steps into the cellar.

It was no longer dusty and empty. There were seven people in it and the rubbishy furniture had been piled at one side near the door leading into the wine cellar. One person was the *maître d'hôtel*, another was the cook. A third, surprisingly, was Filomena. She had her little dog with her and carried a big black string bag filled with vegetables. The other four she had never seen before.

At sight of her, Filomena grinned, delighted with the surprise. They greeted each other and Roxie picked up the little dog which yapped with pleasure and excitement.

Then the *maître d'hôtel* said, "We all belong

here, Mademoiselle. This is Monsieur Dubois, Madame Vladek, Mademoiselle Malkowska and Monsieur Lopez."

They shook hands all around. She was certain that none of the names were real names, but that did not matter. Lopez was obviously French—the plump, blue-eyed blond type of French workingman. The others might be French or might not be. Behind them stood the hand printing press. They had been operating it and there was a smell of ink in the musty air.

She said to Filomena, "How did you get in here . . . not by the front door?"

Filomena laughed and the *maître d'hôtel* said, "No, Mademoiselle. They came in from the rue de Berri—all but the cook and myself. As servants we use the proper entrance."

"But how?"

Monsieur Lopez grinned and stepped to a cheap, battered old wardrobe. With very little effort he pulled it out from the wall.

"See!" he said. "It leads to the garage in the rue de Berri."

It was very interesting. They had knocked a part of the built-up wall inward, into a vaulted passage long ago bricked up, like the passage that led to the wine cellar.

"But what if someone came through it you didn't expect?"

Monsieur Dubois answered her. "We always have a guard stationed at the garage end. If anyone came we could escape from here by the front of the house or the garden."

It was all melodramatic and yet singularly clever. Léon must have explored all the possibilities before he settled on this cellar. Even Nicky had never told her.

Monsieur Dubois pushed back the wardrobe and the woman called Madame Vladek and the man called Monsieur Lopez went back to the press and started it moving. The papers fell off, damp and odorous, printed on one side. It was an old-fashioned press which printed only one side of the paper. It had to be run through twice. A pile of neatly folded copies lay on a broken table salvaged from among the old furniture.

She picked one from the top. It was the same edition which had lain beneath the soiled table-cloth at Maxim's.

Filomena said in her deep voice, "It's beautiful, isn't it? *'L'Eunuque Arrive à Paris.' Quel salaud!*"

"I met the eunuch last night," said Roxie.

"Really," said Filomena with passionate interest. "Tell me about it."

But Roxie could not tell them about it. The unpleasantness was too great. The others came closer to her, all save the two who worked the press. Above the noise they had not heard her remarkable statement.

"It was nothing," she said. "A fat man covered with decorations. But one of these papers was under the tablecloth at the table where we sat."

"Who was *we*?" asked Filomena impudently.

"I went to Maxim's with a major."

"A German?"

"Naturally."

"*Tiens!*" said Filomena. "That's certainly interesting news. Did you discover anything?"

"Nothing . . . nothing at all."

The others listened without speaking. It was as if they wished to remain as anonymous, as shadowy as possible. But Filomena was an old friend.

"When are you coming to our place?"

"I don't know. When I can. Now the revue is open it's impossible to come except early in the evening."

The heavy old press went on clanking in the background. The *maître d'hôtel* was holding out a card toward her. "Have you seen these, Mademoiselle?"

She took the card from him and read it. In simple type, in English, it read only, *"With the com-pliments of the British Secret Service."* She looked at him for an explanation.

"We slip them under the doors of rooms occu-pied by the Boches, sometimes into the pockets of their coats and inside their caps. It is easily done and very effective. The Germans are naturally a morbid people. It upsets them more than the aver-age people. We are constantly thinking up new things." He smiled modestly but with pride.

"Beautiful, isn't it?" said Filomena. "Well, I must get back."

She picked up the string bag filled with pack-ages and a sprinkling of unwrapped carrots and potatoes and a long loaf of bread wrapped in paper. These she emptied onto the table. Picking up the bread, she removed the paper and broke the loaf in half. Then she took up a score of the freshly printed copies of *"France Eternelle"* and rolled them into a tight roll no bigger than the circumference of the loaf. Laying this end to end with one of the half loaves she wrapped the whole in paper and tied it with string. She repeated the operation with the other half loaf and when she had finished there appeared to be two paper-wrapped loaves of bread lying side by side. Then she picked them up and thrust them into the string bag, the end containing the newspapers first. At last she piled on top of them more packages and a sprinkling of carrots and potatoes.

Looking at Roxie, she said, grinning, "You see? Simple, isn't it?"

She took the little dog from Roxie, set it on the floor, fastened the leash to her big wrist, adjusted the rusty black crocheted shawl over her massive shoulders and picked up the string bag.

The *maître d'hôtel* pushed back the wardrobe and Filomena, turning to Roxie, said, in her rolling niçoise accent, "*Au revoir, Mademoiselle! A bientôt et vive la France!*"

Then with the comical exaggerated gait of a concierge she went through the opening into the passage leading to the garage. It was a clown's performance but magnificent. When she came out of the garage into the rue de Berri, no one could possibly suspect that she was a carrier of the awful "*France Eternelle.*" She would simply be a concierge who had been out to do the marketing with her little dog and stopped in at the garage to speak to her cousin who worked there, washing the cars of German officers.

When she had gone and the wardrobe was once more in place, Roxie said, "We'll open wine and celebrate. I'll fetch the keys."

The *maître d'hôtel* went with her as she unlocked the two doors which in turn shut off the wine cellar. This part of the cellar he had never seen and as she unlocked the steel door that shut off the damp cold wine cellar itself, he exclaimed, "What a place! What a tomb! And in the very heart of Paris!"

She let him choose the wine and he selected a bottle of *Vin d'Anjou*, a simple good wine.

"Better take two bottles," she said.

"*Merci, Mademoiselle.*"

He carried out the bottles and she relocked the doors.

After they had all drunk a toast to "*La France Eternelle*," she left them and went upstairs once more, slowly and thoughtfully.

No, it was impossible to defeat a people like that. You couldn't say properly that they were a *people*. Only three of them, she suspected, were French— the "cook," the "*maître d'hôtel*" and "Monsieur Lopez." The Vladek woman was probably Czech or Jugoslav and Dubois Spanish. Her thoughts ran on—and Nicky was Georgian, like Stalin himself, Léon a Levantine, a God-knows-what, and she American while Luigi and Filomena were really Italians. And of course there were all those people with the burning, sad eyes, whom Luigi fed. . . .

It was as if the Germans had raised the whole world against themselves.

Léon came in about five o'clock with his dispatch case. He seemed cheerful, almost gay, because the revue was obviously a success. All that hodgepodge of spectacles and tableaux and old worn-out blackouts having to do with husband and wife and lover, all the old scenery and costumes dug out from other shows, had delighted the Germans.

He said, "As a race, they are real hicks. They think it's all very wicked and gay and French . . . even the officers who should know better." He had been a little worried for fear some of them, like Major von Wessellhoft, would see through what he had done.

His pupilless black eyes sparkled in the ugly face. He was gay, thought Roxie, almost too gay. It might bring bad luck.

"And they went for the girls too. Eleven of them wanted to meet girls." He cocked his bald head thoughtfully on one side. "They are different about women too. They want women the way you take a physic or a liver pill and then when they're bedded they lie there and cry about Gretchen and the children at home in Posen." He slapped his knee. "They are the God-damnest people. They never seem to get anything straight. Everything they do is cockeyed. It's been so all through their history."

There didn't seem to be any hate in Léon just now. With that light of intelligence which often came into his black eyes, he was being scientific, studying these Germans as strange animals.

"What girls did they select?"

"They didn't select them, I did . . . to make sure they got the right ones."

"Did they?"

"Yes."

He laughed. "It's a new kind of pimping. I've never done political pimping before."

"What if one of them falls in love?"

"That's unlikely. I chose the old experienced ones. They understand the difference between love and business . . . There was Yvonne and Félice and . . . you know them all."

She nodded.

"And eight or nine others. They know the difference too between love and patriotism. It's wonderful how whores can love their own country." He lighted a cigar and said, "And your deluxe job? How did it go?"

She told him quietly, describing the strange

evening in great detail. Suddenly she could talk about it, because Léon's approach was different. He made the whole thing seem objective and scientific. She saw it now, suddenly, in the same light and that made it easy.

In the middle of the story he laughed and smacked his knee again. "*L'Eunuque Arrive à Paris*. I wrote that one. So he's a peeper, is he? That's a new one." He leaned a little toward her. "He got a copy of the paper too. We found a way of getting it to him. It was lying in his bathtub when he got up this morning."

"I don't know whether I can go on with it," she said. "I don't know whether I can take it."

He took the cigar out of his mouth. Usually he talked with it hanging from one corner. He only removed it when he sought to invest what he was saying with an air of importance. "You take the wrong attitude. Your psychology is wrong. Look on the whole thing as an adventure, as an experiment. It will teach you a great deal."

"Maybe I don't know how to do it that way."

"You'll learn." He put the cigar back in his mouth. "This guy . . . this Major . . . is he attractive?"

"I don't know. I didn't have any feeling one way or another about him. It was like being out all evening with a ghost."

"He's a good-looking guy."

"I suppose so. I really didn't have any feeling about that either, and I ought to know."

"You certainly should." His eyes narrowed shrewdly. "Nicky wouldn't be getting in the way, would he? He wouldn't be falling in love with you?"

She felt the color coming into her face. It was something which had not happened in many years. "What did you think it was between us?"

"I didn't think it was love, exactly . . . up to now." He leaned forward and this time instead of slapping his own knee he patted hers. "Listen, Roxie. I've never had any woman love me. I've had some who've respected my smartness and some who respected my money. But I've had to buy it all in the long run. So I've got a special interest in love. I'm not talking about *l'amour* now but love. The thing I'm talking about is something special, something you can't buy or win or invent. It's something that just happens. I'm no fool. When you and Nicky first got together it was fine—two good-looking people who had a yen for each other —a couple of wise guys who knew all the answers and weren't playing the wrong numbers and didn't expect any more than they got. But it didn't turn out like that, did it? I mean, not lately."

She didn't answer him and he repeated, "Did it?"

"Leave me alone. It's none of your business."

He leaned back in the chair again. "Okay," he said, "I just wanted to be sure."

"I want to know about the people in the cellar," she said.

He told her. As she supposed, they were not all French, but all of them had lived a large part of their lives in Paris. They were only a part of the whole band, a very small part. Their particular job was the printing press. None of the others knew where it was located. The others received the material and distributed it. The others were everywhere, in hotels and cafés, in apartment houses, in railway stations, in the Métro. Few of them knew each other or that they were working together. Only he himself and Nicky knew who all of them were. In that way there could be no betrayal— even if one of them was arrested and tortured and shot. You could not betray what you did not know. Among them were two or three former communists, two daughters of a former cabinet minister, a countess, a banker, a dozen chorus girls, women in brothels, a Protestant pastor, an ex-member of the Croix de Feu and three Roman Catholic priests. They had one thing in common, regardless of nationality or of station in life. Each one loved Paris and each one would go on until there was no longer a German in the city or he himself was shot.

The band had a name. It was called, *"Les Cos-tauds"* which translated out of Montmartre slang meant "The Mugs" or "The Tough Ones" or "The Strong Arm Squad."

She smiled, "So I am a *costaude*."

He grinned, "Yes. Whether you choose or not."

"I must say I slipped into it."

"And now?"

"And now I don't know. I guess I don't hate enough."

"You will," said Léon. He stood up. "What about going to eat?"

"All right."

They went to Luigi's. None of the refugees were there since it was too early for them to risk coming out of their hiding places. La Biche with her plumes and jewelry was in her corner. There were three girls from the revue. That was all beside themselves.

They had only begun to eat when the door opened and the German officer with the little French policeman came in to go over everyone's papers. He bowed stiffly to Léon and Roxie and ignored La Biche. But the three girls he had not seen before and he crossed the room straight toward them to examine their papers.

"They are all in my revue, Herr Lieutenant," said Léon in German, but the officer did not answer him, nor even give any sign of having heard him speak. In a low voice, Léon said, "They are not so correct. Their correctness is breaking."

As the officer examined the papers of the girls, Roxie observed that Luigi was standing very close to him, apparently absorbed by interest in the procedure. She thought, "He is up to something." And as she watched she saw Luigi take a card from his pocket and deftly, quickly slip it into the pocket of the German officer's uniform. She felt a wild desire to laugh at the comic slyness with which Luigi achieved the maneuver. She knew what was printed on the card. "With the compliments of the British Secret Service."

The officer was satisfied with the papers and when he had finished went out, saluting them on his way. When he had gone, Roxie said to Luigi, "I thought they always came later, at the same hour."

Luigi grinned, "No, they've changed all that. They come at a different hour every evening, hoping to catch us."

Then Filomena came in the door with her little dog.

When Roxie came down the great stairway on

the second night there was no fear in her heart. The panic of that first night was gone and from step to step with the professional gestures and un- dulations which long ago had become formalized she moved downward toward the music and the glow of light. In her descent there was the old as- surance, the curious provocative air of detachment, the indifference that had set her apart from the others from the very beginning. *La Reine des Oiseaux*, as Léon said, did not ogle the audience. She moved with a curious air of pride in the beauty of her own body and face. Tonight, it was the old Roxie, experienced, cool, almost cold, who seemed to say "Here it is, boys!" as the beau- tiful body, clad in a few golden feathers, moved toward the front of the stage. "Here it is! So what? You dopes!"

In every curve of the breasts, the hips, the thighs, in every undulation, there was contempt. On this night there was contempt not only for nearly all men but special contempt for the men who sat there beyond the lights, row upon row of them, in gray-green uniforms with closely cropped heads. Through the hazy rose and amber of the lights from the spots, the heads were like rows of figures in a shooting gallery.

Then as she paraded from one end of the stage

to the other while the commère sang, "*Les Oiseaux! Les Oiseaux!*" in her brittle, piercing music hall voice, she discovered that the Major was there again in the same box and casually she thought, "So, you're catnip, Roxie! So you're the cheese in the mousetrap!" For it was clear that he had come only to see her. The same hungry, almost haggard look was there in the opaque blue eyes.

After the *entr'acte*, Léon came into the dressing room. He brought a card—the Major's card with a note written on the back. Léon had read it already.

He said, "It's not just accident. He wants you to go out with him again tonight."

She put the card on the dressing table. "Tonight I want to spend with Nicky."

"Nicky's gone to Bourges."

"Why didn't he tell me?"

"He hadn't time."

She was silent for a moment and then said, "I wish he wouldn't run around like that. What if they checked up on him. He's supposed to be here every night at the theater."

Léon put both hands on her shoulders. "Listen, honey, you can't keep Nicky in a cage. A falcon won't live in a cage. You're happy and he's happy for the first time. Am I right?"

"Yes."

"You wouldn't give it up?"

"No."

"He's happy because he's found a job he likes, for the first time. If you take that away everything would go to pieces."

"Knowing that doesn't make it any easier."

"No, I suppose it doesn't. But what Nicky is doing is the breath of life to him. Take it away from him and he's finished for good."

She did not answer him directly. "What do you want me to do?"

"Be nice to the Major and his friends."

"I'm no good at finding out things."

"Don't try to find out anything. If you don't try he's much more likely to tell you of his own account. Just listen. Don't forget anything he says."

"I don't like him. I don't like any of them."

He looked at her sharply. "You don't hate them?"

She considered the question and after a time answered, "No. No. It isn't hate. It's boredom and contempt."

"Okay. Then go ahead and do your job."

"All right. Give me your pen."

She took the pen and over the name of Major

Freiherr Kurt von Wessellhoft she wrote, "*Avec plaisir. Je vous attends.*"

It was the beginning now of something which might go on and on. When the door had closed behind Léon she thought, "I should have stopped it now. I should have refused. But she only sat there staring at herself in the mirror, as if she were hypnotized by her own reflection.

They did not go to Maxim's that night nor the next nor ever again. The Major proposed it because it seemed the thing to do. It was where all high-ranking German officers went. It was the favorite restaurant of the Field Marshal. It was the correct thing to do. But when he proposed going there, she said, "No, please. I don't like it there."

It seemed to be the only place he knew, so she said, "I know a place where it is quiet . . . a place on the Champs Elysées."

"Very well. It is for your pleasure."

So she directed the driver, through the Major, to a night club called Tout Paris. It was a dark place and since the Germans came, no longer fashionable. Very likely she would see no one she knew. In the darkness it was difficult to recognize anyone.

She had not been there for a long time, not since

the days after Vienna fell. Then for a time it had been a Viennese café. The musicians, the performers, even some of the waiters were Austrian, all refugees who had fled before the Germans. She had happy memories of the place. For a time it had been gay in the Viennese way, with waltzes and sentimental songs, with now and then a refugee singer or a dancer from among the patrons of the place performing. There among the Viennese she had seen the last burst of hysterical gaiety before the curtain came down. She had come here many times with Nicky. Once long ago it had been owned by Stavisky. That was how Nicky had come to bring her there. For a little time he had operated the place himself. All that story too was bad melodrama, before the end of the world.

As they walked down the red-carpeted stairs into the baroque room she knew how much the place had changed. The difference was something you could smell. Although the lighting was the same, it seemed even darker than it had always been. In the old days when you walked down the stairs you heard laughter coming toward you and the sound of gaiety, even above the music. Now there was music but over it no sound of gaiety. Nearly every table was filled and there was champagne everywhere—Germans were utterly convinced that if you drank champagne you were gay —but it was a dead room. The Austrians had fled;

the Germans were in possession. It was like crossing the frontier from Bavaria into the Salzkammergut in the old days.

She wished suddenly that she had not come here
at all but she thought too, "It is as good as any
place. They are probably all the same now." A
German had only to appear and everything
changed. Was it because they were something sinister or because at their approach other people
chilled with dislike and contempt?

There was a table in an alcove, very dark and
a little apart from the others. She chose the alcove
because she did not want to be seen, not knowing
that the darkness was sought too by her companion.

When they were seated and she had ordered supper he told the waiter to bring champagne. But
she protested. "No, if you please, I should like a
small bottle of Château Margaux."

"Of course . . . with your supper," he said. "I
only thought champagne was gayer." She looked at
him with sudden surprise. He had been in em-
bassies. He had been out in the world but he seemed
no different from the others. Champagne! Always
champagne. It seemed to be the only wine they had
ever heard of. Or perhaps it was because champagne was the symbol of what they had expected
to find in Paris and had not.

Tonight he seemed less stiff, less *correct*. While
they ate he even attempted one or two feeble jokes

and when the last of the food had been taken away he said, suddenly, "Tell me about yourself. Where were you born?"

She said, "Evanston, Indiana." And suddenly the whole thing seemed silly to her and desperately unreal, that she should be sitting here with this Prussian officer. What could he know of a place like Evanston, Indiana? What could the wrong side of the railroad tracks mean to him? What could America itself mean to a man like this?

She asked, "Have you ever been to America?"

"No."

"Then it's very hard to make you understand it." She understood now why the strangeness between them was so agonizing and so profound, why there was really no basis for intimacy or understanding. The barrier was something that neither she nor he would ever be able to destroy. It would be far easier to explain America to a Chinese or even a Hottentot.

"I have heard of your gangsters and politicians, your millionaires and movie stars."

"But that isn't America," she said quickly.

"What is?"

"Never mind. It is much too long a story."

"I should like to hear it."

"No." There would be no use in trying to explain because he was already certain that he knew better than she did herself. She was discovering slowly that that too was a German trait.

"Then tell me about yourself."

She divined that her story would be of very little interest to him because it was not in the realm of the spectacular. It was simply a story of things happening to her, filled largely with humble people. She was perfectly aware that he was trying to establish some basis of intimacy between them. It was something which, despite Léon's admonitions, she did not want to risk. Quickly she thought, "I will make up a story—the kind he'd like to hear." And she found herself inventing for him a preposterous yarn out of whole cloth, as fantastic and unbelievable as publicity men invent for picture stars. If it was bad enough he would perhaps divine that she was mocking him and leave her in peace.

"My father," she heard herself saying, "was a distinguished professor, very well known. Unfortunately he died when I was nine years old and left my mother and myself without any money. She was the daughter of the Governor of Illinois, of a very distinguished family. When I was ten I was sent to a convent and my mother went back to the concert stage which she had left to marry my father."

She told the story coldly and dispassionately, entertained by her own ingenuity. She went on and on, inventing triumphs which had never occurred in the whole commonplace, sordid, record of her existence.

"In New York," she heard herself saying, "I was a great star when I was eighteen. Then I came to Paris to the Ambassadeurs. . . ."

Then all at once she found herself growing bored with the narration. If he did not know by now that she was mocking him he would never know. But when she looked at him she saw with astonishment, that he was believing her tale, word for word. He was enchanted, like a small child hearing a fairy story. There was a softness in his eyes she had not seen there before.

"That's all there is to it," she said. "It's a very simple story . . . really."

"It is very interesting," he said. Instead of refilling their glasses himself from the bottles which stood on the table he sent each time for the waiter to perform the service. It was only then that she saw he had drunk a whole bottle of champagne himself. He ordered another bottle and said, "What blood are you?"

"You mean . . ." Then she understood. She felt a sudden desire to continue the mockery and to say, "Really I am Jewish," but she knew that to say that would very likely destroy at once her usefulness to the plans of Léon and Nicky. So she said, "I am very nearly pure English with a little Scotch blood."

"That explains it," he said.

"Explains what?"

"The look of race. Your perfect hands and small feet and the Grecian quality of your figure."

She felt a sudden desire to use some violent obscene expression. She knew little enough of her ancestry but she knew that she had in her veins Polish and Italian and Irish blood.

"There is very little pure race in America," he was saying. "It is really a bastard race. The French are a bastard race too."

The waiter had returned with the champagne. That, she knew, was good, especially since he had ordered it himself without being urged. It would loosen his tongue. Already he seemed relaxed and more human.

When the waiter had gone she said, "I wish you would tell me about Germany. I know so little about it. I have only been to Munich twice."

"Munich is not Germany. It is Catholic. It is soft. The Bavarians are not really Nordics and they are a mixed race. Most of them—especially the people —are Alpines. Race is a very interesting thing."

"Yes, I suppose so." She thought suddenly of Léon and the odd mess of ancestors who had gone into the making of his ugly little body and his shrewd mind. She had never thought much about race one way or another and the discussion was beginning to bore her.

She saw that, as the champagne began to take possession of him, he had taken to watching her with the same look in his eyes she had seen as he sat in the theater box. There was something disturbing in the fixity of his stare. If he became drunk enough she might ask him indiscreet questions and receive indiscreet answers. And then she remembered Léon's admonition, "Ask him nothing. Let him tell you. It is much better that way." She divined too that the look in his eyes was one of bitter unhappiness.

"I want to be a friend," he said out of the soft darkness. "What has happened is unfortunate but it need not affect the relations between us, especially as you're an American."

"No, I suppose not."

"The French are being very unfriendly. We have tried to meet them more than halfway but they are pigheaded."

She scarcely heard his last remark, for it had occurred to her with a start of surprise that she did not feel American any longer. She did not feel that she was French either or anything at all. She was simply one of those many who found the Germans strange and unpleasant, who were unwilling to accept them, even as friends. This, she found, was a startling discovery.

He went on talking. "What we are trying to do

is to put the world in order, to make it a more decent and orderly place. If people would only understand that we are trying to help them, for their own good."

She did not answer him. She was thinking of the people in the cellar, of Luigi and his family, of Léon and Nicky and the tarts on the bar stools in Maxim's, and the daughters of the cabinet minister . . . they were of all nationalities, of all kinds, but they were all against Germany. She, who had never thought very profoundly, was beginning to think about a great many things. She took out her compact and lipstick and began making up her face. It was extraordinary that the Germans who had always made a mess of everything, should think they could teach others.

He said, "But you're not listening."

"Yes, I'm listening but I don't quite believe what you say."

He sat up more erect, chilling a little. "Then you are like all the others. You detest us."

"No. That's not quite true. I just don't believe as you do."

"That's the trouble. None of you believe in anything. Only Germans have faith nowadays."

"I know what I believe."

"What?"

"That people should be permitted to work out their own salvation in peace."

He laughed. "A fine world that would be! Quarreling, swindling, misery, confusion, no order, nothing correct."

"Still it is better than your way," she answered stubbornly. He said nothing and presently she put away the lipstick and added, "Let's talk of something else. You haven't told me what *your* life has been like or where you come from."

He poured himself another glass of champagne and said, "It's a very different world I come from."

"I'm sure it is."

She was still not really listening, because she had begun to think about Nicky, wondering where he was, what fresh danger he was encountering, wondering why of all people in the world she had chosen him. But, of course, she had not chosen him. It had nothing to do with choosing. It had simply happened.

She thought too, "My friend the Major is inhuman. If somehow he cannot become human I can't go on with this, no matter what Léon wants."

She heard him saying, "It was a big white house, wide and high with small windows because in winter Silesia can be very cold. It had belonged to my family since it was built and the land for a long time before that. When the house was built my family owned the people as well . . . all the people who tilled the fields and lived in the dark pine forests." His voice grew soft suddenly. "The forests . . . they are wonderful . . . black and dark even at noonday. I played in them as a boy. All my ancestors were soldiers till my father. He was born lame. He became a judge. He hated being a judge. He hated being lame. He did not love any of us much—not even my mother. Being lame and not being a soldier poisoned all his existence."

She was aware now that he was a little drunk, not gaily drunk as champagne was supposed to make you, according to German belief, but morosely drunk. He was telling her things that only a tipsy man would tell her.

"My mother was unhappy all her life. We were all unhappy. I was eight years old when I heard that we had lost the war. We didn't lose it fairly. We Germans, we soldiers did not lose it." Bitterness crept into his voice. "We were betrayed by the socialists, the communists, the Jews, the people outside who promised us things." (She thought, "It is the same old thing.") "I was very unhappy. We were all unhappy and then we were very poor and my mother had to sell the big white house and all the land and forests and we went to Berlin to live in a tiny flat. We had to send Lisa away. And after we had been in Berlin for a little time we had a

letter that told us Lisa was dead. I think that was
the worst of all. It was worse even than seeing my
mother go out each morning with a piece of jewelry or old silver to trade for a few potatoes so that
we could eat. It was even worse than losing the
land that had always belonged to us since the
beginning of time. Lisa was something special to
my sister and me. Lisa . . ."

Suddenly Roxie asked, "Who was Lisa?"

He looked at her with a tipsy blank look of
astonishment. "Lisa? But of course you know who
Lisa was?"

"I never heard of Lisa. You had better not have
any more champagne."

He still stared at her in a curious, fixed, unhappy
fashion, "Lisa—" Then he shook his head. "Lisa. Of
course Lisa was our governess. She looked exactly
like you . . . even her body . . . it was like yours.
My sister and I used to share a room with her. We
used to sleep in the same big bed with her. I used
to watch her dress and undress."

She was aware as she listened of that same wave
of distaste she had felt in Maxim's when the Field
Marshal's young men had crowded about her. It
was more, even, than distaste; it was a sense almost
of sexual hostility, not like that she had felt at times
for other women, or even for men who did not like
women. This was a new emotion, instinctive, but

puzzling. It astonished her a little that there should be anything new in the range of her experience. Perhaps this was that complex, tortured German thing which Nicky and Léon talked about, which came out of brutality and sentimentality and at the same time gave birth to them, the thing which made Prussians different from other people.

"Lisa," he was saying, "was the only bright thing in our lives. Silesia is not a soft country. It is hard and dark." He was becoming eloquent, forgetting the policy of "correctness." "The forests were dark and the climate hard. My father hated us and my mother was dutiful—a good mother but Spartan and without warmth. But Lisa . . ." His face softened. The blue eyes went soft. "Lisa was everything to my sister and me. She came from the south. She was Swabian . . . really German but with some mixed blood. She knew songs and games. My mother kissed us good night and Lisa kissed us good night, but it was not the same. Lisa's kisses were warm." He stared at his glass. "I saw you the first time three years ago, before the war. When you came on the stage I felt sick because you were Lisa . . . even with no clothes on you were Lisa . . . and I knew Lisa was dead. I went back again not once but many times only to see you. I tried not to go but I had to. I wanted desperately then to send you my card, to ask for a meeting, but I dared not. I was with the Embassy then. It would not have been correct. But now it is different. This is war and Paris is a conquered city and I am important."

"But still not important enough for me, you bastard," thought Roxie. There was something nauseating in the story which revolted her.

"And all the time I hated Lisa and loved Lisa . . . just as I hated and loved the great white house and the black pine forests. I loved her for being gay and beautiful and making us happy, and I hated her for dying and leaving us. I don't know today whether I hate or love her most. I only know that I cannot escape her. I only know that she is always there between me and any woman I have ever known . . . beautiful and smiling and kind . . . but dead." He poured out another glass of champagne and Roxie, glancing at him, saw that he was crying.

Then suddenly he did a strange thing. He leaned toward her and rubbed his head against her breast. There was in the gesture something puppy-like but at the same time repulsive.

"So you see," he said in a low soft voice, "why it meant so much to me to meet you, to have supper with you."

Roxie picked up her bag and drew the coat about her shoulders. "I think," she said, "you had better ask for the check. It is very late and I have a singing lesson tomorrow."

"You have been very good to me. You are very beautiful . . . in character too . . . very beautiful, *Aber schön und süss.*"

Roxie called the waiter and herself paid the check. The Major, lost in a fog of memories, did not seem to notice. The tears were still in his eyes and he was staring into the glass of champagne that was supposed to make one gay.

At the Ritz Major von Wessellhoft had a bad night. Three times his cries wakened the orderly who slept on the sofa in the sitting room outside the door of the bedroom. Three times the orderly went into the Major's bedroom filled with terror lest some violence for which he would perhaps be shot had come to the Major. But in the light that shone in the doorway he saw that the young Major in his pale green silk pajamas was alone and apparently asleep. The third time, the light wakened the Major and he cried out, "Who is there? What is it?" and the terrified orderly said softly, "It is only me, Herr Major . . . Private Heinrich. You remember me, Private Heinrich?"

"Yes . . . of course."

"You cried out in your sleep. I was afraid of harm."

The Major sat up rubbing his eyes which were

red and swollen "I was dreaming. I had a nightmare. I thought I was a little boy again in Silesia
and was being chased by a wild boar in the dark
forest."

"I know, Herr Major," said the orderly, "I too
have nightmares. It is this terrible wicked place. It
is homesickness. We do not belong here."

"We belong where we are sent. We are soldiers,
Heinrich."

"All the same," said the orderly, "I would like
to go back. I would rather fight."

The Major lay down again. "If I cry out again,"
he said sleepily, "wake me. It is better to be awake."

The orderly closed the door softly again, leaving
the room in darkness, and after a long time the
Major fell asleep once more. He did not cry out
again, and a little before ten he wakened.

Private Heinrich had gone away and in his place
was the lieutenant who also served as secretary.
He was the pink, plump, almost beardless young
man with thick gold-rimmed glasses, whose poor
eyes made him useless at the front. He came in and
said, "There is a message from the Military Governor. He wishes to see you at eleven-thirty."

"Very good, Lieutenant."

The Military Governor lived in a great house
with a garden off the Avenue Gabriel which had

belonged to a Rothschild. It was an imposing house, very beautiful architecturally, and filled with wonderful pictures and furniture. Piece by piece the Governor was sending the things back to his house in Pomerania, quietly without ostentation. Each day the house grew a little more bare. The Germans had produced no great painters since the Middle Ages and the Governor's wife had a taste for French paintings and French furniture. Each time she came to Paris she pasted little stickers on the things she wished to have, and a little later they were sent to her.

A little before eleven-thirty, Major von Wessellhoft entered the great hallway where another aide to the Governor, a thickset man of middle age called Hueffner, told him that the General was engaged and that he would have to wait. Sulkily the Major seated himself and looked about him. He felt dull and sick and inwardly cursed the champagne, and he hated Hueffner who always behaved as if he were closer to the General than the other aides. Hueffner was an upstart, the son of a common rich industrial. Quietly as he watched Hueffner rustling papers on the big Louis Quinze table, he marked him down. Hueffner would have to go one of these days.

The hall, he noticed, was barer than it had been the day before. The space where the Claude Lorrain had hung was bare and the Gobelin on the far wall had disappeared. These things too he marked down in his mind to put in his report when he returned to the Ritz, the report which he kept beneath the mattress of his bed.

He was watching Hueffner once more when the door of the room which the Governor had turned into an office opened and a woman came out. She was an extraordinary woman, elderly and very fat but of a commanding appearance, with an enormous bosom. She was dressed in a commonplace rather shabby fashion and looked like the cashier of a *bistro*. She carried a dispatch case and had a professional manner, rather like a midwife or a female attendant at a public bath. Hueffner rose and went with her as far as the door. When he returned to enter the Governor's office, Major von Wessellhoft asked, "Who is that woman?"

Hueffner looked at him for a moment without answering, haughtily, as if he regarded the question as an impertinence. Then he said, "Her name is Madame de Thonars," and disappeared into the office of the Military Governor. He spoke the name as if it were one which the Major should know, without explanation, and the name echoed for a moment in the Major's brain. He was aware that he had heard it somewhere at some time. Lazily he tried to discover where and how.

Then Hueffner came out again and said, as if conferring a favor, "The General will see you, Major."

"*Besten Dank.*" It was a rude abrupt reply, full of contempt. That Hueffner! With his airs . . .

The General sat at a huge mahogany table, his back to the light of the huge window. The papers on the desk were in disorder and very unmilitary in appearance. The General looked sallow and tired, as if he had not slept.

"Sit down, Major," he said amicably. Then with a shadow of humor he said, "Has Hueffner been annoying you?"

The Major flushed. "No more than usual."

"He can be very officious at times. He confuses money with authority. Authority you must acquire with good reason." He fumbled with the papers, seeming only to add to their confusion. Then he asked, "And how are things going in your department?"

"Well enough. It is very difficult—trying to keep order and still create the appearance of normal life as if nothing at all had happened."

"I can understand that."

"It is growing more difficult."

The Governor sighed. "I am afraid it is only the beginning."

The Major's jaw hardened. "Oh, we shall manage it. These people don't seem to realize they have been defeated. A few, of course, are willing to co-operate."

The Governor smiled. "I wouldn't trust the few. A man who sells out once will sell out again and many times. I don't believe the Führer himself is taken in by them." He pushed a gilt inkwell away from him. It was a heavy gesture accompanied by a deep sigh as if he sought by that simple move-ment of the hand to divest himself of all the duties and responsibilities and doubts which weighed him down.

"There was nothing special you had to suggest?" he asked.

"No."

There was a little pause and the Governor turned in his chair to look out of one of the win-dows. Then suddenly he asked, "Do you believe in astrology, Major?"

"I don't believe or disbelieve. I know nothing about it, Herr General."

"You saw the woman who went out of here?"

"Yes."

"She is an astrologer . . . a very famous one—Madame de Thonars."

Then the Major remembered. He had read the name in the newspapers.

"She has made some remarkable predictions in

her time," continued the General. "She predicted the assassination of the Archduke Ferdinand and Alexander of Serbia and the rise of the Führer himself. She has told me some remarkable things."

The Major felt an impulse to ask, "Why do you meddle around with such nonsense?" but was aware that this was an impossible thing to say to a general. So he only asked, "Good things, Herr General?"

The General did not answer him at once. He was still seeing Madame de Thonars sitting opposite him with her charts spread out on the table—a square, heavy, solid figure with very bright eyes behind the gold-rimmed pince-nez. He was hearing her say, "Do you want to hear what is in the stars, Excellency, or do you want to hear what you would like to hear? What is in the charts is not pleasant. It may displease you. But please understand that I am not afraid of your displeasure. I am an old woman and I have already seen too much. What happens to me is of no consequence." And he had answered, "I want to hear what is in the stars," thinking, "I too am old and what happens to me is of no consequence. I too have already seen too much."

She had begun by saying, "It is very black. It is the ruin of Europe, the end of Germany and the rise of Russia." But even that had not startled him, because, as he was aware suddenly, he had known that all along, since the very beginning.

And now, looking at the man opposite him, whom he did not trust as a good army man, who might even now be spying on him, he said, "No. Bad things. A few good things at first but in the end only black things, blackness . . . blackness." His voice trailed away wearily into silence.

"Probably it was rubbish. She is French. She doubtless was trying to undermine our morale."

The Governor shook his great sheep-dog head. "Perhaps. There is only one thing which worries me."

"What is that?"

"That we have all the world against us, even the defeated, even our allies. Somehow we are always hated."

"The master race is always hated."

The General did not answer him. He stared at the table for a long time as if he were hypnotized or had fallen into a trance. The Major's cold eyes watched him, thinking, "He is an old, tired, sick man. In spite of all his decorations, all his fame, he is finished and useless."

Then as if he had pulled himself together suddenly, the General sat up stiffly and said, "There is one more thing." He spoke very slowly almost with difficulty.

"Yes?"

"I understand that you have taken a mistress."

The Major felt the color rising in his face, "No, Herr General."

"Who is this dancer?"

"She is a performer at the Alhambra . . . very well known. She is not my mistress."

"Would you like her to be?" asked the General, and then added, "Forgive me for asking you intimate questions. It is only because these things affect the efficiency of my administration."

"Yes," said the Major.

The General smiled. "I take it that she is being difficult."

"No." He hesitated for a moment. "It isn't that exactly. I can't quite explain it. She is not French, you know. She is American. American women are strange and difficult."

"I have heard they are spoiled. I myself have had no experience," said the Governor. "Please don't misunderstand me. I was merely going to suggest that mistresses are sometimes dangerous."

The Major interrupted him. "She is not dangerous. She is rather stupid and vain."

"And you still find her attractive?" There was a twinkle now in the eyes of the older man.

For a moment the Major was floored. He could not tell the long story of Lisa to the General. After a little time he said, "One does not choose a mistress for her brains, Herr General."

"Well, that is a question. Fashions change. I only wanted to suggest that it is better in time of war to take it where you can find it rather than become attached to one woman. They tell me she is handsome."

"Yes, Herr General. That is true."

The General stood up and rang a bell at his side. "Well, good luck to you. I shall be interested to know how it comes out."

The Major thought savagely, "You won't be here to know how it comes out." He saluted and went out. In the doorway he passed Hueffner who looked at him arrogantly, smiling. He might just as well have spoken the words, "So you have had your backside smacked."

The Major brushed past him thinking, "And you too, you pig! You and your factories! You too are going! Go on, grin! Grin and remember Thyssen who simply disappeared. The time is almost ripe."

All the way back to the Ritz he felt furious and depressed. He thought, "It's that damned champagne. I talked to her too much last night. I don't even remember what I said to her. Maybe the old man is right. Maybe I ought not to see her again. But he can't be right. She is American. She's a dancer. She's stupid. What does she care what becomes of these bloody French."

In his own room he locked the door and took the report file from beneath the mattress of his bed. It was a file bound in brown cardboard and tied with a brown string. He laid it on the table and was about to untie the string when his hands ceased to function. It happened without his knowing it for his thoughts actually were elsewhere, on the Governor and his doddering nonsense about the astrologer. His finger tips had divined that there was something strange about the knot. They were aware that it wasn't the same knot they had tied a few hours before when he had hidden the file away beneath the mattress.

He looked down at the file. His fingers had been right in their discovery. It was a different knot from the one which he always used. Long ago in the dark forest old Herman, the forester, had taught him a special knot, very difficult to accomplish, which since then he had always used. The knot which had alarmed the tips of his fingers was a simple affair, amateurish.

Someone had opened the file. And the same someone had not been able to tie again that special knot.

He stood for a long time staring at the bit of string. The discovery might mean many things—

that a chambermaid had been satisfying her curiosity, that someone French had been spying on him, or, what was worse, that one of his own people had opened the file and read it. He had been sent to Paris to spy upon the army and now perhaps someone was spying on him.

He unlocked the door and called his aide. The young man with the thick glasses came in.

"Yes, Herr Major."

"Has anyone been here since I left?"

"No, Herr Major. Absolutely no one." He shrugged his narrow shoulders. "Only two chambermaids who came to do the room. Why, sir? Is anything wrong?"

"Someone has been tampering with my affairs."

"I doubt that it was the chambermaids, sir. The door was open. I keep an eye on them. One cannot be too careful."

"You swear it could not have been the chambermaids?"

"I swear it, sir."

The Major looked at him coldly. "Have you ever seen this file before? Look at it."

The Lieutenant looked at it and then at the Major. The eyes behind the thick glasses were honest. He could not lie. He was too stupid.

"No, sir," he said, "I have never seen it before.

I see only what you give me to do. I swear I have never seen it before."

"Very good. Thank you."

He closed and locked the door again and opened the file. Inside everything was in order, in too good order, exactly as he had left it. This he did not like. If the file had been only the victim of a chambermaid's curiosity, the papers inside would have been put back hastily and carelessly. There would have been some evidence of tampering. But there was none—save only the knot which the intruder had been unable to duplicate. Someone who knew his business had gone through the papers and replaced them skillfully.

He sat down and set to work on a new sheet of paper. At the top he wrote "Report on His Excellency, General Albert von Heinrath, Military Governor of Paris." The report did not come easily. He had unfortunately, a fondness for the old man, for his frankness, for his occasional fatherly interest in himself, for his weary dignity. But these things he did not allow to get in the way of his duty. The old Governor did not understand what this war was about. He did not understand nor support the hard beautiful ruthlessness of the Party. In his own special way he represented something of that lost softness which had to be exterminated, cut out like a cancer, from the character of the

German people. He was like many other officers, past middle age now, who had been in the last war. They were tired. In their hearts they did not believe that triumph was worth all this suffering over again. They did not really belong to the new Germany or the Party. No, the General would have to go, either willingly into retirement to his estates in Pomerania, or unwillingly, in an accident or by a sudden mysterious illness. He was in the way, useless. He might be experienced and wise, but wisdom was not always a virtue, not when it softened you.

Resolutely he went to work writing his report of the General's weariness and illness, of his defeatist talk, of his consultations with the female astrologer. All these things, he stated in the report, were directly related to the growing resistance and disorders in Paris. The Parisians had not chosen to co-operate; they had refused to see the peace, the order, the efficiency which had been offered them. The policy of "correctness," of co-operation, was not proving to be a success. A strong man was needed, preferably a party man, a younger man. *The general weaknesses of the policy of the Military Governor*, he wrote, *are reflected in the members of his staff, notably in the case of Captain Hueffner concerning whom a separate report, No. 487 M, is attached.*

He looked at the last sentence and he saw suddenly Hueffner's round arrogant face and the look of mockery in the bloodshot eyes. Hueffner. . . . Did he know something about this file? Had Hueffner been appointed to spy upon *him*? Was it Hueffner who had told the General about Roxie Dawn? Was it the fingers of Hueffner or of one of his subordinates who had untied the knot and been unable to retie it? Was Hueffner on the *real* inside, nearer to Borman than himself?

The knowledge caused a sudden chill along his spine and he thought, "No, that is impossible. It couldn't be like that. I mustn't think like that. It's going in circles. It's madness."

Yet the image of Hueffner's face would not go away, nor the knowledge that inside the Party such things could happen. They did happen.

He returned the papers to the file, carefully pinning them together, top and bottom. Then he closed the file and tied the string in the same complicated knot old Herman had taught him long ago. This time he did not put the file beneath the mattress. He placed it inside his military trunk and locked it carefully.

All at once he felt tired and confused. His hand trembled and again he cursed the champagne, thinking, "Whoever thought champagne made you gay?" A drink at the bar would make him feel better.

He unlocked the door and went into the sitting room, carefully leaving the door open. The Lieutenant was working over some papers, peering at them through the thick glasses. He said, "Lieutenant, I am going out. I shall return in a half hour."

The Lieutenant stood up respectfully. "Did you find any clue, sir, as to who had been meddling with your papers?"

"No. It must have been the chambermaids. In any case, it was nothing serious. However, I suggest you move your table over there, facing the door to my room. Leave it open so you can see if anyone comes in."

"Very good, sir."

He was about to leave when he turned and asked the Lieutenant, "Do you know anything about astrology?"

"Not much, sir."

"Do you believe in it?"

"I don't know, sir. My mother has always believed in it. She rarely does anything important without an astrologer. And the Führer. He believes in it. My mother believes his great success has come from consulting the stars."

The Major considered this for a moment. "There is one more thing. Will you look up in the tele-

phone directory the address of a Madame de Thonars?" He spelled it while the Lieutenant wrote
down the name. "She is an astrologer. Make an
appointment for me—let me think—yes, Thursday
afternoon."

The Major started toward the outer door when
he heard the Lieutenant's voice behind him. "I
beg pardon, sir. There is something I forgot."

He turned to see the Lieutenant coming toward
him holding out a card. "I found this under the
door this morning when I came in. I am not familiar with English. I can't quite make it out."

The Major took the card. On it was printed a
single sentence which read, "With the Compliments of the British Secret Service." He frowned,
crushed the card in his hand and said, "It is nothing important. Only a bad joke," and went out the
door.

Nevertheless the thing got on his nerves. Probably the card was no more than a bad joke played
by a servant of the hotel or even one of his fellow
officers. Then he thought suddenly, "Maybe it was
an agent who got into the file." The thought re-
lieved him. There would be nothing in it of value
to a British agent. It was much better that the intruder was a British agent than one of his own people. But that idea made no sense. If a British agent
had been in his room he wouldn't leave a card

tipping off the visit, because he would want to return. No, it couldn't be that . . . Hueffner, that damned Hueffner.

The whole thing was beginning to be a nightmare. As he got out of the lift he thought, "It's all crazy. And that girl is the craziest of all. Maybe the General was right. I'll forget her. I won't see her again."

But that night he was back again in the box at the Alhambra.

On Thursday in the afternoon the Major went on foot to the house of Madame de Thonars in the Square Chauseé d'Antin. The elderly chambermaid opened the door for him and showed him into the dusty room with the naked light bulb which threw a hard, uncompromising light upon the face of all Madame's visitors.

"I will tell Madame you are here," the chambermaid said, and withdrew closing the door behind her.

Then he sat alone for a long time, troubled because he had come here at all, ashamed because he half-believed such rubbish, telling himself that he had only come because it was necessary to have a complete record of the Military Governor's behavior. He found the room disturbing, with the hard light falling on his face and hurting his eyes. The room, with its mixture of dust and sloppiness and practicality (the businesslike file) disturbed his sense of correctness. No German woman—even a fortuneteller—would have a room as untidy as this.

Then he saw the dusty verdure tapestry move and from behind it emerged the squat figure of Madame de Thonars. She nodded to him and asked, "Major von Wessellhoft?"

He stood, "Yes, Madame."

"You speak French?"

"Yes, Madame."

"You understand it easily?"

"Yes, Madame."

She sat down, "You have come for a reading?"

"No, Madame, not exactly." He was ashamed because in his heart he *did* want "a reading."

She looked at him directly, with frank surprise, and he explained, "I have come on a very complicated mission. I will try to explain." He coughed, as if a little uncertain how to go on. "I am an aide to General von Heinrath, the Military Governor."

"Yes," she said, "I know that."

"It is about him. The General means a great deal to me. He is almost like a father. I have been worried about his health . . . it is very difficult to say exactly what I want to say. I have been warned not only of his physical health but his mental health as well."

He was annoyed by the intensity of Madame de Thonars' gray eyes. She sat opposite him, like himself in the full glare of the naked bulb. Her face was old and fat, the sallow greasy skin shining in the brilliant cold light, but the eyes were ageless and searching and bold. They did not waver. It was as if they were seeing inside him, through him, absorbing his vitality, draining his self-assurance, as if they explored the depths where all the perversity, the cruelty, the torment, had been thrust out of sight, even out of his own consciousness. His voice faltered and he coughed again. He felt the blood coming slowly into his face.

"I thought you might be able to tell me something of what he is thinking . . . what he is worried about, why he sent for you. It would perhaps help me in being of use to him. I want to do my best to serve him."

She waited, still staring at him, as if she expected him to go on explaining. At last he said, nervously, "I hope you understand why I came."

Then, thoughtfully, after a long time she answered him. "I cannot tell you those things. My own rule has always been never to betray the confidence of people who come to me. I had thought you were coming to consult me about yourself."

"I don't believe in such things."

"That is a mistake. They are still in the realm of the disputable but no one has proven that prophecy, or clairvoyance or astrology is unsound. No one has really explored these things scientifically. It is foolish to mock at what we do not understand and have not investigated."

The chair creaked as she shifted the weight of her squat, heavy body, and surprisingly she said, "I can tell you this much in confidence. You need not worry about the Military Governor. He will be out of your way within three months."

"How?"

"That I cannot tell you. He will no longer be Governor of Paris. He will no longer be alive." She took the gold-rimmed pince-nez from the little hook by which they were attached to her huge bosom. "I would let him have peace. It is only for a little time."

While she had listened to him she had been watching him as she always watched a new client. She had been remarking the fact that he was well built and possibly intelligent within the limits of his education and that he was handsome in his peculiar Prussian way. She had had great experience with all sorts of people but mostly with worried and frightened and neurotic ones, and she divined almost at once that this young man, despite the outward appearance of health, was troubled and frightened and neurotic. That was typically German. The Germans were the only people whom neuroses did not betray themselves in outward physical signs, perhaps because the whole nation was in a peculiar fashion neurotic. Her own power of clairvoyance, her luck, whatever it was, frequently astonished her but she was not without doubts, even of herself. At this moment, however, she was not exercising the powers of a seeress but those of a diagnostician. From her experience, her observations, she was able to divine many things from the physical aspects of her clients which aided her enormously in the field of divination.

While she listened to him without much interest in what he was saying she studied the face, analyzing it carefully, partly with her mind and partly with the instinct and intuition which was her genius. She saw in the rather large but tight, thin-lipped mouth the defect of a nature that was sensual but baffled, twisted and defeated. There was cruelty there too, a kind of mad cruelty, supplemented by the blank staring quality of the eyes. And in the chin, rounded, with a faint cleft, there was softness and weakness which, tormented, produced a kind of desperate, mad and unpredictable action. The straight nose was too thin, too over-bred, denying the vigor of the outwardly healthy body and in the eyes there was the look of one whose inner consciousness was obsessed by hidden things, things which were frightening and so were thrust back deep inside away from the light. They were in a way beautiful eyes, clear blue, but the staring expression she had seen before many times in the eyes of drug-takers and clients whose twisted, fearful lives led downward into the most sordid parts of the Paris underworld.

Watching him while he talked with increasing uneasiness beneath her steady gaze, she saw that inside the perfect erect young body there was darkness and confusion and defeat. She was perfectly aware of the treachery behind the hypocritical words he spoke. He had come to her for information because he sought to destroy that sick old man who governed Paris. The sick old man was bad enough. This apparently healthy young one was far worse, far more evil, and quietly she thought, "This is the ultimate Germany. This is everything German pushed to the limit of its development. It is ruthless and treacherous and cruel. It is also so neurotic and so obsessed by fear and by evil that the neurosis has been transmuted into a positive characteristic and become a sense of virtue." That perhaps was what Hitler had accomplished. That perhaps was the Führer's greatest achievement—that he had persuaded the Germans that evil was good, that their weaknesses were strength. It was a curious inversion of moral values become fact and logical and in the German mind justified.

And then into her crafty old mind came another thought, "I could destroy him. I have the power. I could lead him to destroy himself." And she felt a brilliant sense of satisfaction. "They will always destroy themselves in the end. It is a race in love with violence and death and somehow with them death and corruption are implicit in love and the very process of procreation. German children commit suicide. Nowhere are crimes of sex so morbid and intricate as in Germany."

Aloud she said, "I could tell you a little of what I told him. He wanted to know about the future of Europe . . . about the future of his own people." She waited for a moment and then said, "Of course what I found in the stars may not interest you, since you think all of this is rubbish."

He moved forward a little in his chair. His expression was now one of great interest. She knew that in order to accomplish what she meant to accomplish he must be curious. He must *want* to hear what she meant to tell him. If he *wanted* to hear he would believe it despite his own reason. And he must believe so that the festering doubts could be planted in his deepest mind and spirit. For that, she knew, he would only have to believe a little.

"No," he said, flushing a little, "I am only an agnostic. I don't say flatly that it is rubbish. I simply don't know."

"The Governor wanted to know what I saw in the future of Europe. Would you like to hear that? It is quite impersonal. It has nothing to do with the life of the Governor or yourself."

He swallowed and stiffened his body a little as if his answer cost him a great effort. "Yes, please."

"It is not very pleasant."

"Very little is pleasant nowadays."

"You understand I cannot change what is written. I cannot change what is revealed."

"I understand that."

She leaned back in the swivel chair and closed her eyes. She did not want to look at him while she spoke.

She heard him saying, "I really would like to hear." He was like a little boy now, wanting to be told a secret, or a frightened neurotic woman hoping to be told something that would relax the agony of nerves.

Her voice came out, suddenly sharply, a different voice, deeper and more mellow. It seemed to come from a great distance and to possess a curious timbre of dignity and authority.

In this sibylline voice she said, "There is great darkness and confusion. There is smoke and fire everywhere and destruction and war everywhere between nations, between neighbors, between brothers. Death rides in the skies. And out of the East under a red star come hordes of men in machines bearing fire. And everywhere in every corner there are men fleeing, from fire and from sword, from hanging and death and mutilation. Everywhere they try to hide—in forests, in houses and in caves. Everywhere they are dragged out and beaten and killed." She pressed a fat hand against her eyes. Then she shuddered slightly, "The ones who run, who cry out in terror are all dressed alike. They are in gray . . . no in green . . . no it is a gray-green like the dead corn that has been blighted in the field."

His voice broke in upon her: "You are lying! You are a saboteur! An old witch! You lied to the General and you are lying to me! There is only victory ahead for us!"

With her eyes still closed she went on, as if in the depth of a trance she had not heard the hysterical outburst, "And there is a great blackness . . . over everything. Everything dissolves in smoke. I can see nothing beyond. The curtain has come down."

The heavy eyelids fluttered a little and then opened but the eyes were rolled back in her head so that only the whites of the eyeballs appeared. (It was an old trick learned as a child which could be at once impressive and terrifying.) For a full moment she kept her face with the sightless eyes turned toward him, aware of the horror of her appearance. It was like being looked upon by death which is blind.

Then slowly she allowed the eyeballs to resume their normal position. For a moment she appeared again to stare past the Major, through him, as if he were not there at all. Yet she saw him, dimly out of focus; she saw that he was sitting stiff and up-right with an intense expression of anger and terror on his face. She shuddered and then pressing her hands against her eyes she leaned over the table.

"There is more," she said. "More is coming. It concerns yourself. There is something you want . . . something you are afraid of, which tortures you . . . something you try to put away from you. You must not be afraid. You must be strong. You must throw off fear of yourself. There is an obsession you must satisfy or it will destroy you. You must kill it by yielding to it. You must put shame from you. You must realize yourself . . . your desire."

Then she groaned and said, "Oh . . . Oh! That is all. That is all!" The sweat stood out suddenly on the tallow greasy skin. She leaned back in her chair as if exhausted.

She heard him say, "Madame, you are a liar! You should be thrown into prison. You are evil and dangerous." And she affected not to hear what he said. She thought, "I have planted there what I wanted to plant. He will never escape it now . . . he will never again be free of doubt. He will never again have any peace." There was an obsession, she knew now for certain. What it was she did not know. The Germans were peculiar and their obsessions sometimes twisted and incredible. Of its existence she was certain.

Then she opened her eyes and he said, looking at her, "Why did you tell me all that?"

"I do not know what I told you."

"It is rubbish and you are lying."

"I warned you. I shall have to leave you now. Afterward I am always exhausted."

He rose. "I am sorry," he said coldly, "that I troubled you . . . and myself. I have wasted a good hour or two of valuable time."

She watched him go out the door. When he had gone she put her desk briskly in order, switched off the naked bulb to save money and went in to her supper. She was having a *poulet de Bresse*—a whole *poulet*—all to herself, with a bottle of Chablis and some fresh pâté. You could live well even in conquered Paris if you knew where and how to buy.

In the hallway as the chambermaid held open the door for the Major to leave, she said, "It is the custom to leave something for Madame with me."

Quickly he thrust a fifty-mark note into the outstretched hand. Outside it was already dark and cold. An old woman passed him in the archway leading from the square and although he did not know her, or had not even seen her face, he cursed her, and all these people who got under his skin, who would not be defeated, who did not understand that they were already crushed, forever.

The fog came down early that autumn as if Nature sought to hide the suffering of the proud city. At night the streets and squares turned chill as soon as darkness fell. "Paris Toujour Paris!" ran on and on behind the blind darkened façade of the Alhambra.

Then late one afternoon about the hour the chill descended on the city, Léon left his office early to go to the house in the rue Washington. He had his own key and at the sound of the closing of the outer door, Roxie appeared at the top of the stairs. At sight of him she said at once, "What is it? What's happened?"

"Something bad. Give me time to get my breath."

"Something has happened to Nicky?"

"No, nothing has happened to Nicky."

In the sitting room he took off his coat. "It's Luigi. They've arrested Luigi."

"When?"

"At noon today. They raided the coal cellar but found no one."

"How could they know about that?"

Léon shrugged his shoulders. "One of the refugees must have squealed."

"Which one?"

"How should I know that? He may have been an agent or a spy or he may have been arrested and tortured. The Boches are capable of anything."

She had never seen Léon so serious. His face was a gray color like putty. He had not shaved and the blue blackness of his beard stood out against the gray.

"What does it mean? Do they know about this house—about Nicky?"

He took out a cigar and lighted it. His hand

trembled a little. "I don't know. I don't think they know anything about anything but Luigi and the refugees. I saw Filomena. She swears Luigi knows nothing about what is going on here. She swears she has never told him where she got the papers and cards. I believe her."

"Then they can't force it out of him."

"There is one great rule in conspiracy," he repeated, "a man cannot betray what he does not know."

"And Filomena? They didn't arrest her?"

"No. She saw the soldiers outside and went away and came straight to me."

"And Maria?"

"They didn't bother her. They told her that if she wanted Luigi to be all right she must keep the restaurant open as if nothing had happened. They are probably hoping the refugees will return and they can pick them up one by one. Filomena wanted to go to Maria but I forbade it. Filomena *knows* about this house. They could torture it out of her. They must not pick her up. She is at the flat of my secretary."

"And what if Nicky goes to Luigi's?"

"He is safe. He has papers. He has his special permit. They won't be suspicious of him. We must go there now as if nothing had happened, as if we knew nothing about the refugees . . . as if we thought they were simply customers." He knocked the ash off his cigar. "It is the only way to play it . . . boldly. Don't forget we have every reason to go to Luigi's. It's near the theater. We have dined there nearly every night for years. There's nothing unusual about our going back. And if Nicky comes back we shall be there."

"He'll come here first."

"Then we can leave a note."

"I'd rather wait here till show time."

"If we don't go to Luigi's it will arouse suspicion. That will be bad for Nicky . . . for all of us."

She considered this for a moment. "Yes, that's true."

"There is only one thing to do. Behave as if nothing has happened. Filomena has managed to warn some of the refugees. She knew where two or three of them were hiding. La Biche will help too. They think she's crazy and won't bother her. She's not so crazy about some things . . . a lot less crazy than they think. Filomena and La Biche will stay near the restaurant tonight and try to warn the others before they come in."

It didn't occur to her to say, "I knew this would happen. I knew I should have forced Nicky to go back to America." She was long past all that now. For the first time she felt a little of the excitement which Nicky and Léon experienced.

"Where have they taken Luigi? We ought to help him if possible."

"I don't know. I doubt they have told Maria anything. If it is possible I will ask her tonight if she knows anything." He stood up. "We had better go at once. From our side everything must look as usual."

She wrote a note to Nicky. It said merely, *"Come straight to the theater. If we are not there, wait for us. We are not going to Luigi's."*

She put it in a large envelope and left it lying in the middle of the Argentine's bed in the room with the pink satin curtains. Nicky would come there to have a bath and change his clothes. He could not miss the white envelope against the violent pink of the bed cover.

When she came out, Léon said, "There was one other thing. They killed Filomena's little dog. It yapped at them and they kicked it to death."

At Luigi's they walked in the door casually as they had done a hundred times before. The room was empty save for a German officer and a sergeant eating spaghetti and drinking a bottle of Chianti. The officer was the one who had come regularly each night to inspect the papers of everyone in the restaurant. He nodded to them without saluting and scowled. The "correctness" was gone completely now. He knew now that night after night the people in Luigi's had made a fool of him.

Léon said to Roxie, "Sit down." As he helped her off with her coat he said, "Leave it to me."

They sat down and took up the menu cards written in purple ink. After studying his card for a time Léon turned toward the kitchen door and shouted, "Luigi! Luigi!" There was no response to his call and again he shouted, "Luigi!" Still there was no answer and the German officer turned and said, "Luigi is not here. He has been arrested."

"What for?" asked Léon.

"That is our business," said the German rudely.

"And his wife?"

"She is in the kitchen, I suppose."

Without saying anything more, Léon rose and went through the door into the kitchen. Roxie knew that was what he wanted—a chance to speak to Maria alone.

She continued to study the menu, aware that the German officer was watching her. After a little time she heard his voice asking, "You come here often, Mademoiselle?" To her surprise he spoke almost respectfully.

Looking up at him she said, "I have been dining

here for ten years every night before I go to the theater."

"It is a pity your friend Luigi is in trouble."

"What has he done?" she asked and this time the man gave an answer.

"He has been sheltering spies—communists and Jews."

Very quietly she said, "It is a pity he is in trouble. He is a good man."

"There are many misguided people nowadays. You are very fortunate to be an American and out of all this."

She gave him a sharp quick look to discover if he had any suspicion and was mocking her. But there was no sign of anything but a casual sincerity.

Then Léon returned and said to her, "We had better go somewhere else. Maria asks us to."

Without answering she rose, put on her coat and they left. As they passed the German officer Léon said, *"Bon appetit!"* and once the door closed he added, "you son of a bitch!"

He did not speak until they were away from the door. Then he said, "She does not know where they have taken him. She wanted us to go away . . . I don't know why."

"If we knew where he was," said Roxie, "we might be able to do something."

They walked slowly for it was a moonless, overcast night and the darkness was like velvet. He did not answer at once. Presently he said, "I think you might be able to find out where they have taken him."

"Me?" said Roxie. "How could I discover?"

"Through your friend, the Mayor."

"It's too risky."

She heard Léon laugh, "It isn't risky at all. He knows all about you. He knows you dine at Luigi's every night. He knows much more than we think. All you need say is that Luigi is a friend, that you have known him for years and would like to know where he is."

"How does he know that I dine at Luigi's?"

"Very likely you've told him for one thing. For another thing your friend is a great deal more than he appears to be."

"How?"

"He isn't just an aide-de-camp to the General. That's only a cover for other things."

"How do you know?"

"I don't know for sure, but I think I've made a very good guess. He's working for the army only at second hand. His real job is with the Party."

"I still don't see how you know."

"What one doesn't know, one can't betray," said Léon. "Otherwise I might tell you."

She wished that she could see his face as he

spoke. It was always important to see Léon's face when he spoke. If you knew him well enough, his face told you many things his mouth did not say. But it was dark.

They were near the end of the block now and as they turned a corner Léon ran full into someone. He called out, "Hey! Look out!" and out of the darkness came the hoarse laugh and voice of La Biche. *"Ah, c'est toi, Léon!"*

She was at her post watching to warn any of the refugees who turned into the alley. On the opposite corner in a doorway Filomena stood on guard, alone, without the little dog. She and La Biche had planned their technique: when anyone passed, they deliberately bumped into the passer-by in the dark. If he was German they excused themselves: if it was one of the refugees they were sent away. The officers and the sergeant sat waiting all the evening in Luigi's for the mice to come into the trap, but none came.

He was there again in the box and after the performance he came again to her dressing room, looking rather sallow and haggard, as if he had not slept for a long time. Remembering what Léon had charged her to do, she spoke with a kind of false intimacy, saying, "You look ill tonight. Is there anything wrong?"

Her interest appeared to please him. He said, "No. Nothing. Only work and responsibility. It gets worse all the time. Another of our men was killed tonight. There will have to be violence and reprisals."

She thought at once of Nicky and said, "Violence is always foolish. That kind of thing only makes everything worse." And she found a sudden pleasure in the hypocrisy of the speech, just as she had found unexpected pleasure in the prospect of danger. It occurred to her for the first time that there might after all be some satisfaction in playing Mata Hari, that she might even have a little talent for the part.

He held her coat for her as he had done on the first night. "I am glad to see that you are becoming reasonable."

Then for the first time he took her hand and gave it a sudden pressure that was painful in its violence. "You are always the same . . . always beautiful." And she was aware of a change in him, something that had nothing to do with herself, her sudden friendliness and hypocrisy. He smiled at her. It was, she thought, the first time she had ever seen him really smile.

"Come," she said, "I'm hungry."

They went again to Tout Paris. It had become the fixed place since it was as good as any other and dark and unfashionable. He now kept the table in the alcove reserved each night until midnight.

He ordered champagne and when she said, "The last time it did not make you gay," he replied, "It is to celebrate. I am going back to Berlin tomorrow."

She felt a quick sense of relief.

"Are you sorry?" he asked.

"Yes." Again the excitement rose in her. "I am always sorry to say good-by to a friend."

"I shall be coming back."

"When?"

"That I don't know. My sister is being married. I go back for the wedding. There will be other business too. When it is finished I shall come back."

She raised her glass, "To a good trip," she said and then thought, "I must not overact."

She asked what his sister was like and whom she was marrying.

"She is very handsome," he said. "Tall and straight and blonde. And she is making a very good match considering that she has no inheritance whatever. She is marrying a colonel. He is older than herself but his family is very good. He was a neighbor when we lived in the big white house. His family had been in Silesia as long as our own. They have known each other always. It is a very correct, a very solid match. She is a quiet girl, very intellectual. She works with the educational division teaching the new philosophy and religion. The Führer has already honored her with a ribbon. In Breslau in 1938 she was chosen the perfect German girl."

He talked for a long time about her, prideful and a little homesick, and slowly Roxie began to see the young woman quite clearly—straight, tall, rather stiff, with blonde hair braided tightly about her head.

As he talked of her he grew soft, with a curious softness that was very near to hysteria. The very quality of his voice changed. It was the first time she had ever seen him happy and a little relaxed, and it occurred to her how terrible it must be to live always in a state of exaggeration, of caricature, in which all one's emotions were distorted.

She watched now and listened, while he drank more and more champagne, thinking, "When he has a little more I will ask him." Her own head was strong and experience had taught her long ago to keep a clear head. There was nothing more helpless, more defenseless than a tipsy woman.

He ordered a second bottle and she said impulsively, "There is something you could do for me as a kind of going away gift."

"I have brought you that," he said quickly, and took from his pocket a small box. He gave it to her and opening it, she found inside a ring, a great aquamarine set in platinum. "I've had it for days," he continued, "waiting for the opportunity to give it to you. One's mood has to be right for such things." He grinned at her and it was a curious empty, sheepish grin, somehow chilling in its quality. He laid one hand on hers and she felt the trembling of the nerves in the long bony big-knuckled fingers.

"It is very beautiful," she said.

"It goes well with your eyes," he said, with an air of pride. "I thought of that. If the size is wrong, they will change it for you."

"It is very kind of you. I've done nothing to deserve it."

"You've been very kind to me. You've spent a great deal of time with me." He was a little drunk now and again saying things that were indiscreet. "I couldn't think why. It puzzled me." Then he looked at her with directness. "Why did you?"

"I liked you," she said. "It was very simple. There are so few friends in Paris now." She felt the thing slipping away from her. To get his help to save Luigi the mood must be exactly right. She thought, "Perhaps I had better say it now." She looked at the ring, hating it, and said, "I have a friend who is in trouble with your people."

The blue eyes grew suddenly wary. "How in trouble?"

She told him about Luigi, saying that she had known him for many years because she had dined in his restaurant night after night. "He is a good man," she said. "If you could help him it would be more to me even than the ring." She felt herself acting now, as if she had no control over herself. She became wistful, thinking at the same time, "Perhaps after all I am not so bad at my job."

"What is your friend accused of?" he asked.

She told him and he said, "That is very serious, but I will do what I can. I have heard nothing of the case."

"It would be a help if I only knew where they had taken him. Even his wife doesn't know."

He stiffly took from his pocket a small notebook and wrote in it Luigi's name. Then he replaced it in his pocket. "I am going away in the morning but I will leave orders for a report to be sent you as soon as possible."

She turned the ring round and round on her finger. "That is very kind of you. Could I have more champagne, please?"

He beckoned to the waiter to refill her glass and

when the waiter went away he said, "The ring wasn't all. When I come back I shan't be living at the Ritz. I've taken a flat in the Avenue Foch. It is big and quite splendid. It belonged to a rich American woman. You Americans have taste in such things. It is much too big for me. I was wondering whether you would share it with me?"

It was a courtship unlike anything she had known in all her rich experience, puzzling because of its curious cold correctness and lack of all intimacy or gaiety, its lack of any physical attack despite the intensity of the desire which she had felt in the background since the beginning. He was drinking champagne again in order to destroy the barriers which shut him away from her.

And now it had come—the thing she had dreaded. She saw that in his mind he had regarded her from the beginning as a woman of a certain class, pigeonholed, ticketed. In his world there were no shadings, no gray colors, but only black and white. She was aware now that she had become an obsession with him, not because she was herself, but because slowly she had become Lisa, the Swabian governess. And suddenly she was afraid of him for the first time because it seemed to her that he was mad to be obsessed by love for a woman who was dead. And he was drunk now and the odd thing was that only when he was drunk did he seem normal and human. Only then could she feel any warmth toward him.

"I don't know," she said, "I could not answer you now."

"I think it would be easier for us. It would be different that way. We should never have to come to these depressing places. You are very beautiful. Whatever happens to you, I shall never be able to forget you . . . not until I die."

She knew that he was not talking to her but to the dead girl.

He put his hands suddenly to his face, pressing the eyeballs as if he were in pain. "Yes, it will be much better that way."

"I am not altogether free," she said.

"Do you have a lover?" He looked at her.

"Yes."

"Where is he?"

She began to invent again, craftily, with a skill and ease which astonished her, taking pleasure in the invention. It was better to lead him away from the trail of Nicky.

"He is in Marseilles," she said. "He is a lawyer, older than I am. He is married but unhappy. We have been together a long time. I do not know what will happen now. He cannot return to Paris.

He was compromised with the Reynaud government."

"Do you love him?"

"Yes . . . very much."

"That is a pity. Still you might change."

"Yes. I might change."

"I could give you a good deal. Not much in jewels but a great deal in privileges and honor. You could even have a car of your own."

Again she knew he was thinking of her as pigeonholed, as a tart. Very likely he had never known any German woman like herself, who had made her own life, living like a man. Very likely there were none. . . .

"Yes. It is very good of you. I understand all that." And again the strangeness of the courtship startled her. In this man there was obsession perhaps, and passion, but no love. She saw the vein in his forehead throbbing. She, like Madame de Thonars, was in her way a diagnostician. In a way, diagnosis had, by necessity, always been a part of her business. It was a part of the necessary equipment of any woman who on her own succeeded in the world.

"You will give it your consideration?" he said stiffly.

"It is not a thing to be turned down easily." And

she wanted suddenly to laugh, thinking this was the strangest of the many propositions she had received, the coldest and at the same time, the most passionate and tortured.

When they had finished the second bottle of champagne she said, "I think I had better go now."

He was quite drunk now. He stared at her, smiling. "You are so very beautiful," he said. "So very like Lisa."

She smiled back at him. "Have you ever thought," she asked, "that if Lisa were alive she would be middle-aged and probably fat and very dull?"

He seized her hand, the hand with the ring on it. "Don't say that! It's not true. She could never change! It's not true!" There was a terrible strength in the hand which grasped hers. The force of it drove the ring into her flesh, bruising and cutting the skin. She cried out in pain and he released her.

"I beg your pardon," he said, "I have hurt you. I beg your pardon." He raised the bruised hand and kissed it. "Forgive me! Forgive me! I could not help myself." Then he began to cry, the tears coming into his eyes. "It is not my fault. Forgive me!"

"You are forgiven," she said. "And now I think I had better go home."

Again the champagne had not made him gay.

Champagne, thought Roxie, is a drink for Americans and French but not for Germans.

Nicky had not come back. The sitting room was empty and the lonely envelope still lay in the middle of the pink silk bedcover. She who rarely knew weariness or depression was suddenly tired, more tired than she had ever been in all her life. She thought, "It is only because of what happened to Luigi and all the strain and the way the major behaved tonight."

She looked down at the ring. It was a beautiful ring. Taking it off her finger, she turned it from side to side and held it against the light, watching the lovely cold blue and green lights, calculating that in the old days it would have cost at least ten thousand francs. What he had paid for it she did not know—perhaps nothing at all, at most a handful of that useless paper with which Germans bought everything—perfumes and silk stockings, pâté-de-fois-gras and diamonds, champagne and sables, all the things which in their minds were symbols of the luxury and beauty of Paris.

Her impulse was to fling it from her, to throw it out of the window or put it down the toilet, but experience said, "No. Keep it. Some day it may be of use." Money meant less and less except these bits of paper with which the Germans paid you, holding a pistol at your head, telling you that the bits of paper were worth ten marks or fifty marks or a hundred marks. That was "the new order." For such a system to work they would have to conquer all the world. No, money soon would be worth nothing, but you could always bribe with a clip or a ring or a bracelet. You could buy food and shelter and loyalty or betrayal.

She crossed to the opposite side of the room and, pulling aside the pink satin, opened a small wall safe and took out her jewel case. She put the ring inside with the bracelets and clips, necklaces and brooches. Then for a moment she sat on the edge of the bed looking down at the case, thinking how wise she had been to put money into jewels now that money was worth nothing at all. All the francs in the bank were shrinking hour by hour, minute by minute. And she was glad too that when she had moved she kept the jewels here in the house rather than at the bank. Now any day, if things went wrong, she might have to disappear suddenly. It was well to have them here.

Then she put them away and undressed and went to bed but she could not sleep for worrying about Nicky. Somehow in the course of the evening, she had come to identify him with the violence that was breaking out everywhere in Paris, in the middle of the city, on the outskirts, in the Métro, in the *banlieues*. He would never tell her. Like Léon he believed that what one does not know one cannot betray. It was her knowledge of Nicky which made her know that somehow, in some way he was associated with the violence and the killings. His recklessness would never be satisfied with so simple a business as the printing press in the cellar. Nor would his hatred be satisfied. To him, she knew well enough, death did not mean very much, even his own death. That was perhaps something that people like herself, brought up in a civilized world, could not understand. That perhaps had been the weakness of the French—that they could not believe in the reality of violence or the efficacy of death. They were afraid of it because it was shocking and put an end to pleasure. To be without fear of death one had perhaps to have faced it many times, to have been wretched, to have suffered, to have learned the ultimate sum of values.

Perhaps the lack of fear in Nicky more than any other thing stood between them. Perhaps that was why he had been a scamp, a mocker, cynical and jeering at all law. And now he had an honest excuse for lawlessness, it had become justified. Making war upon existing law had become a normal way of life in this grim, half-dead city in which they lived.

It might easily be that he had not gone to Marseilles at all—that all the time he had been here in Paris in hiding, coming out only after darkness to attack and kill. Perhaps he was the one who, as leader of *les costauds*, planned all the campaigns.

And in the darkness, for the first time in many years, she felt a sudden desire to pray. It was a profound desire, as if she had become aware that she no longer had any control over her existence, as if somehow she must put it at last in the hands of God imploring Him to help and preserve Nicky. For he had become slowly, she knew now almost with bitterness, the beginning and end of her existence. She was no longer free and alone, no longer possessed of the safety and strength which comes with a lonely life. If you really loved no one, there was no one you could lose. If you were alone you could not be hurt through another, and that she knew now was the only hurt which could in the end be enduring and of importance.

She thought, "I will go to mass again and confess and then perhaps God will listen to me." But in her heart she knew that the determination was born only of fear. Out of fear she had gone to see Madame de Thonars. She knew now what it all meant—the things Madame de Thonars told her. It was all clear enough.

Toward morning she knelt beside the bed and prayed as she had not prayed since she was a small girl in Evanston. She had prayed then because she was terrified of what the Irish priest had told her about hell. She did not believe any longer in hell; she had not believed in hell for a very long time, because it seemed to her a silly improbable place and because she had seen worse things than hell all about her, in life. She did not pray now in fear of hell, but for Nicky, for God to save him from his own recklessness. In a curious way she had become a little girl again with the simple faith of a little girl.

And she thought, "Some day all this will be over. Some day the nightmare will be finished and we can be happy again and safe and can love each other."

In the morning Filomena came through the passage from the garage in the rue de Berri into the cellar. She sent word that she would not come upstairs and asked that Roxie come to the cellar to see her.

She was a changed Filomena. She had come with

the basket to carry the copies of "*La France Eter-nelle*" out into the city; but the old spirit was not in her. She stood by the wooden wardrobe, big and grim, the basket over her arm, alone without the little dog.

There was no news of Luigi. The Germans, she said, were there in the restaurant all day and all night, sitting at a table playing skat and drinking Chianti. But they had caught no one, because she and La Biche had managed to stop the refugees and warn them. The word had been passed on to others. Poor Maria wept all day, saying that she wanted to die, terrified of what the Germans were doing to her good-natured Luigi.

At the end Filomena swore a great ornate, baroque Italian oath. "We will kill them all, Mademoiselle, if it is necessary," she said, and then lifting aside the vegetables in her basket she said, "Look!"

Beneath the vegetables lay a sharp new knife, long and newly polished, the sort of knife used by the men in the slaughter houses for killing steers.

"You see," said Filomena, "I have prepared myself. In the darkness it is very easy to operate. Nowadays they only go in twos but I am a strong woman." She flexed her right arm and patted the biceps. "I am a strong woman. I can do for two at a time if the knife doesn't get stuck."

Her voice took on an edge like that of the knife itself. She said passionately, "Why did they come here? No one wanted them. Why couldn't they have left us alone in peace?"

Then quietly she unpacked the vegetables and went to work rolling up the papers. In the bottom of the basket, when the vegetables had been removed, Roxie saw the leash of the little dog.

While Filomena worked Roxie went to fetch wine. The lock on the outer door was rusty and gave her trouble so that the little man called Monsieur Lopez came to her aid. He went with her into the chill vaulted passage which led to the wine cellar itself. The second door, made of steel with the spring lock, opened easily. Monsieur Lopez went into the wine cellar with her. The sight of so much fine wine moved Monsieur Lopez. Tenderly, with deep respect, the pink-cheeked little man picked up one bottle after another, taking out his spectacles to read the stained and dusty labels. Then he looked about him and said, "What a fine cellar! The old monks built well. You could be shut in here and no one on earth would know you were here." He turned to the steel door and tried the spring lock, saying, "It needs oil, Mademoiselle. I'll go over it for you."

While the others drank to the defeat of the Boches, the little man set to work with the loving care of a good mechanic to put the locks in order. When he had finished he pulled aside the wardrobe and Filomena went out alone, back again through the garage into the city with her rolled up newspapers.

Roxie watched the departure, moved by the dignity of the big Italian woman. There was in the Latin people a great capacity for emotion and acting. The exit of Filomena was magnificent, dignified and tragic. It was as if vengeance itself had left the cellar in a sortie upon the city.

When the wardrobe was in place again, Roxie left the workers and went slowly up the stairs. She wished with a sudden passion that she might have peace, that all the misery, the violence, the dark conspiracy would end, that there might be once more that lazy, quiet life which was the Paris she had always known. Little Monsieur Lopez followed her and closed and barred the door behind her.

Then as she climbed the great stairway leading to the second floor, she knew all at once that Nicky had returned. It was a curious inexplicable feeling as if in some way her whole body and spirit had grown sensitized to his nearness. He was there in the house. She *knew* it.

She began to run up the wide stairs and as she

reached the top she called out, "Nicky! Nicky!" and in a second she hear his voice answering her.

He came out of the salon, hurrying toward her, and she saw at once that something had happened to him. One hand was bandaged and the side of his face was bruised and discolored and he limped —but it was more than that. There was in the dark face something which had never been there before.

She managed not to cry and said quietly, "What is it? What has happened to you?"

He grinned, "They caught me . . . but only for a little while."

It happened, he said, at the border between the two zones. He had a Spanish passport, not a very good passport for it was full of flaws, but it had served on other trips. They had arrested him and questioned him and when his answers did not suit them they had begun to beat him.

"It was pretty bad," he said. "I am still stiff. You should see my back. There were four of them. I took it because I had to but I kept thinking, 'I must get out of this. I must get out of this,' and then the leader of them stood up and came toward me and I saw my chance. I seized the chair he was sitting on and swung it over my head." He grinned again. "It was wonderful, cleaning up that room. I killed the leader—smashed his skull and knocked out the others and then I jumped through the window. I am strong . . . but I never felt so strong before. I was a giant, a terrific fellow. I have not had a fight like that since I was a kid."

After that, he said, he had hidden in a haystack for a day and then a farmer took him in and hid him until he felt able to make his way to Paris.

"And now," he said, "I shall have to hide out here until my eye gets better and my hand is mended. They'll be looking for me. They must have known what they did to me."

She felt happiness stealing over her, like a slow pleasant glow of warmth in a chill room. Now he would be hers for a time. Now he would be safe. He could not escape her. As he talked she watched him, discovering a strange new quality in him— that the beating, the torture, the anguish had been nothing to him. He exulted in them as if somehow they contributed to his strength. It was the battle itself which delighted him. He described it all, his spirit rising, even to the sound the chair made when it smashed the head of the German officer.

"That," she said, "is the Russian in him," and she remembered the story of the child born on the edge of the battlefield while his father fought and his mother hid in the forest near by. "That," she thought grimly, "is not in me."

When he had finished she told him about Luigi

and he said, "I'll find out where he is. We might even be able to rescue him."

"No," she said, "you mustn't try that. I'm finding out where he is."

"How?"

She told him about the Major and his promise of a report, and as she spoke she saw the pupils of his eyes contract and knew with a preverse rush of satisfaction that he was jealous.

"And this Major," he said. "What has gone on between you two?"

"Absolutely nothing."

"Because that must not be . . . no matter what happens. Even if it was a question of saving my life, it must not happen. If you were unfaithful with a German, even to save me, I would kill you afterward."

She thought again, "He *is* a savage." All this was something she had heard of but never believed because all her experience argued against its truth.

He came to her and put his arm about her. "You are to go away," he said. "I've thought a lot about it. It is serious now. It is growing worse all the time. It does not matter that you have been guilty of no particular act. You have been a cover. You have been a front. If they caught you they would treat you like all the others." His face seemed old and serious suddenly. "No, you must go away while you are still safe." Then he looked at her and she knew that at last somehow, in some way she could not understand, the thing had happened. There was no more mockery, no more barriers. The thing in which she had never been able to believe had happened.

She thought, "I must not be a fool. I must not spoil it. I must not cry because I am happy. I am a tramp. I deserve none of this. I have done nothing to earn it. Thank you, God!"

She heard him saying with shyness, "I think it would be better if we were married before you went away. It would make it more certain, more legal. I would like it better. It would make me more certain of you. Perhaps such things are *bourgeois* but just the same I would feel different."

Again she felt called upon to stiffen her body in order to exact control of herself. After a moment she was able to speak. "It does not matter. I cannot go away . . . not now."

"There is nothing to hold you."

"I cannot go away . . . I cannot . . . not now. Can't you see that? Can't you?" It was all she could manage to say but her spirit cried out again, "Oh, thank you, God! Thank you, God!"

When Léon saw her in the dressing room he said, grinning, "You see. I told you he would come back. He was in a tough spot but he is a tough guy."

"Just the same . . ."

Léon's shrewd, pupilless eyes were very bright, glittering a little like jet. He said, "I must say I never expected to see it happen to you."

"Do I look like that?" she asked.

"It's sticking out all over you." Then the brightness went out of the eyes and they turned soft and he said, "Do you know the most beautiful thing on earth?"

She divined what he meant to say but held her tongue, "No."

"It is a woman who is in love and happy and satisfied." The speech finished with a faint uncontrollable sigh. He said quickly, "You'd better get on with your undressing," and left her.

While the golden feathers were fastened on her naked body she thought, "It is not right to be so happy," and superstition claimed her suddenly and she was afraid, but when her call came the fear had gone out of her and *la Reine des Oiseaux* descended the stairs toward the glow of light pridefully in a kind of triumph. The box where the Major always sat was empty tonight, completely empty.

When the curtain came down at last and she returned to the dressing room, the maid was waiting for her with an envelope bearing the stamp of the Hotel Ritz. Opening it she found inside a bit of plain paper on which a message was typewritten in German. She could read none of it but among the intelligible words she saw a name, written with an official air all in capitals—it was Luigi's name.

To the maid she said, "Go quickly and find the boss."

In a little while Léon came in. Without saying anything she handed him the note and watched his face grow dark as he read.

Then he said, "The sons of bitches! Luigi is dead!"

The note was brief and simple. It read, *At the request of Major Freiherr Kurt von Wessellhoft, I am sending you a report of the case of Luigi Salvemini, proprietor of a restaurant at No. 4 Impasse Galatée. The prisoner in question was killed when he jumped from a window while being questioned at the Military Barracks at Joinville.*

Lieutenant Gottfried Hessell.

Léon said again, "The sons of bitches! It has only begun!"

He went with her to spend the night at the house in the rue Washington. They were crossing the square before the theatre when out of the darkness came the sudden murmur of voices penetrated by a sudden sharp cry. Near them, quite close, was a crowd, shapeless and mysterious, in the thick darkness. Then someone in the crowd switched on an electric torch and the circle of light from the torch, directed at some object lying on the ground, silhouetted the figures near by. Out of the dim refracted light the figure of a French policeman appeared quite near them and Léon asked, "What is it? What has happened?"

The light was switched off again and out of the darkness came the voice of the policeman, "They have got two more of them . . . a lieutenant and a sergeant. The lieutenant is dead. They were stabbed. *Nom de Dieu!* It is a dirty business!"

Then Roxie remembered Filomena saying, "I am a strong woman. I can account for two!" This was the corner where she kept watch with La Biche, alone now, without the company of the little dog.

Léon took her arm and dragged her into the thicker darkness toward the entrance of the Métro, away from the group crowding around the dead lieutenant.

After the attack on the lieutenant and the sergeant the Germans closed Luigi's little restaurant and nailed up the door, and Maria went away, back to her own country in the south. They would give her no papers but Nicky helped her across the border between the two zones. He had many friends along the border—peasants and priests and schoolteachers and working men. Maria had to be sent back to her own country since, with Luigi gone, she had made up her mind to die and it was only kind that she should die among her own people. She grieved not only for Luigi who was dead but for what they had done to him before he died. That she could never really know. So Maria believed it easier to die than to go on living.

Some of the refugees they were still able to help because Filomena and La Biche had somehow kept in touch with them. But these too slowly, one by one, disappeared—perhaps picked up by the German police, perhaps by suicide. What became of them no one knew—the lonely homeless, weary acrobats and professors, workingmen and physicians, singers and politicians. Simply they disappeared.

The spring came early in a sudden rush of green over the tops of the chestnuts along the Champs Elysées and the poplars along the Seine, in a green carpet wherever there was a garden or a patch of grass. It came in the strutting and cooing of the pigeons which each day grew a little fewer in number because for one day at least a hundred or so citizens of Paris had meat. Spring came into the garden behind the house in the rue Washington lighting the candles on the chestnut trees turning to purple and white the plumes of the lilacs. Their perfume drifting in at the windows in the early evening, made Roxie again see the grimy brown house on the wrong side of the railroad tracks in Evanston. In the trodden, soot-stained earth of the yard, a single lilac tree had flourished—a miracle each time it bloomed to the hard, resourceful, sad-eyed little girl she had been long ago. The scent of the lilacs involved no happy memories save the glory of those white blossoms against the grimy liver-colored clapboarding of the house. All the rest was better forgotten. Whatever strength, whatever experience, whatever resourcefulness she had learned in that far off childhood had cost too much. She knew now, in the sudden discovery of so many things she had never known before, that they had kept her from happiness she should have known long ago but for her own hardness and self-reliance.

She thought, "But for all that I would have had all these years some other answer to living than 'Oh yeah!'" She had a different answer now. She accepted and even welcomed a great many things, like loyalty and devotion and even perhaps suffering.

The spring came quickly to Paris but it brought with it none of the gaiety that had always been spring in Paris. Chairs and tables were set out under the chestnut trees but Parisians did not sit at them— not real Parisians who loved Paris to the death, but only nameless shabby creatures who had betrayed her and felt no shame at sitting side by side with their enemies. The blooming trees, the cooing pigeons, the sudden carpets of green, brought no gaiety to the hearts of people who were in prison. Misery is easier to endure in miserable surroundings than in gay and brilliant ones, and spring this year was gay and warm and brilliant as if nature herself were mocking man and saying to him, "Have your wars! Kill each other! Destroy what you have built! I will carpet the graves and the battlefields made by you fools, I will clothe the shattered walls with green! Spring will return even when there are no more men on earth!" There was about this spring in Paris something derisive and triumphant and bitter.

In a strange fashion, Roxie in her own small happiness, was aware of all this. There was no reason in her nor any power of putting things into words even in her own mind, but the brilliance of the spring sometimes frightened her, and the sight of the lilacs and chestnut trees in blossom left her feeling sad with a dread that came over her from time to time, suddenly, like a recurrent illness.

In the streets the poor people grew more sallow and thin despite the sun which warmed the stone of the white and gray façades. There seemed for each blossom, for each new leaf, some new sadness, some new tragedy.

And then four months after the Major had gone back for his sister's wedding the tired old Governor who shipped the tapestries and pictures back to Pomerania was sent in disgrace to his estates and a new Governor arrived—the new kind of soldier, younger, with a hard narrow jaw, a small receding chin and small cold blue eyes behind pince-nez. He was the new sort; he resembled a shark. His name was simply Herrhauser. His origin was obscure.

It was Nicky who came in with the news, baffled and angry.

"I know about him," Nicky said. "A killer! A sadist! A criminal! In Hamburg he shot with his own hands three women in the water-front quarter because they had spat on a Nazi poster. It is bad. It will be like Prague before we are through."

She tried to calm his anger by saying, "Paris is not Prague. They would not dare."

He looked at her quietly, fiercely. "It makes no difference to them. In the end if they cannot hold Paris they will try to destroy it! They are like rats.

They will turn and die with their teeth bared because this time they know there is no mercy for them anywhere in the world." He put his hands on her shoulders. "You do not know. You still do not believe me or Léon or Filomena or a million others. They are abominable. They are not human. Until you hate them you will never understand. Until you hate them they will lie to you and betray you and cheat and steal and kill. Until you hate you are helpless as a child against them. Some day you will know!"

"Don't say that! Don't say that!"

He walked toward the window and looked out into the garden, not answering her, and as she watched him she felt a chilling sense of dread taking possession of her body. It was a physical sensation beyond all control. The black hate in him had shut him off from her again.

She thought, "If I could feel hate I would be one with him, with Léon and Filomena. I am still outside."

He went away from her then without speaking and threw himself down on the bed, burying his head in his arms. Quietly she sat down on the bed beside him, running her hands through his thick dark hair, but he did not speak again. He made no sign that he was aware of her nearness. It was as if he were frozen. And in a little while, exhausted, he fell asleep.

She left him only when she heard the voice of Léon, calling from the salon.

He was there with his dispatch case and a newspaper, looking sober and pale. He did not say anything. He only held the paper out to her and when she took it she saw at once what it was that disturbed him. It was one of the collaborationist papers which even in its headlines groveled and licked the boots of its barbaric conquerors. It stated simply that the new Military Governor had decided that the policy of conciliation and "correctness" had been a failure. In order to cope with the plotting and violence of Jews and communists, fifty hostages would be shot in reparation for the death of every German soldier.

She asked quickly, "Does Nicky know this?"

"I don't know. I don't know what he will do."

And she was afraid again. But Léon distracted her fear by saying, "I was right about your friend, the Major. He was even a bigger shot than I believed. He got the old General sent away. He is responsible for the new bastard who thought this up."

"How do you know?"

"I know all right. He is back in Paris."

"He hasn't been at the theater."

"No, but he is back. He has been back for three days. He no longer wears a uniform. He dresses now in English clothes and has a flat in the Avenue Foch."

"I know about that. He wanted me to share it when he came back."

He smiled grimly. "You haven't lost him, have you?"

"I wish I had." She remembered Lisa and knew that so long as the obsession for Lisa endured she would never be free of him. She said, "There is no triumph in it for me. It is not me he wants but a woman who has been dead for more than twenty years."

And then she told him the story of Lisa. When she had finished Léon said, "The dirty Boche! They are all nuts! That kind of thing happens only to them." And for a moment she felt again the same cold hatred in him that she had felt a little while before in Nicky.

"He will turn up again. He is crazy," she said.

At that moment Nicky came into the room looking tired and grim. She had not the strength to give him the newspaper or to speak of what was in it. He looked at them and at the paper, then picked it up and read what they had read, slowly without speaking. When he put it down he said wearily, "That changes everything. All the killing will have to stop. It is not possible to be responsible for the slaughter of innocent people." After a moment he added, "They are beyond anything."

"How will you stop it?" asked Léon.

"I shall have to see every man and woman and argue it out with them. With people like Filomena it won't be easy to stop the killing. We shall have to find something else—dynamiting bridges perhaps, blowing up their trains, thinking up violence and death which appears to be accidental. We shall have to go on fighting somehow. I shall have to go away again." He turned to Roxie. "It will only be for three or four days. It will have to be done at once."

"Don't go tonight, Nicky. Tomorrow." Just one more night together . . . it was not much to ask. She could not tell him what it was she feared. He looked at her. "They may kill more soldiers even tonight." His eyes were kind and she thought, "He is mine again. He has not gone away."

"Just tonight. Tomorrow will be soon enough." She could not keep the anguish out of her voice and for one horrible moment, watching his eyes, she thought, "I have told him. He himself knows now."

Then he smiled at her and put his arms about her. "All right, I'll go tomorrow."

When she turned to speak to Léon she discovered that he was not there. The little man had gone away. She thought, "He must have seen what was in my eyes," or it may have been that what had happened between herself and Nicky was unbearable to him whom no woman had ever loved. It was something which she would never know.

Nicky did not go with her to the theater. There would be work for him to do. He would wait for her.

That night on the great stair, in her golden feathers, *la Reine des Oiseaux* was magnificent. There was a radiance about her which brought cheers from the rows of green-gray uniforms. The theater was still filled, night after night, but nowadays most of the tickets were no longer paid for even with pieces of paper that had no value. Now Léon received a daily order to reserve a great bloc of seats for the entertainment and recreation of the ordinary soldier and for the tourists who came upon "strength through joy" tours. It was a lumpish audience but bedazzled by the lights and the gaudy, shabby scenery.

At the bottom of the stairs, *la Reine des Oiseaux* moved toward the glow of light and then quickly, more quickly than usual, toward the box on the right side of the stage. The box had for her a terrible attraction. Twice earlier she had gone to the peephole in the curtain to survey the box and twice she had discovered it was empty. And now she hoped that she would find that he had come in late and was sitting there as usual. She had been almost happy while he was away but now she wanted him back where she could see him, where she would know a little of what he was doing. It was worse to know he was in Paris without seeing him.

The box was empty.

After the *entr'acte* she met Léon in the wings. He said, "Two of the girls didn't show up tonight."

"Were they with us?"

"Yes. Félice and Margot. They sent no word."

"What could have happened?"

"I don't know." He shook his head as if to clear it. "Something is going on. I don't know what it is."

At the final curtain she found Nicky in the dressing room and at sight of him she forgot Léon and Félice and Margot and all the other worries.

In the Métro she thought that a small man in a green hat watched them too closely, but at the Concorde station he stayed on the train when they left and she thought, "It is only nerves. It is nothing. I'm beginning to imagine things."

The evening was warm and the rooms of the house in the rue Washington were filled with the scent of late summer. Roxie thought, "If I died tomorrow, it would not matter now."

He left in the morning a little after daylight, saying, "I'll be back on Friday. If I do not come back, then don't worry. Many things can happen but I'll find a way out."

When he had gone she found the house unbearable so dressed herself and went down into the cellar. They were all there, the little people—working like moles below ground. She worked with them for a while, doing small things which she was able to do. She folded and piled fresh papers as they came off the creaking old press. She took a broom and swept the thin paper cuttings into a pile near the heaps of broken furniture. This was only the first morning and yet the waiting was unbearable. It would grow worse and worse as Tuesday turned into Wednesday and Wednesday into Thursday and Thursday into Friday.

"I must be reasonable about it," she thought as she swept. "I'm thirty-two years old and should have some sense. He knows what he is doing. He is bold. He is clever. He is filled with hate." But he might be too bold. He might hate too much. He might take terrible risks.

Then she saw Monsieur Lopez push aside the wardrobe and unbolt the door behind it and Filomena came in with her basket. It was the first time Roxie had seen her in a fortnight and she was much changed, even to the style of wearing her hair. She looked thinner and taller and there were deep lines in her face. The black hair was drawn back severely from the face and streaks of gray were in it. She had a new kind of beauty, classic but almost cold and a little astonishing. At sight of Roxie she smiled but there was no gaiety in the smile. In it was simply the recognition of an old and tried friend.

She said at once, "I have seen your Nicky."

"When?" asked Roxie.

"Only just now. There is a strange man working in the garage. The others say they know him but I don't like it."

Monsieur Lopez was listening, "Did he see you come here?"

"No. The others saw to that. All the same I do not like his looks."

Monsieur Lopez smiled. "You are losing your nerve."

She gave him a furious look out of the great black eyes, "I do not have nerves."

Roxie went for the wine and Filomena with her basket came with her through the two doors into the cold damp room where the wine was kept. She said, "Your Nicky says I am not to kill any more."

"You agree?" asked Roxie.

"No," said Filomena. "I will kill and kill Germans even after the war is over and there is peace.

And not I alone but the Czechs and the Jugoslavs and the Norwegians and even the Italians." The look in the black eyes was quiet in its intensity.

"I have already attacked six," continued Filomena. "Four are dead. With the first two who lived I was learning. Now I know how to do it." Under the hard light of the naked bulb overhead the grim face had a special beauty as if it were carved from marble. "I know now the trick. It requires a great strength and a steady arm." She grinned suddenly. "Do you know where I work now?"

"No."

"I am the femme de ménage in the house of a German colonel. I come in on Thursdays to clean. The Colonel has been very ill lately. They cannot find out what is the matter with him. This Thursday I will not return. It won't be necessary. The job is finished." Then Filomena shivered suddenly. "It is cold as a tomb in this wine cellar. Let's get out of here. It is not healthy."

As Roxie closed the steel door and the lock clicked into place, Filomena said, "But that's neat. It works so easily. Nobody could get through that to steal your wine."

"It was an Argentine who thought of it. He owns the house. I bought the wine when I rented the house."

In the cellar under the vaulted roof the printing press was stopped and the moles raised their glasses, "*A bas les Boches*," said Filomena.

Wednesday came and Thursday and Friday. In the garden the lilacs were gone, the gay plumes brown and withered. Beneath the chestnut trees the fallen petals lay in fading drifts of pink and white. In three short days the carpet of grass changed from the lettuce green of early spring to the deep emerald of summer. It was as if in three days the whole world had changed . . . three long interminable days.

Roxie saw Filomena again but Filomena said little. She still did not like the newcomer in the garage. Her hate had become, it seemed to Roxie, an all-consuming passion, something for which she lived. She ate and slept only to feed and restore her hatred. Roxie, watching her, thought, "They have not only killed Luigi. They have killed Filomena as well." For what was left of the Filomena calling out to them from the darkness on the night Nicky returned? All that remained of that boisterous, Rabelaisian Filomena was the great heavy body daily growing more gaunt and ravaged.

Filomena went away and Friday came and the

hours of Friday were each as long as the days of the week had been, for Nicky did not return. In the evening at the theater Léon said, "There's no need to worry. He always comes back. He told you that himself."

She asked abruptly, "What about Félice and Margot? Have they come back?"

"No."

She waited for him to say more, to hint at least at what he thought had happened to them, but he said nothing.

"Will they talk?"

Léon frowned. "There is nothing they could tell about anyone but me. They don't know about any of the others."

"And if they come for you?"

Coldly he said, "I am prepared for that. They'll never be able to question me."

She went into her dressing room without answering him. You could not tell Léon that with Nicky it was different this time because of something inside of you. To anyone as hard-boiled as Léon, it would mean nothing. Then as she walked into the wings to climb the ladder to the top of the stairs, the figure of Léon emerged from the darkness and he said, "He is in the box again. He just came in."

She heard the voice of the *compère*, "*La Reine*

des Oiseaux" and out of the darkness she stepped into the glare of light. Her slippered feet felt uncertainly for the steps. Her naked legs trembled. She thought, "I mustn't fall. I must not faint . . . not now." Beyond that she was aware of only one thing, that the Major had returned and was sitting in the box. After all he might be useful now. Now, if anything had happened to Nicky, she would need his help. She would do anything he asked her to do. It did not matter what Nicky had said. It did not matter if he never saw her again so long as he was saved.

Dimly she was aware that she had reached the bottom of the stairs. She thought, "It may be in earnest now. It may be that I shall have to play Tosca and Mata Hari whether I choose to or not." It was all melodrama, bad melodrama. But somehow, without her wanting or knowing it, her daily life had become like Léon's history of Europe for the past twenty years, bad melodrama.

She heard the shrill brave voice of the *commère* singing, *"Ah! Qu'elle est belle! Qu'elle est brave! La Reine des Oiseaux! L'Aigle d'or!"*

The box was emerging now out of the rosy glare of the lights and in it alone sat the Major. He was not in military clothes but in a suit of brown tweed, well and loosely cut. That was what Léon had meant when he said, "He is wearing English clothes." But they suited him less well than a uniform. They looked strange and grotesque on him. His neck seemed longer and thinner, the face narrower and sharper. He had an awkward countrified look sitting there alone in the box. And then on an instant she was no longer aware of anything but the eyes with the look of madness and the hard line of the tightly compressed lips. The clothes made the rest of him seem gawky and insignificant.

"*Oh, les Oiseaux!*" sang the *commère*, "*Les beaux Oiseaux!*"

It was all old stuff—this *oiseaux* business. She was sick of the whole thing, of the whole picture. It stank with dullness and falsity. And suddenly she was aware that he was smiling at her, a curious smile with a quality of artificiality and fixity. She pretended not to have noticed the smile, and turned back toward the great stairs, thinking, "He is certainly crazy—crazy as a bedbug!"

The curtain came down and she was back again in her dressing room without remembering quite how she got there. The maid was pouring a glass of brandy and saying, "You are shivering, Mademoiselle! Drink this. It will make you feel better." And while Roxie drank the brandy the maid went to work stripping off the golden feathers. As usual she laid them in a cardboard box on the shelf and as Roxie watched her she felt a sudden inexplicable impulse to say, "Don't bother saving them! Throw them away! I'll never wear them again!"

She poured herself another drink of brandy and began to feel warm again.

Each time she went on until the end of the show, he was sitting there in the brown tweeds. Each time she passed the box he smiled at her through the yellow glare of the footlights. She thought, "He's damned pleased with himself. He never smiled before."

At the end of the show she ignored the curtain calls and went back to the dressing room. When she opened the door, Léon was standing there, his back to the mirror, his swarthy face grave and the eyes very soft. The moment she saw him she knew, with a curious feeling of having lived through the whole scene before in some earlier existence, what was coming. Before he said it, she heard him saying, "I have bad news," and heard herself saying, "It's about Nicky . . ."

"They've arrested him."

She closed the door. "Where have they taken him?"

"I don't know."

"How much have they found out?"

"I don't know. Certainly he won't talk."

She sat down because she could no longer stand.

"They may try to make him talk. They'll do any-thing."

He put his hand on her shoulder. "You mustn't be hysterical. You've got to keep your head now if you ever did in all your life. He's coming back-stage to see you. If he asks you to go out with him you must go. He's much more powerful than we thought. I think he knows all about Nicky."

"About Nicky and me?"

"I don't know. I should think it wasn't likely."

She pressed her hands against her eyes and heard him saying, "Tonight is the time to use him if you can."

"He's not a man. He's not human. I'm afraid of him."

Léon did not answer her. He waited as if to give her time to think what she must do. Presently she said, "There is one thing he wants of me."

"Yes?"

"If it were simple . . . what he wants, but what he wants is awful. It's no simple thing he wants. It will be horrible. Nicky said he would kill me . . . if he ever knew, he might do it."

"That is something you will have to decide. It is a small thing—nothing at all—or it is a monstrous thing. It depends on the point of view."

"I haven't any choice . . . if it will help Nicky."

There was a knock at the door and when Léon opened it he was standing there in the brown tweed suit looking awkward and insignificant. He said, "Good evening. I have come back. May I come in?"

She was glad then of the brandy and she thought quickly, "I can only go through this if I act . . . if I give a performance. I must act so that he'll never know or even suspect what I am feeling."

She stood up and held out her hand for him to kiss. "I'm glad you've come back," she said. "I thought you were never going to return to Paris. It's been very dull without you . . ."

"You are looking very beautiful . . . more beautiful than when I went away."

They went as usual to Tout Paris to sit in the dark alcove. It seemed the best thing to do—to behave as she had always done, as if she knew nothing whatever. In the darkness he could not see her face too distinctly. She herself asked for champagne and after they had drunk a glass apiece she said, "I think I would like to dance."

He did not dance well. He was awkward and stiff like one who neither understood dancing nor liked it, but he seemed pleased and excited, as if the contact of their bodies brought a new vitality to him. She thought again, "I must act! I must act! It is the only way I can go through with it."

When the music stopped and they returned to the table he seemed changed, less dead, less stiff, less correct. He talked almost with excitement of his visit to Berlin and his sister's wedding.

"My mother is very pleased," he said. "It was what she wanted."

He had been to the opera in Berlin. He was, he said, very fond of opera, almost as fond of opera as of the theater. It was good to see her again, he said. He had missed her very much. He had returned to Paris three days before, but there were many things to do and so many responsibilities he had been unable to come to the theater.

"I heard you were here," she said, without thinking.

He looked at her quickly. "How could you have known? No one knew I was here . . . at least only one or two people."

She had to think very quickly. "I don't even remember," she said. "Someone at the theater said, 'Your friend the Major is back.' I don't even remember who it was. I suppose someone who saw us out together."

He poured himself another glass of champagne and said rather like a sulky boy, "It is very strange."

"Would you like to dance again?" she asked.

"I am not a good dancer. Ordinarily I do not like dancing, but with you it is different."

She smiled at him and said, "Thank you."

"I am only sorry I am not a better dancer."

"I think you do very well."

This time while they danced he seemed to come completely alive and he said, "You know I am very much in love with you."

"Thank you. That is very pleasing for a woman to hear."

"And you . . . how do you feel?"

"I don't know," she sighed.

"Do you like me?"

She laughed. "Of course I like you. I wouldn't have risked being seen with a German if I hadn't liked you."

"It was not for any other reason?"

"No. What other reason could there be?"

"It is wartime. There could be many other reasons."

She laughed again. "So you think I am a spy. I'm not clever enough for that. In any case there would be no point in it. I am an American. This is none of my affair."

Then for a while they danced in silence while she thought, "I must be very skillful about it." And doubt answered, "But how?"

The music stopped again and when they returned to the table he said, "You are not wearing my ring."

"I never wear jewelry when I go out alone. It isn't safe."

"I suppose that's true, although we do our best to make Paris a safe and orderly place."

"It is a very beautiful ring. Everyone admires it."

He ordered another bottle of champagne and she noticed that the vein in his forehead was swollen and throbbing. She thought, "He suspects me. Perhaps he even knows everything. He really hates me but that crazy thing about the governess will give him no peace."

They danced a third time and a fourth and had more champagne and she thought, "It is getting late. I shall have to do it somehow quickly. It's just possible that if I'm clever enough it can be done."

Abruptly he asked her if she was still of the same opinion about the flat in the Avenue Foch.

"Yes. My situation hasn't changed."

He said, "It is a pity. It is a beautiful flat. We should be very comfortable there—perhaps very happy too. It would be so easy for us to go there directly tonight . . . so easy and convenient."

She was thinking all the time of Nicky. If only she could get him out of her mind, if she could somehow, miraculously, forget him, it would be easy. It astonished her a little that she put such value upon faithfulness; but now it was not simply an idea, it was a reality, a necessity, unless being unfaithful was the only way of saving him. She was aware that the Major was becoming loathsome to her, beyond anything she had felt about him until now. It was extraordinary that inside the handsome body there was no soul at all, no warmth, nothing that any woman could really love.

But Nicky would not leave her in peace. He was in prison. They might be torturing him now, while she was sitting here trying to discover how she was to do what she must do, trying to find a way . . .

She heard him saying, "You seem very preoccupied tonight."

"I thought I was being gay . . . I'm sorry. Perhaps it's because I'm tired. The show has begun to be a terrible bore. It's been going too long and it's not really very good."

"No," he said, "it really isn't."

She thought, "Now is the time. I must do it now . . . now . . . not later." And she said, "No, it's really not true that I'm tired. I am very worried about a great friend of mine who is in trouble."

He grinned. "You seem to have a great many friends who get into trouble."

"No more than anyone else. After all, nearly

everyone is involved some way or other in the whole thing. I have a great many friends in Paris."

A sly look came into the dull blue eyes. "Is it the *bourgeois* lawyer?"

She had hoped that all the champagne would dull his mind and stimulate his desire, but somehow it had failed to work as she had planned. She said, "Oh, no. He is still in Marseilles. It is simply a great friend. We grew up together."

"A woman."

"No. A man. His mother and mine were great friends." And almost at once she saw that she had made a mistake. He would scarcely believe that her mother who lived in Evanston, Indiana, was a great friend of a woman who lived in Paris.

He said, "I was sorry about the other. It was too late to help him. He had already committed suicide."

Somehow she had not thought of Luigi all the evening and now the mention of him chilled her. She managed to say, "I suppose there was nothing you could have done. I appreciate your sending me the report."

"What is the name of this friend . . . the man?" he asked.

Quickly she said, "Pierre Chastel. He worked at the theater as secretary to the Manager. I'm sure there is some mistake. I'm sure he's guilty of nothing whatever."

"What did you say his name was?" He was watching her now.

"Pierre Chastel."

"And he is French?"

"Yes. His mother was Russian." She tried desperately to piece the story together, but somehow she seemed only able to make things worse. The papers Nicky carried said that he was of French parentage, his father a consul in Cairo.

"You are sure it is not the *bourgeois* lawyer?"

"Absolutely. Why, don't you believe me?"

He did not answer her directly. He said, "I do remember the name. I think he was picked up yesterday."

She kept thinking, "I must act. I must pretend I'm playing a part." And she said, "Do you know what he is charged with?"

"Sabotage and suspicion of murder."

Quickly she said, "Would you be able to help him? Is there anything you could do. It would make a great difference to me." She knew now that he did not believe in the story of the lawyer and had never believed it.

"Perhaps. How great a difference would it make?"

She did not answer at once. She was certain of

what was coming. She thought, "The time is here. I must decide." It did not matter now what Nicky felt or wanted. Nothing at all mattered but to find out where he was and to save his life. It did not matter even if he killed her afterward or never saw her again. It was all very clear. She said, "The greatest difference in the world . . . the very greatest." She tried to control her voice but she was not a very good actress. She had never been and she knew that even while she was speaking she had told him everything.

"You could do something for me too," he was saying, and she was aware that his voice was trembling too.

"Yes . . . anything you wish. Anything at all . . . any bargain if you will help me now."

"Your house is not far . . . only around the corner. We could go there to arrange the terms of the bargain. It is not exactly correct to do it here in a public restaurant. Does that suit you?"

"Yes . . . whatever you like."

He called for the check and they went out through the dancers and the people at the tables as if nothing at all was happening. In the street they walked in silence but in the silence there was a strange feeling of sadness which she could not explain to herself, a sadness that was profound and enormous, even greater than either of them, so great that they were dwarfed and insignificant. Now that a decision had been reached the sense of tension was abated.

He spoke only once. As they turned into the rue Washington he said, "It is a beautiful night. See, the stars are shining."

The words hung in the night, repeating themselves over and over again in the sad silence, "The stars are shining! The stars are shining!" And as they reached her door, she remembered why the words haunted her. "The stars are shining!" It was the aria from the last act of Tosca which Mario sang before being shot.

Inside the door she switched on the light and looked at him quickly but the face was blank. "Perhaps," she thought wildly, "it was only a coincidence, an accident. Perhaps it means nothing." But she remembered too what he had said of the opera a little while before.

Upstairs in the sitting room, she threw off her coat and said, "If you'll excuse me, I'll bring some champagne."

"Have you no servants?"

She remembered the lie she had told him long ago about the servants and thought, "I must be careful. I was nearly caught again." Quickly she said, "This is the night they spend at home."

"You are here alone? Aren't you afraid?"

"There are not many things I am afraid of."

The curious look of utter madness which sometimes came into his eyes was there now and she thought, "Perhaps he means to kill me." But she still was not afraid. On the contrary she experienced a quick sense of exhilaration.

She went to fetch the keys to the wine cellar from the drawer of the brass and marquetry table and as she reached the table she saw in the circle of light from the lamp a plain white envelope addressed in Léon's handwriting. It was unmistakable, the small precise handwriting of a clever, calculating man. She thought, "There is something inside that envelope that I must know at once."

He was watching her now with the look of obsession in his eyes, but he appeared to attach no importance to the envelope. She picked it up and walked out of the sitting room into the pink bedroom. There, closing the door behind her, she tore open the envelope. Inside was a card advertising the Alhambra Music Hall—"*Paris! Toujours Paris!*"

She turned it over. On the back was written the message. It read: *I could not stay. Nicky is dead. You must get away tonight.*

She stood there for a long time staring at the

card, feeling nothing at all. In the words written by Léon there was only an abstraction which at first did not touch her.

Then she sat down on the bed and thought wildly, "He knew all the time that Nicky was dead. That is why he came to the theater tonight. He knew Nicky was my lover. He only wanted me really after Nicky was dead." And again there swept over her the feeling of horror and disgust she had felt the whole evening at Maxim's. They were horrible people, more horrible, more perverse than Léon and Nicky had said . . . Nicky! Nicky!

She rose and crossed the room to the big mirror. She was thinking, "When I return to the other room, I must look as if nothing had happened, as if I knew nothing at all." She had to appear cool, for now there was something to be done that must be done if she was to go on living.

In the mirror she did not look any different, save perhaps for the expression in the eyes. There were no tears. What happened to her now did not matter. She was not even thinking of Nicky now. She was thinking of something else.

The first idea that occurred to her was the revolver beneath the pillow, but this she rejected almost at once. She barely knew how to fire it; if she missed him he would disarm her and then she would be lost along with all the others. The revolver could serve only as a last resort. "No," she thought, "there must be some other way." Quietly she sat down at the dressing table thinking how strange it was that she should be sitting here, planning to kill. The project filled all her being. It was as if she had become herself a weapon of vengeance and destruction, a steel blade like the one Filomena carried or a phial of poison.

Quickly she tore the card with d'Abrizzi's writing into a thousand small pieces. These she disposed of in the bathroom. Her heart cried out suddenly, "Nicky! Oh, Nicky!" But she thought, "I must not think of that now." She had a new strength she had never before known—the strength that was in Léon and Nicky. And then as she opened the door into the sitting room she knew what it was she meant to do. It was much cleverer than merely shooting him. It was a plan worthy of himself, of all those Germans at Maxim's. The sense of playing a role returned to her. Opening the door, she made an entrance, like an actress coming onto the stage. It was easier like that. It made the whole thing objective.

He was standing by the window holding in his hand one of the heavy gold cords which tied back the brocade curtains. The sight puzzled her for a moment until she saw that he had fashioned the heavy cord into a sort of cat-o'-nine-tails. The pocketknife with which he had cut the cord was still in his hand. In a flash of intuition she understood. "He means to beat me," she thought, "because Lisa escaped him . . . because she was older and died and he was never able to make love to her. He means to punish her through me, to make me pay for all his suffering." It was as if with these Germans death and love were always grimly near to each other. She would have been frightened by the look in his eyes if she had not, consciously, been playing a part as if she were on a stage.

She said, quietly, "Well, what is our bargain to be?"

He smiled but the eyes remained unsmiling, "The bargain is very simple. You are to tell me everything you know. You are to do what I wish for tonight. I will arrange it so that he will be let off and you yourself will be able to escape. For the others of the band I can promise nothing."

"The others," she repeated. "What others?"

"Who have worked with you to make Paris impossible for us . . . who have worked at treason and sabotage and murder. There is a long account to settle."

A voice inside her kept saying, "You must keep your head! Now, if ever, you must keep your head!" So she went on acting.

"It is a filthy thing you're asking," she said.

"I am asking very little." He sat down on the

arm of a chair, braiding and unbraiding the gold whip as he spoke. "You thought I was a fool. You meant to use me. As it turns out, it is I who am using you."

The voice inside kept saying, "Keep your head! Now you know what it is to hate. Nicky is dead, but there are others to be warned and saved." She leaned against the edge of a table and said quietly, "There is a great deal you do not know but a bargain is a bargain. Do you know what goes on in this house?"

He looked at her sharply. "What goes on?" he asked.

"You seem to know a great deal but do you know about the cellars beneath this house?"

"No."

"Come. I will show you."

He looked at her sharply, suspecting a trick but she said, "There is no one there. They have been warned and have gone away."

He asked suddenly, "Was that what was in the letter you picked up?"

"Yes."

"Where is it?"

"I destroyed it." And she told him what she had done with Léon's card.

She turned and took the keys of the wine cellar and the outer door of the gallery from the drawer of the table. Very casually she said, "In any case the champagne is down there. We cannot enjoy ourselves fully without champagne. There is no ice any longer. The cellar is very cold."

Quietly he put down the whip of gold cord and took a revolver from his pocket. "I do not mind shooting. It can easily be explained."

She smiled. "You talk like a bad melodrama."

For a moment she was afraid that he would not go into the cellar and she thought, "I must get him there! I must! If I never again achieve anything."

So she said, "Would you like to see the presses of *'France Eternelle'*?"

"*'France Eternelle'!*" he shouted. "Where are the presses of that filthy paper?"

She smiled again. "In this house! If you don't believe me, I will show you."

"Come," he said. "I think you are lying."

She led the way down the stairs and through the narrow door which led into the cellars. Behind her she heard his heels click as they struck the stone steps. In her wild guess, she had been right. The cellar was empty and in darkness. They had all gone away, warned by Léon when he left the note.

At the turn of the stairs she switched on the light and there beneath the vaulted ceiling stood the hand press, the type rack, and near them a pile of freshly printed copies of the terrible paper. At the bottom of the stairs she said, "Now do you believe me?"

"Yes." He walked over to the stack of papers and picked one from the top of the heap. For a long time he stared at it, and when he looked up, he said, "I have been more of a fool than I believed!"

She went to the wooden door opening into the vaulted gallery that led to the wine cellar with the steel door. As she put the key into the lock she saw that he had not followed her but was still staring at the hand press and the pile of papers. She thought, "He is suspicious." As she unlocked the door she said casually, "I'm afraid you'll have to help me. The champagne is in the high racks."

Then he turned and came toward her and she said, casually as a guide lecturing tourists, "These cellars are very interesting. They were once a part of a Benedictine Monastery. They run on and on under the garden and into the hotel beyond. The people who worked here didn't come in by the front door. They came through a passage from a garage in the rue de Berri."

He was still apparently fascinated by the whole cellar. While she spoke he stopped again and looked about him. After a moment he said, "That explains everything. No one ever came in the door but the servants, d'Abrizzi and your friend."

So now there were no more pretenses. He too

was telling her everything, that the house had been watched, that he knew all about Léon and Nicky. She had a strange feeling of being at the end of the world, of utter finality in which there were no more secrets, no more conspiracy.

She pushed back the door and at the sound of the heavy oak striking the stone he turned again and followed her into the vaulted gallery as she switched on the light. He was still carrying the revolver. The look of madness was no longer in his eyes. He was alert now and curious, like a detective. It was almost as if he felt admiration for her.

She said, "You must admit it was a good hiding place in the heart of Paris?"

She came to the steel door and slipped the key into the lock little Monsieur Lopez had oiled so carefully. The door swung back easily. She switched on the light and said, "We might as well be gay about it. We'll have the best Lanson of the best year. There's very little left of it in the world."

He followed her in and she said, pointing, "There it is in the top rack. You might as well bring two bottles. It will make it pleasanter."

He stepped past her and thrust the revolver into his pocket.

It was the matter of a second's timing. If she had not been a dancer she might not have been quick enough to achieve her purpose. She moved with the quickness of light, while he still stood on tiptoe reaching upward for the bottles. The rest was the matter of a second. She was outside and the steel door had swung shut. The lock clicked into place.

Then quickly, moved by anxiety, lest someone should enter the house before she had finished, she went through the vaulted gallery, shivering a little with the damp and chill, to the outer wooden door. She had gone half the length of the gallery before she heard the sound of kicking against the metal door and the very faint sound of shouting. By the time she reached the wooden door, the sounds were scarcely audible.

It all happened quickly, to the very end, as if she had planned it with intricate care well in advance. She closed the wooden door and fastened the lock and then stood listening with her ear pressed against the wood. She could hear no sound whatever. It was silent as a tomb.

Quickly she crossed to the wardrobe of wood and bamboo that covered the door opening into the passage which led to the rue de Berri. She managed to tilt it on its side then up again, then on its side toward the door leading to the wine cellar. With each step of the operation she gained a few feet. She was strong and the wardrobe was less heavy than she had imagined. At last she set it upright before the door, close against the wall, and stepped back to survey the effect. The door was completely hidden. Unless one moved the wardrobe, the existence of the door would never be suspected.

But the task was not quite finished. Quickly she moved a great pile of furniture around the wardrobe so that it would appear careless and casual to any stranger coming into the cellar. After that she picked up the broom and carefully obliterated all traces of her activity that remained on the stone floor. When she had finished, she stood for a moment looking at her handiwork and thought, "He will disappear. No one will ever find him. He can shoot himself if he likes, after their fashion—the way they do to their own prisoners—a cell and a revolver, or he can drink himself to death. After all, there is all that wine."

As she turned away to climb the stairs she felt a faint pang of pity for him, not because he had to die, for death no longer meant much to her and perhaps very little to him, but for the sad thing he was, and what he had been since the beginning— twisted, perverse, defeated and inhuman. It passed quickly for they had left her no time or place for pity. When she thought of Nicky and Luigi, the old Jewish doctor, the sad-eyed refugees and Filomena's little dog. . . . No, there was no time or place for pity.

Upstairs on the table lay the whip he had fashioned out of the curtain cord. She stood for a moment looking down at it and then, smiling suddenly she pushed it to the floor. After that she went to her own room, took out the jewel case and two fur coats and changed into street clothes and put on a hat. Then with the fur coats over her arm and carrying the jewel case, she turned out all the lights one by one and went down the stairs. At the bottom of the stairs, she turned once and looked back and her heart cried out, "Nicky! Oh, Nicky!" Then opening the door she stepped into the street.

She was going underground now, like the others. There was a new strength inside her, a deep, rugged strength born of all Nicky had seen—the dead children, old women along the road, the murdered priests, the driven, tortured Jews, the starving and dying from one end of Europe to the other. She knew now what it was—that thing they talked about, deep inside you, that never died but burned steadily and forever. . . .

The night was black but overhead the stars were shining.

THE END